Five Frozen Pekingese

Stefan Gadnell

There is no time, everything is just a
mass of atoms in motion

This book is a work of fiction, and any resemblance to persons, l
living or dead, or places and events is entirely coincidental. The characters are products of the author's imagination and used fictitiously.

Five Frozen Pekinese

Publisher Ymershorn, Sweden
www.ymershorn.se
Cover by Stefan Gadnell, www.gadnell.com
ISBN 978-91-989402-0-6

Big thanks to:
Kule Palmstierna
Albin Berglund
Margaretha Stjernefeldt
For your proofreading and tips
that have made the book what it is

First book

Is everything an illusion?

1 TRAVELING WITHOUT A DESTINATION

"Actually, time travel is impossible. When you travel in the usual way, you go to places that exist, that exist right now. Thailand exists all the time, even if we are not there at the moment. The woman standing by the petrol drum preparing your lunch has grown up in Thailand and has been there for over twenty years, until you arrive and order a Pad Thai, a true classic. When you return to home, the young woman will continue to toss her noodles, day after day. If you were to go back later, after several years, it is entirely possible that you would be served by the same cook. Hopefully not the same noodles and nuts, but the woman has lived her life all the time you've been apart. However, time travel is not possible; those places, or rather, those different points in time, do not exist. Since they do not exist, they are, of course, not accessible. When you flip through the latest edition of the Time Travel Brochure, it is empty of destinations, and it will be forever."

The university auditorium was full of listeners, all eagerly watching Professor Harriet Hanson as she flipped through her papers to visualise a charter-loving time traveler. Despite her age of over fifty, she was considered attractive by many of the young students. Her small upturned nose made her resemble Nefertiti, but the light ponytail diminished the queenly effect somewhat. Occasionally, a student would flirt with her, but it was something she neither noticed nor understood.

"How would it work if someone traveled to a time when you were eight years old? Would you suddenly be created? Or would you, who exist now, become aware that another version of you is suddenly created, as an eight-year-old? Would your body be generated just because a time traveler arrived? Would the memory of this event appear in your mind ten years later? Or do you exist forever as an eight-year-old if someone from the future wants to pay a visit?"

Harriet nodded lightly to the audience.

"Imagine if all moments are preserved in some hidden multiverse, and one could travel to any time and start time there. It sounds too incredible. Unreal. Totally impossible. Is there a time coordinator somewhere deciding that now we must start on November 5, 1776, because a time traveler is appearing there right now?"

With a brusque expression, the professor mimicked an imaginary coordinator. The corners of her mouth down and eyebrows crossed, then she shook her head.

"That can't work, too unthinkable. But it's very exciting to fantasise about time travel. It's fun. It tickles the mind, doesn't it? Of course, entertaining stories can be created about someone traveling in time. Someone preventing their father from meeting their mother, and then making it even more exciting when that person tries to restore everything, just for their own existence. What wonderful paradoxes that would be. But that's all it is, a thrilling story, completely impossible in reality. But is there really no way to move through time at all?"

Another pause. Harriet smiled slightly.

"One could say that we are traveling forward in time at a speed of sixty seconds per minute, or twenty-four hours per day if you prefer. What we call time. All we need to do is simply sit and wait."

Here, Harriet made a long pause. After a while, a muffled laughter and some giggles were heard from the audience.

"If you want to move forward in time faster, you can try taking a nap. It's a straightforward and very cheap way to travel in time. You could also consider freezing your body and then waking up in the future, after several years. Theoretically possible, and maybe it will work... in the future. One thing applies to both sleep and freezing. You can't go back, never travel back!"

With her hand, Harriet indicated a backward movement.

"One theory is that time machines will be invented in the future. But... is it perhaps that the future is the present moment? Do we exist so they have a place to travel to? We exist in this moment only because someone from the future happens to be here paying a visit? An entire universe exists right now, just for a time traveler to stop by the toilet at Burger King in Portsmouth?"

Harriet fell silent for a short while and noticed that some in the front row were smiling.

"If the future exists, or has existed, one might wonder why there are no time travelers with us right now? Why haven't they revealed themselves? Anyone?"

The professor took another pause. With her hand above her eyes, she scanned the audience. Glanced at the balcony.

"One could wonder why there is no time traveler with us today? Perhaps our time is uninteresting to visit. We wage wars and rape. Abuse each other and the little children. Eradicate thousands of animal species every year. We abuse and deplete the Earth of its resources. Our mobile phones look ridiculous. Large, heavy, and run on batteries. Must be charged every night. We watch TV, with loads of TV channels, or we get stuck in some video game. Who would want to visit us, brutal, antisocial, and quite boring? Perhaps we are an uninteresting and dull destination. For a long time, last-minute trips to our time have been randomly assigned, but no one from the future wants to visit us. Fortunately for us, someone is currently visiting Portsmouth, otherwise we wouldn't exist at all."

Harriet shook her head.

"Time travelers from the future would probably prefer to go to more exciting events like the crucifixion of Christ, or even better, his birth. The three wise men might have been from the future? They had unusual clothes, and it is said that they came from afar? Maybe it's that there are plenty of time travelers around us anyway, but no one dares to reveal themselves. Because then the infamous time police will come. Security guards who ensure that everyone adheres to the Big Rule Book Regarding Time Travel. Because there are certainly people who behave as if they come from the future, and perhaps even more likely from the past."

Now Harriet took a sip of water and moistened her throat.

"Nostradamus was a philosopher who, in the 16th century, wrote verses and prophecies that are said to have predicted the future. Perhaps he was a time traveler from the future, a rebel who did not follow the big rulebook on time travel? His verses can be interpreted in any way you like. You can easily find a passage that fits an event that has already happened. However, no one has succeeded in predicting an event using his texts. No, Nostradamus probably did not come from the future, and it was probably fortunate for him. The thing is that if you travel in time, you end up in a completely different place, probably out in space. Earth rotates and travels around the Sun, which in turn moves around the centre of the Milky Way. The Milky Way moves at high speed in the Universe, which means that the Earth is never in the same place. It might be easier to understand if you imagine yourself on a road trip. After many hours, you realise that you took a wrong turn; you should have turned two hours ago. You should have turned off at Petersfield, towards Portsmouth."

Harriet's hand pointed to the left.

"But you are fortunate and have a time machine built into your car. You simply travel two hours back in time to correct your mistake."

Harriet made a short pause.

"Did you think so? But what happens when you set minus two hours and press the button on your magical machine? You stay in the same place, of course, but the clock on the car's dashboard shows two hours earlier. You did indeed travel in time, but not back to the place you were two hours ago. But don't despair; you have a little extra time to find the right way. It's easy to think that you would also travel back to the same place you were two hours ago? But how would that work? A journey in time also involves a displacement. It can take a long time if you want to go back to the same place you've been before. A trip twenty years back in time would place you far outside our solar system. An attempt to travel to see dinosaurs would place you even further away, perhaps outside the Milky Way. If you were to travel in time, the Earth and everything around you would be far away, in an entirely different place. You would end up in the black space, swell up like a balloon, and boil away in the vacuum of space. You wouldn't get to see any lizards because they would be several light-years away. Far away!"

With her whole hand, Harriet pointed out the window.

"Very short intervals are the best choice if you want to travel in time. Perhaps a few minutes, or preferably only seconds. But it will still be risky. We and the Earth move in the Universe at a fantastic speed, about six hundred kilometres per second. Earth is a perfect spacecraft, maintaining a good pace on its journey through space. Together with the sun, we are a completely self-sufficient system that has traveled for many billions of years. The Earth has moved four hundred light-years since humans began walking on it, which took about two hundred thousand years. If we wanted to travel back two hundred thousand years, we would have to move four hundred light-years. It's far."

The professor crossed her arms.

"If we were to travel back in time just one second, the Earth would end up sixty miles away, or rather, where the planet was a second ago. You can surely calculate which way we are moving and make sure you find Earth after this short time travel. Don't count wrong, or you could easily end up somewhere among our satellites. Or worse, a few kilometres inside the Earth. For safety's sake, we aim a little above the Earth's surface. Therefore, you should have a parachute on you."

The professor emphasised the last part.

"After making all the calculations, we send you back one second in time. The Earth's surface is then in a different place, sixty miles away, and you end up over a mile in the air. The parachute unfolds. You hover. When you land, you may not have noticed the time travel you did in one second. But you can proudly show off your wristwatch to your friends. The question is whether anyone will believe you just because your clock shows one second wrong?"

Here, Professor Hanson held up her wristwatch. It had an extra-large dial, selected specifically for this gesture, on this occasion.

"A parachute could be a way to prepare, but one could think one step further. We know that we would end up far out in empty space if we traveled back one year in time. Specifically, twenty billion kilometres away. That's five times farther than Pluto. It's far. Unfortunately, it takes ten years to travel to Pluto with our current spacecraft. It would take fifty years to travel to the place where Earth was one year ago. So go away in your youth, to the right position in empty space, far beyond Pluto. Fifty years later, you are in place to enter the right date on your time machine."

The professor took a pause and looked up at the balcony. A student sneaked in with a cup of coffee. Carefully, he sat down at the back. Harriet continued, with a raised voice.

"With the typical sound of a time travel, Earth appears outside your spacecraft. It's just a matter of descending and landing. Extremely easy. Here, you might meet your twenty-year-old self. Maybe persuade them to do something else with their life than spending fifty years alone in a spacecraft?"

The professor glanced at the front row to see if they understood.

"Instead of time travel, one could look back in time by somehow accessing the light that was emitted from Earth a long time ago. The light from England in the 15th century is moving at the speed of light through space at this very moment. We know that for sure. We simply take a very fast spacecraft, go far away, look back at Earth, and see the light that left Earth five hundred years ago."

Here, Harriet clasped her palms together in front of her mouth.

"But it is impossible to travel faster than light. It's impossible. But the light might pass close to a black hole, thus altering its direction, and then one could deflect the light and catch a glimpse of Henry VIII and all his wives. A moustache-adorned man with puff sleeves and plumes in the hat. How awesome it would be to see in a super-telescope how feathered and colourful dinosaurs hunt prey at sunset. Telescopes like that we have not yet manufactured; we can't even see a planet orbiting a star four light-years away. We have to settle for looking at the moon and seeing one second into the past. When you look at the sun, which you shouldn't, you actually see something that happened eight minutes ago. When you look at the stars, you see several million years into the past. But it's, of course, not time travel. In fact, there is only one *now*. If one could travel in time, it means that there are several *nows*, and that is not possible. It doesn't work like in science fiction movies where photographs change, and texts on gravestones disappear. Talking about different timelines is just an attempt to bring some kind of logic to something entirely illogical."

Harriet adjusted her papers on the lectern; her lecture was approaching its end.

"A journey in time involves a very long journey in space. Six hundred kilometres for every second you want to travel. One could summarise the dream of time travel like this: The future is not yet created, and all old moments no longer exist, they do not exist. Even if one of you were to create a time machine, there are no destinations. Unfortunately."

2 GRANDFATHER PARADOX

"In the movie Back to the Future, a sports car is used, which must reach a certain speed to time travel."

The confident voice belonged to one of the older students at the school. His gaze moved across classmates before finally fixing on the professor. "Does this have anything to do with it? That you also have to move to travel through time?"

Professor Harriet Hanson looked down at the floor, took a few steps to the side. She knew this question would come.

"You mention a fantasy product; the movie, of course, has nothing to do with science. It's a coincidence that this sports car, a DeLorean DMC-12, has to reach a hundred and forty-one kilometres per hour to achieve time travel. It may seem strange that the vehicle is also cooled, as if it has been in space for a longer time, but that's a coincidence. That it sometimes even flies is just a stroke of luck from the director, Leonardo Zemeckis."

The professor waited for a few seconds, letting her excellent knowledge sink in with the audience.

"To travel thirty years back in time, as they evidently do in the movie, means you have to go to where the Earth was thirty years ago. It becomes a very long journey and, excuse the humour, an extremely time-consuming journey. Almost two hundred billion kilometres. Fifty times longer than the distance between Earth and the outermost planet in our solar system. That's the distance Earth has moved in space during the thirty years that have passed. It took our space probes twenty-five years to reach the edge of our solar system. It would take us more than fifteen hundred years to travel to the place Earth was thirty years ago. The crew could, of course, be frozen during the long journey, but the big problem is that you don't have a functional time machine when you finally arrive. But of course, they might have a DeLorean in the cargo hold?"

There was a faint chuckle in the room. Harriet smiled. This was the perfect response after a well-executed lecture.

Among the audience sat her nephew Samuel. He remembered talking about Back to the Future with her once, but at that time, she knew nothing, not even what a DeLorean was.

There weren't many empty seats in the auditorium at the Department of Astronomy and Theoretical Physics. Harriet was relatively new to the university, and her lectures often filled the auditorium. Samuel looked proudly at his aunt. He had met her sporadically during his upbringing, but since a month ago, she had been living with him, or rather, he was living at home, and Harriet had moved into the house. This happened after Samuel's parents had died in a car accident.

"What if you were to go back in time to kill your own grandfather before your father was born? What happens if you succeed?"

A first-year student with curly hair stood up. The professor was well-prepared for this question.

"You have prevented your own birth, so you won't be able to travel back in time and commit the murder. A paradox, simply. It's called the grandfather paradox. A popular explanation is that it creates an alternative reality or a parallel universe. You live in one reality and kill your grandfather in another reality, in a universe where you won't be born."

Silence filled the room. Many began to think about relatives and friends who had passed away and might still be alive somewhere, in another universe.

"Another, more humorous explanation is that you will miss every time you try to shoot your grandfather. You simply cannot kill him. You stumble just at the moment of shooting and miss. The weapon might click. The bullets don't work, or maybe a time traveler pops up in front of you and gets in the way of your shots."

Laughter echoed in the room again. Harriet closed her eyes briefly. That response was perfect.

Another hand went up in the air. Harriet wasn't prepared for this and hesitated. She nodded briefly to the young aspirant who stood up. She recognised this guy, a real troublemaker.

"But many famous professors and scientists research time travel; they talk about quantum physics and entanglement, about wormholes and curved time? These are very intelligent people with long education and serious research. Does the professor claim they are wrong?"

This was a dig; it felt in the way the question was formulated. Of course, one would rather believe in men talking about curved time than a woman saying it's impossible, thought Harriet.What surprised Harriet was that the student managed to produce such a long and coherent sentence.

"It's about money, like so much else in this world. You don't become famous or get research funding by saying that time travel is NOT possible. That would be unwise, and as you said yourself, they aren't."

The young man retorted, "But maybe one can predict the future in some way. There are people who claim to be clairvoyant?"

"Earth moves in the Universe at a speed of six hundred kilometres per second. That means tomorrow we'll be in a different place, twenty-five million kilometres away. It's as far as halfway to Mars. It is impossible to see if someone falls into the water or drives into the ditch from so far away. We can't even see the moon lAndrew on the moon with our telescopes, let alone see any numbers on a lottery ticket at an even greater distance!"

Harriet thanked the audience after her retort; she didn't want another unprepared question. Samuel followed her with his eyes as she packed up her things. He thought about his parents, who had also lectured at the school, mom and dad.

Alice and Leopold Hanson had both worked on research at the university. Two months ago, they had taken the car for a weekend by the sea. A much-needed break, a few delightful days of relaxation. During their journey, a drug addict crossed over to the wrong side and collided head-on with them. It happened fast. He had been driving at a very high speed. Alice didn't make it, but Leopold survived the crash. After a few days in the hospital, Leopold wrote a will asking his sister, Harriet Hanson, to take over the house and help Samuel until he grew up. Leopold knew he didn't have much time left, and that evening, the day after, he closed the blinds for good.

Harriet was shortly thereafter employed at the university and simultaneously moved into the house with Samuel. The villa was situated high in a popular area, at least popular for older couples with relatively grown-up children. The house was large, with a basement, and Samuel had his own room and bathroom for as long as he could remember. It was close to both the city centre and the university, which all family members had appreciated.

But now they were gone.

The fact that Harriet resided in the house should have been advantageous for the young man. Frequently, older boys also require solace.

But when the worst tears began to subside, it turned out that Harriet was preoccupied with her work, planning lectures, research reports, reading books, and flipping through magazines. Often she walked around the house with a folding rule.

Samuel's aunt found it challenging to get close, to show warmth and understanding. A pat on the shoulder wasn't much comfort. Hugs weren't Harriet's thing, evident. If you got closer than a meter, she would become paralysed, drop the folding rule, and hang her arms. When Samuel stepped back, she picked up the folding rule and looked at Samuel, but not in the eyes, a bit more diagonally, more at his one ear.

"How are you?"

Samuel mumbled. No one expected an answer.

One of the large rooms on the ground floor quickly filled with moving boxes. Boxes that Samuel absolutely wasn't allowed to touch, except they had to be arranged in the right order. Harriet couldn't stand that box number five was after number seven. It was incorrect, she insisted, and must be corrected.

Harriet had significant renovation plans underway. Just a few weeks after Harriet moved in, a bunch of guys started tearing down a large closet in the middle of the house. The entire room was covered with concrete and steel. Worse than the worst bomb shelter, Samuel thought.

The construction workers worked for several weeks and installed all sorts of technology. Along the concrete-clad steel walls hung colourful cables like the worst reggae hairstyle. A reinforced door marked the entrance to the closet, next to it stood a small white pillar with a glowing fingerprint reader on top. Harriet told Samuel that he had no access here. Never, ever!

The door remained closed, and Samuel had no idea what was in the boxes Harriet had brought in. It must be very valuable, thought Samuel, something much more valuable than the cost of the renovation.

Harriet was wealthy, he knew that, but he didn't understand why she was renovating in this way, at this enormous cost. Clearly, it wasn't a shelter for him and the neighbours.

Harriet was single, but it hadn't always been that way. A few years ago, she had a relationship with a man, a young and handsome gentleman. They had both visited Alice and Leopold, and they had all gone to a restaurant. There were crystal chandeliers, white tablecloths, and waiters in tails. Harriet had paid for the whole feast because she was a multimillionaire, as Alice had told Samuel. It had been nice, and Leopold could be seen happy that his sister had found a life partner, even though the young man seemed a bit strange. He never listened to anyone but himself, and Leopold was annoyed that the man kept starting new dialogues all the time.

"It's like talking to an answering machine," Leopold yelled when they returned after eating lobster and drinking wine that cost five thousand pounds.

But only a year later, it ended between Harriet and the answering machine. Somehow, Harriet knew it would happen. She said she had tried a hundred times to get him back, but each attempt hurt so much that she gave up. Samuel didn't quite understand what she meant by that.

Afterward, Harriet chose to live alone. Samuel reminded himself that Harriet had called his mom and dad on the morning of the fateful day when his parents were hit. She had warned them not to take the car. Something terrible would happen. Leopold had laughed and called her silly.

"Have you become clairvoyant in your old age?" He had laughed loudly. "Have you started reading horoscopes? You always say that stuff is bullshit."

Harriet had called several times and tried to stop them, but Leopold didn't care.

Did she know what would happen? Samuel wondered.

Often, Samuel got the feeling that she really was clairvoyant. But that's impossible; that's what she's trying to prove in her lectures?

A strange incident was when Harriet woke Samuel up early one morning and explained that Samuel couldn't take the bus to school.

"Car?" Samuel wondered.

"We're walking!"

"Have you thought about how strange it is that the municipality charges people for taking the bus?"

A few leaves swirled around on the sidewalk, the sun shone through the trees, it was a beautiful morning.

"What do you mean? That's not why we're going to university today?"

"No, it costs money to take the bus to work. It's a small punishment, charging, I mean. Taking the bus should be free, or even better, people should get paid when they take the bus."

"Paid, so dumb, how would that work?" Samuel shook his head and looked hesitantly at his aunt; she rarely jokes.

"Simple, when you get on the bus, the driver gives you a coin. Then we would have considerably fewer cars in the cities, and the municipality wouldn't have to build new wider roads, costly intersections, and other roadworks. The municipality could surely afford this and still make a profit."

"But then people could jump on the bus just to make money. How would that work?"

"Yes, but you have to get off to be able to jump on, and then you have to wait for the next bus."

"Maybe you could arrange it so that you only get paid twice a day?"

"Punish people for taking the bus, so incredibly dumb!"

Samuel looked at his aunt, and he realised she wasn't joking.

As they approached the school, Harriet looked more and more at her wristwatch.

"Some things are inevitable," she suddenly said, and Samuel wondered what she meant. Shortly afterward, a car came at high speed and crashed into the bus, the bus Samuel was supposed to have been on. A truck had trouble stopping, swerved away, and ran over a small sports car. Several cars collided from different directions, turning the entire intersection into a tumult of vehicles and running people. Screams mixed with revving engines. In the distance, screeching tires and another bang were heard.

Harriet sighed and dialled 112. She reported that there were five dead and over thirty injured. Then she walked straight across the street to a small Skoda that had been badly squeezed. She opened the back door. That's when Samuel saw the child crying in the back seat. Without looking at the front seat, Harriet unfastened the child and held it tightly in her arms. Samuel ran up to the car.

"The mom is dead," Harriet said. "We'll leave the child at the school's reception. The little boy's name is Joe, and the woman in the car is Ellen Coghill. We can't do anything more. Ambulance and police will soon arrive and take care of all this."

Samuel didn't know anyone named Coghill and asked if Harriet knew Ellen and the child in any way.

"No," she replied shortly, almost a little surprised. "Why? The woman is dead."

Harriet never got sick or injured for that matter. It was as if she knew what would happen and avoided those places. She could suddenly take another route to work or not go to work at all. Shortly afterward, you could hear on the traffic radio about queues, sometimes accidents, and other stops. But it also happened that Harriet was in the right place at the right time. Once, she ran into Richard Gere when he got out of a taxi at the airport. Once she was on the beach, and Brad Pitt showed up to film a short scene by the docks. There stood Harriet, looking not at all surprised, just devoted.

3 The Flying Yellow Taxis

At the end of a lecture, a student asked Professor Hanson about the speed of light.

"If I travel in a spaceship at the speed of light while dropping an atomic bomb behind me, shouldn't I increase the speed even more?"

A distant muted cough was heard in the crowded room. Harriet knew that many of her students struggled to grasp Einstein's theory of relativity. They had simply learned that it is so and didn't really understand. If they were to whisper that, they would appear ignorant, so it was especially quiet when this question came up. Admirable of the student to have the courage to raise the issue in front of all their classmates.

"Imagine that everything in the entire universe is static, nothing can move. Every molecule is immovable. Everything is frozen, everywhere. Nothing is happening. Moving is impossible; not even radio waves can move. It's as if time stood still. There is no time. Light stands still. The water droplet in your kitchen faucet hovers in the air. The high jumper floats a centimetre above the bar; not even the pants flutter. The waves in the sea have solidified, with the foam floating around. The Earth has stopped in its orbit around the sun. Not even the black holes can suck in anything; everything is frozen in a moment."

Professor Hanson stood still for a few seconds before continuing.

"That's how the universe would look if the flying yellow taxis didn't exist."

A few muted uncertain laughs were heard.

"When you want to move a finger, the taxis quickly pack up all the parts of your finger, throw them in the back seat, and drive away. Drive a few centimetres to the place where you wanted the finger. Then they quickly unpack everything, so fast that we don't notice anything. The same thing happens when you cycle. The little taxis disassemble and assemble, both you and your bike, for every meter you move. They are fast, incredibly fast, but they can't drive faster than three hundred thousand kilometres per second. That's the maximum the little yellow taxis can handle. Without them, we wouldn't be able to move, nothing would happen. The universe would never have existed, and there would be no time. The Big Bang would have just been a frozen lump, a single large motionless singularity."

Harriet took a sip of water. The student who asked the question had long since sat down.

"If you were to travel in a spaceship at very high speed, you push your little taxis to the limit. They can't move you and your ship faster, even if a supernova were to explode behind you. That's why nothing in the universe can move faster than the speed of light. Even light uses the little taxis. It's thanks to them that we can move. Think. Love. Exist."

Harriet unscrewed the cap of her water bottle and filled her glass. After a while, whispers began, and Harriet continued, this time a bit improvised.

"But progress is fast. If we were to tell a person from the 1600s about our paved roads and cars driving at a hundred and fifty on five-lane highways, they wouldn't believe it. Think of our mobile phones; they would have been entirely unthinkable a hundred years ago. Therefore, it can be challenging to know what will happen in the future. Perhaps we can create a new material that is not composed of our atoms. That material would be in another dimension and not be bound by the natural laws of our world. They wouldn't have yellow taxis to move everything. Instead, they have small blue jet planes that go much faster. If we built a spaceship with that material, it could move faster than the speed of light. At least faster than our light."

Harriet looked at the students sitting closest to see if they understood. Doubtful, she thought, and continued to explain.

"I have no idea how to create such material. And how would we communicate with the ship? It could travel to the Andromeda galaxy in a few seconds, but how does it find its way there? And it would have a hard time finding its way back to us. We wouldn't see the ship either; it's as if it didn't exist. We'll have to make do with our little yellow taxis; they do an excellent job!"

4 Is Everything an Illusion?

One evening, Harriet was determined to go to the hospital. Samuel was to accompany her; it was crucial. Upon arrival at the emergency room, she insisted that they monitor her. She claimed that she could have a heart attack at any moment. The nurse asked about the symptoms Harriet had experienced, what made her suspect a heart attack. Harriet responded irritably, casting threatening glances at everyone in white coats.

"I haven't come here for any symptoms; I'm here because I'm going to have a heart attack! Don't you understand? A heart attack!"

After providing the necessary information, the nurse asked Harriet and Samuel to sit in the waiting room.

At 8:03 PM, Harriet was placed in a room. The nurse checked her blood pressure and then connected an EKG.

"Wait here; I'll be back shortly," she said and left the room.

At 8:32 PM, the heart attack occurred. Thanks to Harriet being on-site, the medical team quickly assisted her. Samuel was not as surprised as the nurse who had admitted the professor.

Harriet recovered quickly and was already home after a week. Short walks were a way for her to exercise.

"I'm going to start exercising," she said on several occasions.

But just a week later, she had to visit the hospital again. They had discovered a brain tumour, a malignant cancerous tumour. Samuel thought that the tumour was something Harriet couldn't have predicted.

Despite her cancer, Harriet wanted to continue her lectures at the university, and within days, she was back on the podium in a packed auditorium. She was greeted with warm applause.

"What I'm about to tell you didn't happen in reality, and some details may seem illogical. But I urge you not to get stuck in the details. The important thing is to follow the story and create an image of the world that I will try to visualise."

The professor rounded the lectern and stood in front.

"We are mostly made of emptiness. If my body were placed in a black hole, I would be compressed and become so small that you wouldn't be able to see me. Atoms are mostly empty space, with a force field that repels everything—light, sound, and even if you touch them. Without that force field, we could easily pass through each other. If we stood up, we would slide down through the Earth's surface, straight through the floor, and simply disappear. Did you know that if an atomic nucleus were the size of a pea, the first electron shell would be five hundred meters away? That's how vast the emptiness in your body is. Enlarge an atom and place it in Paris. Put the atomic nucleus pea a bit above the top of the Eiffel Tower, and the electron shell would be at ground level. From the ground, you wouldn't see the atomic nucleus, the tiny pea, floating far above the tower's antennas. Everything would look completely empty. This applies to you, me, and all the other atoms in the entire universe."

Back at the lectern, Harriet looked down at her notes.

"You may have heard of New Kiruna in northern Sweden? Beneath the city lies a massive ore deposit that mining companies want to start exploiting. Therefore, they are building a new city nearby. When the old city is destroyed, and the residents have moved, mining will begin. One of the companies forced to relocate is Kiruna Screen AB. They have delivered screens to Apple and Samsung for many years. They are simply the world's best at screens. Most recently, they have created a production line with extremely high-resolution screens for TVs, phones, and laptops. The resolution is nearly at the molecular level. The production line is as wide as a football field, and with it, they can produce screens of all sizes. They can make a high-resolution screen that covers an entire building."

Harriet looked up at the high ceiling of the auditorium.

"Unfortunately, multinational companies are not interested in such an exclusive screen... yet. They don't want development to happen too quickly. They must always have something better to offer, release a new technicality one at a time, only one per year. It would be foolish to sell the best screen already, as the CEO of Apple replied when Leonard Fors, the research chief at Kiruna Screen AB, demonstrated the screen's excellence."

Here, Harriet took a short pause before continuing the story of the peculiar northern city.

"As a result of mining, Kiruna now has an abandoned football stadium. No matches are allowed there due to the risk of collapse. And absolutely no audience. Leonard Fors, the research chief, managed to rent the facility for a grand experiment. The big printer, which creates these high-resolution screens, was placed in the stadium. Then a thin layer of high-resolution screen was rolled out over the entire grass field. Another layer was added on top. The unrolled screen is thin, super thin, only three hundred micrometers. Layer after layer was laid out in the stadium. It took a few days before the thickness could be seen, even though the printer was very fast. The screens were connected to supercomputers placed in the stands, one computer in each seat."

The professor pointed and pretended to count the seats in the hall.

"A year later, the football field was covered with screens to a height of 8 meters, several million layers. All seats, and even standing places, were filled with super-fast computers. Ten to the fourteenth pixels are a lot to keep track of."

Harriet drew a ten and fourteen in the air with her finger.

"Then the experiment began! The computers kept track of the pixels on the screens, the colours they had around them, on the side, above, and below. Then rules were created for how they related to each other. Some colours clumped together, really stuck together, while others repelled each other. A dark pixel has more mass than a light one; the coloured pixel is harder to move to a new pixel. Energy was transmitted through the pixels, much like light and electricity. Bright pixels sent the energy forward, darker pixels absorbed the energy and gained an energy value, as if they could store heat. It became an artificial world, but one that couldn't be controlled. It's essential to emphasise that this wasn't like a computer game where designed characters make pre-programmed movements. Here, there was nothing predetermined, just a bunch of coloured dots jumping between pixels, keeping an eye on the light points next to them. That's all."

The professor waited for a while before continuing.

"Now the light points began to cluster, forming advanced formations. The hope was that some bonds would start reproducing. This became another dimension of a molecular soup. Here, the researchers had some parameters they could change and experiment with. A very significant finesse was that they could control time in the model. They could simply speed up the pace of all interactions, as if time were going very fast. In a week, they could simulate several thousand years. This was not noticeable in the virtual world, much like we don't notice time passing a bit faster when we are at high altitudes. This was made possible by optimising interactions, where a pixel that wasn't in motion didn't update as often. A stone lying still doesn't require much computing power. A pixel-fish swimming requires more computing power. Initially, there were no stones, just a weightless soup. The researchers changed the parameters gradually, and eventually, they produced small groups of pixels that could reproduce. The computers knew nothing about this; they only handled colour, energy, and the position of one pixel at a time. The living clusters were something that occurred beyond the computers' actual influence.

Curiously, the researchers slowed down and took screenshots to try to create a three-dimensional image of what was going on inside. All they found was a soup of light in different colours. But with several images in a row, they could see that some light points were connected and moving."

Harriet's pause created some tension in the room.

"The researchers then continued to run the facility at high speed. After millions of years of development in the large cluster of screens, they found something resembling plants. Shortly after, detached shapes appeared, moving in the soup. Glowing clusters that seemed to swim, eating small energy-filled light groups. Other pixel-fish ate smaller pixel-fish. Still, everything was just light somehow connected. But remember, there were no polygons and AI like in our video games. Then it was time to program and apply gravity. Darker pixels were pulled downward; the brightest pixels strove upward, other pixels were not affected at all or only slightly by gravity. This increase occurred slowly and over a long time, several thousand years in the cube. Soon, creatures were created that wandered in something resembling forests. Something passed at the tops of trees, flew; others crawled among the dark pixels at the bottom. It is fascinating to think that the compact mass of screens contained life and movement. The screens were a compact mass of several thousand tons, totally impossible to penetrate, yet birds flew easily at high speed inside, in their dimension."

Harriet mimicked a bird with her arms, slowly, like a gliding eagle.

"At one point, everything stopped. No life, no movements could be registered. The researchers had no idea what had happened. There was speculation about over establishment of some species; others talked about a mysterious disease, a virus? After months of troubleshooting, they gave up; they found nothing that could cause this mass death. But everything was still. What would they do? The project had been going on for several years. Would they be forced to start over from the beginning? Then someone came up with the brilliant idea of reversing time. Just as they could control the speed and even stop time, they could, of course, run the virtual world backward."

It was quiet in the room; everyone listened with excitement to the professor's story.

"Already in the first attempt, after a while, they could see movements again, this time backward. The thought struck them that when they turn time in the right direction, the mass death will return. They had to influence something. Make a change. But they had no way to prevent events in the world. It was like another dimension. Inaccessible."

Here, Harriet fell silent and looked down at the floor. Found her bag at her feet. There she had her water bottle. It was plastic, and it didn't matter when she deliberately dropped it and let it roll a bit away from the podium. It was only when it stopped that Harriet began to move toward the bottle.

"As you have probably already figured out, they could change gravity. It was an easy way to affect the artificial world. The moment the researchers turned time back in the right direction, they increased gravity, but very slightly. What would happen now? It can't really affect so much, one might think, but it would turn out to cause extensive changes."

Harriet picked up the bottle, opened it, took a sip.

"At first, the large birds had difficulty taking off from the ground. Their prey animals quickly increased in number. The ground-dwelling predators had plenty of food, both small animals and birds that couldn't fly. Even the predators increased, although they couldn't run as fast as before due to their new weight. Evolution quickly corrected this change; soon, there were flying creatures again, but the most important thing was that this time, there was no sudden mass death. After millions of simulated years, the researchers could sense a creature that seemed capable of communicating with its kind. One could say they were small human-like figures. Short and robust because the researchers chose a slightly higher gravity than on Earth. The researchers found two of the creatures that often seemed to stand and talk to each other. They were named Frodo and Sam."

Harriet looked out over the audience. It was silent. At the back, there were some empty seats. Everyone looked at her, and she wanted everyone to have the vision of this experiment in their minds as she continued the story.

"Now we come to your part in this experiment. This can be very challenging, but I urge you to try. Those who get stuck in small illogical details will not understand, but that's just a shame for them."

Harriet waited for a short while.

"Imagine that you are Frodo or Sam. The two creatures who grew up in this pixel world after several generations of evolution. Can you see them in front of you? You are in this world, which has looked like this since you were born. You know nothing else. The world is square because you've heard that there are those who have walked to all corners of the world. You've also observed that there are corresponding corners up in the air. You have no idea what's outside. Sam tells Frodo that he believes the world is not as it seems. We are just small light points, charges, and not as compact and heavy as we perceive ourselves to be. Weight is an illusion. Everything is just light. Frodo laughs and thinks Sam is ridiculous. How can he believe something so stupid? He asks him to pick up a stone next to them on the ground. A pixel-stone. Sam picks it up. It's a fairly large stone, and Sam feels its weight in his hand; it is compact, and it is pulled strongly downward. There is a force. Frodo continues to laugh and wonders how he can believe that it's just light points; he can feel the weight, the stone is hard, compact. If he lets it go, it will fall straight down. It can't just be light points; it's utterly absurd. Absurd idea!"

Harriet squatted down and put the water bottle back in the bag. She wasn't in a hurry; everyone would have time to think through everything that had been said. When she stood up again, she continued with a serious tone.

"Now look around in this room. Look at your fellow students. What do you see? Is the world really as compact, heavy, and stable as you perceive it? We know that most of it is empty space. Could it be that we consist only of some kind of force field-laden light points? Weight is just an illusion? We know that Sam was right, but he couldn't convince Frodo. Who are you yourself, Frodo or Sam?"

5 HARRIET ON TV

"Tonight, we welcome Professor Harriet Hanson, researcher, scientist, and lecturer in theoretical physics at Oxford University."

The red lamp outside the door had lit up, and the fifteen people in the audience had squeezed into the simple chairs. It was crowded. Fortunately, Samuel had secured a seat in the front row. Darkness filled the room behind him, but on the stage, it was bright. On a small podium sat Harriet. She looked surprisingly calm and relaxed. The red dress was a departure from Samuel's expectation of her usual jeans attire. On the other side of the minimal table sat the host. A large black beard sprouted below the black-rimmed glasses. Dark brown shirt, slightly too small.

"You've been in the media lately for refusing to take an intelligence test. Tell us! What happened?"

Harriet looked at the man and wondered if all people, women and men, had beards before, and for some reason, women lost that genetic trait. No one wanted to be with a bearded woman; they simply didn't have children. Or was it that no one had beards during the Stone Age, and suddenly hair began to grow around the mouths of men? A punishment from the gods? Perhaps for hitting women on the head with their wooden clubs?

"IQ tests focus on specific skills, not how intelligent a person really is. It shouldn't be called an intelligence test; rather, an SS test, Special Skills test. We all have a hundred percent skills, distributed differently, but still, a hundred percent. So, some are good at counting, others have strong willpower, memory, endurance, musicality, artistic ability, compassion, etc. The brain is like a car; some models have a lot of horsepower and are super fast but can't be driven off-road. If you take a sports car on a road trip, you only bring a toothbrush. In the motorhome, you can fit everything and more, but it doesn't behave like a Ferrari on the racetrack. While there are numerous models available, no single car excels in every aspect. What car do you drive yourself?"

The beard stiffened at the unexpected question.

"Hmm... I don't have a driver's license!"

"Well, there you go," laughed Harriet. "That's also a variation."

At this point, Harriet paused and took a sip from the glass of mineral water on a small table between them.

"Making a simple calculator that calculates super fast is relatively easy; it doesn't require many transistors. But making a calculator feel understanding and compassion for another calculator requires much more. Much more. This is not included in the so-called IQ test.

Just the fact that those with a certain IQ score form a club suggests that they have too much of one thing and lack a lot of something else."

"Vanity is strong in some," mumbled the beard.

"Yes, unfortunately, that's the case. IQ companies, because they are profit-driven companies that create IQ tests, thrive on selling their tests. So, it was in their interest for me, as a professor of theoretical physics, to take their test. But it won't prove anything. The interesting thing is that if I were to take their test, I couldn't fail."

"Ha ha, that's a bold statement. What makes you think that?"

"After all, the peppers at the IQ company aren't completely seedless. If I did well on their test, over a hundred and fifty, it would be useful in their marketing. If, on the other hand, I scored only ninety, they would either hide the test or simply come up with a better result. I'm popular in popular science; many assume I have a high IQ. A test showing that I have a low IQ would be dEvestating for a company that relies on IQ tests. So, I simply declined."

"Hmm," mumbled the beard, but before he could open his mouth, the professor continued her monologue.

"An even number is chosen as the norm, one hundred, and it's interesting. The intelligence level of humans is very unique. It's at a very specific level. About two hundred thousand years ago, a mutant was born somewhere in Africa. The little child had an enormously large head, not like the other children but a grotesque lump of a skull. However, the child had a good upbringing and much love from its parents. It quickly became apparent that the large brain was no disadvantage; the child was both clever and smart. The girl secured a good position in the group and, as an adult, had many children. A new species had been created on Earth. If the intelligence level of that species had been a bit lower, the species would have continued to live in paradise, collecting its fruits and hunting piglets at sunset for several million years thereafter. The species would have coexisted with the other animals on this planet. However, if the intelligence level had become higher than it did, they could have foreseen what would happen when the first farmer started digging into the earth to plant crops, the first worker. The others would have told him to stop trying. Look around, everything is here, the Earth belongs to us all. If you start farming, collecting more than you need, you will create something called money and work, and thus also poverty and unemployment. A few will have a lot, but most will have little or nothing. This will not only cause injustices and corruption but also world wars, weapons of mass destruction, environmental destruction, and mass deaths of Earth's animal species. We will live in huge concrete blocks, several thousand people in the same place. Work and more work, diseases, dirt, and pollution. We will eventually destroy the entire planet."

Harriet stood up. She put her hand on the host's shoulder, surprising Samuel. She leaned forward and looked him deep in the eyes, surprising Samuel even more.

"Stop your work, my friend. Come with us to the campfire instead. We've killed a deer. It hangs over the fire and will be ready when the sun goes down. Then it's party time."

The host didn't know what to say and turned, smiling, to the audience. The pimply boy with the applause sign also became uncertain but still displayed his sign. Harriet sat down and waited for the applause to quiet down before adding.

"If humans were a bit smarter, they could have foreseen what might happen and convinced the first farmer to stop his work. Humans became exactly so unintelligent that no one understood how to prevent him, unfortunately."

"But we wouldn't have hospitals or doctors? Should we let all the sick just die?"

"Healers and medicine women were very knowledgeable in the past; we don't understand how amazingly much they knew about the human body and nature, something that is completely forgotten now. The small group of hunters and gatherers took care of the sick and elderly, they were allowed to help, everyone was needed. In contrast, we place the unfit in a room, give them food, and change diapers, totally undignified for both humans and animals. Most of our diseases, moreover, we have created ourselves through environmental toxins, unhealthy environments, poor quality of life, and bad living habits. Our civilisation kills people daily in traffic accidents, workplace accidents, and people living in misery created by our technological revolution, not to mention all the weapons. Our youth commit suicide; they didn't do that a hundred thousand years ago, I can assure you.

Harriet fell silent for a moment, allowing the thought to sink in.

"For the majority of the two hundred thousand years that humanity has existed, we lived in harmony with nature, functioning as an integral part of Earth's cycle. The planet was cleaner, water was pure, the air crystal clear—no pollution, no environmental toxins. Of course, people died in nature, a natural death due to injuries and lack of advanced healthcare. However, when compared to the casualties in our high-tech civilisation—caused by carcinogens, environmental toxins, car accidents, murder, suicide, wars, and other horrors—it's a stark contrast. It's not just humans suffering and dying; animals also endure the consequences of our civilisation. To say they suffer is an understatement; animals are tortured to death, and we are causing the extinction of thousands of species every year. But if we lived in harmony with nature, these diseases and deaths wouldn't exist. Of course, we would face other causes of death. The question is, what leads to more suffering and mortality? It seems that Earth can no longer tolerate us. If we lived with nature, humans could continue to live and exist for hundreds of thousands, perhaps millions of years. Imagine how many people could live then. Now, we have many people alive, but only for a short period, as a mass death approaches, affecting both humans and animals!"

The unsettling topic made the host nervously shuffle through his notes to find another subject to discuss.

"Hm... they say that if dolphins had thumbs, they would rule the Earth. But the latest research report shows that the intelligence of these animals is clearly exaggerated."

"Yes, I read that report. Dolphins struggled with our IQ tests, quite a challenge for them. The creature that performed the best was the starfish. But it wasn't clear if it only succeeded in answering some questions because of its shape or if it genuinely thought through the answers. Later, I heard that dolphins conducted their own IQ test on humans, where humans performed poorly, a very weak result. Dolphins swam, jumped, twisted, made noises, and wriggled in various logical patterns, but their trainer saw no correlation —he just whistled and pointed with his whole arm, seemingly not understanding anything at all."

"Ha ha," laughed the host. "But that's not why you're here?"

"Exactly, that's not why I'm here."

"Tell us."

"I've always been healthy, never been hospitalised. But not long ago, something happened in my brain. I felt that something was off. Something was wrong. Besides dizziness and short bouts of headaches, there was something more—a thought that was active simultaneously with my thoughts."

"That sounds strange. Were you about to become schizophrenic?"

"No, nothing like that. I am fully aware and have no difficulties with it. The problem is that it turned out to be a brain tumour. Something that created new pathways in my brain. It opened up my perception, my vision of the world. Now I can see how the world works, how everything looks, from the smallest detail to the entire universe."

"What do you see then?"

"There is no smallest particle. The smallest we will find is a large unit filling the entire universe—that's what we float around in. We hover. I can also say that the universe is not as vast as it appears. The universe has a diameter of only 4.65 billion light-years. It's still unimaginably huge but significantly smaller than what we've been taught."

"But... how is that possible? I thought we could see farther with our telescopes?"

"Yes, it may seem strange, but the universe is an enormous sphere, and there is nothing beyond it. It's actually incorrect to say *beyond* because there is nothing there, and *there* is, therefore, incorrect to say. No time, no void, nada!"

"Oh?"

"It's very difficult to imagine; I never understood it myself before, but my brain tumour gives me an image that makes it comprehensible. This sphere reflects everything—light and radio waves, 100% reflection. The light from a galaxy travels through space, reaches the sphere's end, and everything reflects back. What we see in our telescopes is a reflection of the galaxies around us. Just a few billion years ago."

"Okay," hesitated the host.

"The fascinating thing about this is that we can see how all galaxies have moved until now, how they collided and merged, and sometimes just brushed against each other. With good telescopes, we will see the Milky Way, our own galaxy, from a distance. We will find several versions out there, at different ages. We will be able to see the Sun and perhaps the Earth spinning around. With a super good telescope, we will see dinosaurs. For real. It's amazing!"

The host couldn't quite keep up towards the end. He nodded as if his glasses were about to fall off.

"Yes, that would be amazing."

"We will also discover that the universe is only 79 minutes old! 79 minutes and 7.356 seconds to be exact."

"Oh, that can't be possible. The professor must be joking?"

"Our bodies are adapted to our life here on Earth. It's no coincidence that the amount of oxygen in the air is perfectly suited to our lungs, and gravity has the right intensity in relation to our bone strength. The same goes for time. We have optimised our experience of time to fit us perfectly. Maximised for our survival. A fly has a different perception of time. It sees a hand approaching in good time, leaps into the air to flap away calmly. It turns around in the air, flies backward, and sticks out its tongue. But there's something we don't have time to see. Imagine two ants meeting on a tree trunk. With their antennae, they tell each other about what they had for breakfast, tomorrow's weather, and the best lunch spot for the day. For us, the meeting is over in a tenth of a second. The perception of time is individual. If we flew at very high speed past Earth and decided to have a video call, people on Earth wouldn't understand what we were saying. We would speak so slowly, and the image would almost stand still. However, we would think that people on Earth were rushing around like in an anthill. Super fast. The voices would be so high-frequency that it would create a whistling sound. Completely impossible to understand. Time is individual; it changes depending on our speed and position but is also different for different creatures. Both here and on other planets."

The beard turned his note with the question he planned to ask in case the guest turned out to be laconic. No notes were needed here.

"But 79 minutes?"

"Big Bang is not something that happened a long time ago. Big Bang is something happening right now, and we are right in the middle of it. We are in the midst of a large explosion, which we experience very slowly, on the verge of petrification!"

The host looked anxiously around. "Sounds dangerous. Please explain this in more detail so everyone understands."

"A small firecracker goes pfutt, a dynamite stick goes bang. A supernova doesn't make a sound, but compared to dynamite, it might sound something like; spadoooffffowshsss. Larger explosions take longer. Then we have the biggest bang of all, the Big Bang. It's an enormous explosion, but in ultra-rapid. First, gas is propelled away at high speed. It ignites like a massive firework. Stars light up and go out, twinkling, like glitter, everywhere. Light is thrown around, flying around each other, at tremendous speed. A fantastic sight. But the shimmer slows down, quickly fading away. It thins out. What remains is darkness and black holes that can't decide whether to drift off into the darkness of emptiness forever or fall back to possibly create another bang. Dynamite went off in a tenth of a second. Big Bang took two hours. The biggest explosion of all."

On the small table between them were two glasses of water. Harriet picked up the glass and took a sip, making a grunting sound to signify that she wasn't finished.

"We slow down time and zoom in. Go back halfway, just over an hour into the Big Bang. A galaxy flying at high speed collides with another, tearing them apart into a cloud of stars. A gas cloud compresses on its periphery. A star ignites. The gases and dust around it clump together, forming small balls spinning at high speed. Then the star swells, captures the dust balls, and then shrinks into a withered lump. A short while later, it drops into a black hole, on its way to infinity and beyond."

The beard probably doesn't have children, Harriet thought when she saw that the man didn't react to the last sentence.

"That was still too fast. We missed a tiny speck rotating at full speed around a glowing ball, like an electron in an electron shell. We slow down time even more, so time almost stands still. Then we see that it wasn't a tiny dust particle but a planet, and there are plants resembling mould on cheese. There is life. We find several similar inhabited rocks. On another, there are creatures calling themselves intelligent, and they have developed tests to prove this. But they have a problem; they can't understand that nothing can move faster than light? For them, time almost stands still, and they can observe how light propagates through space. What they see is a light in motion; they have even specified its speed. But we know that Big Bang is over in two hours, and the speed of light is instantaneous. Nothing can move faster. It simply depends on there being no time; time is nothing, everything is just a mass of atoms in motion."

The host smiled uncertainly, but it was hard to see through the beard. He thought he would watch the interview later and try to understand it then.

"Individual time or not. I still see that our program time here is coming to an end. But we have time for one more short question."

The man read from one of his many notes.

"Is there life in other places in the universe?"

"Of course, there is life. There are several million planets with different types of life. Some have only bacteria, others are filled with mollusks, there are also planets with huge animals, as large as dinosaurs, and there is plenty of intelligence out there. But we won't find high-tech civilisations, like the one on Earth. These are far too short-lived and exist only for a few hundred years. Perhaps we can make contact with their robots that take over after them. They can exist for a longer time."

There was silence for a while, a long time for TV.

"We thank Professor Hanson for this scientific insight, or should we say outlook. Do you have anything you want to add? Something brief?"

Harriet turned to the camera and smiled, a little slyly.

"Some say the universe is infinitely vast. That would mean we would be infinitely small. But we're not."

6 HARRIET'S FINGER

The tumour prevented Harriet from continuing her teaching. A couple of days after her TV appearance, she was admitted to the hospital and given her own monitoring room. Samuel visited her every day after school.

"Hello, how are you? The whole school sends their regards!"

"I'm doing okay, at times the pain is quite intense. But the staff here is wonderful."

"But will you be okay? How is it going to turn out?"

"There's no turning back. Death is waiting for me."

"But... are you saying!"

"It's okay. I know there's nothing after death. And thankfully so. Some believe in an afterlife, but oh, the hell one would have to endure if that were true!"

"What do you mean? It doesn't sound entirely wrong!"

"Imagine floating around and witnessing all the injustices, atrocities, tortures, child abuse, and animals suffering without being able to do anything about it. Like a restless spirit floating around, witnessing all the horror that goes on, for all eternity, without being able to do anything about it. The only pleasure would be to haunt a house and say boo!"

"Yes," laughed Samuel. "Spirits seem to have a bit of a hard time communicating with us!"

"It feels good that when this is over, there will be nothing more. I won't haunt you, wake you up in the middle of the night, and stand in some doorway whispering your name."

"Thanks, that wouldn't be very pleasant!"

"Imagine floating around among people and all you manage to do is slow down the speed of a spinning bottle during a boring séance meeting. I don't believe in such things. Luckily, everything turns black when you die."

"But... I have to ask about the secret room."

Harriet suddenly became serious.

"You must not go in there. You cannot go in there!"

"No, I just want to know. I think you can foresee events with something in there. Mom and Dad's car accident, you knew it was coming. The mass crash at the school as well, you somehow understood that it was going to happen!

"No, it just happened...!"

"George Clooney... how did you know that he... and your heart attack! You can see into the future!"

Harriet's face twisted in pain, but after a while, a short laugh followed.

"The future... this time tomorrow, Earth will have moved beyond the planet Mars. It's impossible for me to see what will happen at that distance."

"But there's something about that room, what do you have in there?"

"Nothing... soon... it's very dangerous... everything will be destroyed. If something happens to me, my lawyer has the right to take custody and destroy everything I keep in there. It's safest that way. It's too dangerous; it absolutely must not come out."

"But... what is it?" Samuel wondered.

"Life-threatening, world-threatening, a danger to the entire universe."

"But a lawyer... you've never liked..."

But Samuel was abruptly interrupted.

"No, that's true, but it's mostly what lawyers symbolise that I dislike. The fact that they are needed at all is an expression of the weaknesses and flaws of the human race. We are the only animals on this planet that need lawyers. All animals have orders and rules, but they don't need lawyers, but humans, these intelligent beings, can't do without these parasites. Moreover, they profit from crime; criminality makes them rich!"

"But I can take care of everything; you can trust me."

Harriet pondered for a moment and looked at Samuel.

"It's very complicated... it took me many years to realise that if you move a small stone, a grain of sand, it affects a lot of other things, in time and eternity. Perhaps an entire continent a few hundred years later. You can't have the weight of the world on your conscience. No human can live with that."

After the cryptic answer, Samuel chose not to ask more questions.

But he had a plan.

The tumour grew with each passing week. Harriet could no longer stand, and having a coherent conversation was no longer possible. Samuel visited her in the morning, before school. This time, he brought some things in his bag.

It was surprising that there was a bed in the small room; it felt more like a storage space for various equipment, thought Samuel as he sneaked into her room. He placed the bag at Harriet's feet. She looked like she was asleep. Her skin looked soft in the dim light. There was a calmness in her face, completely unaffected by all the messy displays and blinking lights. How beautiful she is, thought Samuel, taking her hand. It was warm and dry.

What am I getting myself into? How can I do this? But at the same time, he knew he would ponder this his whole life if he didn't complete it now. This must be done, no matter how much he loved his aunt.

What am I doing? Am I insane? A part of him wanted to drop everything and walk away. Another part compelled him to stay.

The pruning shears had a lock that held the sharp blades together. Clicking it off was a way to gather his thoughts. With a small click, the blades flew apart, and Samuel placed the shears around Harriet's left ring finger. As he pressed, he saw the skin pinch together on the delicate finger. Harriet didn't flinch.

What am I doing? I must, I must. This is the only opportunity I have to find out what Harriet has been up to. Forgive me, Harriet, forgive me, dear aunt. Then Samuel pressed down. His hand started shaking again. It was difficult at first, but then there was a crack. The shears had cut through. The detached finger stuck to the blades. Samuel winced, and despite his trembling hands, he managed to ignite the torch. Blood pulsed onto the towels and the sheet. By squeezing tightly around the base, he stemmed the flow.

As he held the hand high, he moved the burner over the wound. The smell of burning flesh filled the room, and Samuel began to feel nauseous. I can't stop now, I must continue.

"UIHHHH!"

A persistent wail echoed in the corridor outside. A sprinkler was positioned directly over the bed. Water sprayed on Samuel's neck and ran down his back. The Cream Brulee burner's metal edges sizzled as Samuel hastily stowed his belongings in the bag. Two nurses, both wielding umbrellas, stormed into the room just as he deftly rolled the fingertip into a towel.

A wet Samuel looked at them in surprise. One nurse pulled out the plastic curtains from behind the equipment and carefully covered the machinery. The other nurse shared her umbrella with Samuel.

"There's a glitch in the system, it's oversensitive. We sincerely apologise," she shouted, trying to drown out the noise. "It has happened before!"

Samuel didn't listen but was busy concocting an explanation.

"Harriet wanted one last smoke, I didn't think and lit a cigarette for her."

No one heard what he said, but the nurse nodded happily

The wailing in the corridor stopped just as the sprinkler in the ceiling sputtered and only managed a few drops. Samuel held Harriet's hand; the wound looked fine, but all the blood and water had turned the bedding pink.

"Um, I was cleaning the wound she got when we arrived. She caught her finger in the car door, as you may recall."

Together, they bandaged the remaining stump. Harriet then got a clean and dry bed."

7 Lawyer Dayton Secures the House

When Samuel returned home, he placed the fingertip in the fridge next to the liverwurst. He wouldn't have time for breakfast and went straight to school.

Tense from the morning's events, he tried to keep up with the morning lecture. How would it go for Harriet? How could he do this to her? What had he done? What madness! Cut off a finger from his sick and dying aunt?

At lunch, two police officers entered the cafeteria. After talking to some kitchen staff, they approached Samuel's table. Thoughts raced through his mind. What has happened? Harriet? I wouldn't have cut off the finger!

He was asked to follow and left his half-eaten lunch sausage on the table. Classmates looked at him in surprise as the two police officers walked on either side of him. Like a criminal, he was placed in the police car, still without explanation. When the car entered the hospital area, Samuel became certain that something had happened to Harriet. But why police officers? Had she woken up and reported him? Or was it the nurse? No, what have I actually done?

At the door to Harriet's room, one of the policemen stopped to guard the corridor. The other pushed Samuel into the room and closed the door.

It was dark. Warm and stuffy. Next to Harriet's bed stood a small man who introduced himself as lawyer Dayton, Andrew Dayton. Hair was absent from both his face and skull. The brown pants looked peculiar against the light jacket, as if he had been dipped halfway into a well of some strange sludge.

On Harriet's table were an electric light and a Bible. Harriet would never have placed that book there.

Samuel understood that she had given up, couldn't take it anymore. He felt sad and desperate, but forced himself to push away the selfish thoughts and focused on Harriet. The painful time. The pain and suffering. This was still the best for her.

"Now you'll see," said the man with the brown pants, casually throwing Harriet's blanket aside. He tore open Harriet's hand where one finger was missing.

"And what has happened here?"

Harriet looked fine lying there. They had dressed her in her favourite blouse, the colourful one. Her face was smooth and fine. She was beautiful. Silent, except for the little man who held her hand straight up in the air.

"Harriet had severe cancer..." Samuel began but was quickly interrupted.

"I mean the finger, of course, it's gone!" The lawyer shook Harriet's hand, making the fingers flutter back and forth.

"She caught her finger in the car door when we were on our way here. She was confused, and..." Samuel was interrupted again.

"But where is it then, HER RING FINGER!" The lawyer pulled Harriet's arm, making her whole body seem to move.

"The finger fell on the street; a dog took it and trotted away. I thought about following, but couldn't leave Harriet alone. She was bleeding heavily from the wound," Samuel answered.

The lawyer grinned; he didn't like what he heard and looked deeply into Samuel's eyes.

"This is, in fact, a special finger that Miss Hanson uses... on special occasions." The policeman at the door snickered, and lawyer Dayton realised his somewhat clumsy wording.

"The finger is of great importance to my investigation as her lawyer," he corrected himself and fumbled for the alarm button. When he finally found it, he proudly pressed the button. A red light came on. A faint beep was heard in the corridor outside.

It didn't take long before a nurse came in. Samuel recognised her. She was the one who helped him with the wound when he cut off his aunt's finger.

"There's a missing finger here," the lawyer said loudly and shook Harriet's hand in the air again. The man was so excited that his voice cracked, as if he were going through puberty.

"We've taken care of the wound as best we could," the nurse apologised.

"When did the finger disappear? Where is it?" The lawyer spat in the air as he shouted.

"The hand looked like this when she was admitted. She apparently got stuck in a door. Isn't that right?" The nurse looked questioningly at Samuel. The Crème Brulée torch must have made the wound look older, he thought. What luck.

The lawyer smiled irritably; he felt deceived. The mumbling that followed was barely audible, as if he were thinking out loud to himself.

"But I don't need that damn finger,... the codes, I have the codes."

With that, Samuel had to leave the room. When he closed the door behind him, he could hear the lawyer screaming at the policeman.

"There's nothing more to find here. This unfortunate woman has passed away, and her damn finger is missing. Now we must act swiftly!"

No police car was in sight as Samuel approached home. Sweat ran down his back after running almost the entire way. There was no time to change the shirt because now it would happen. Now it must happen. He would enter the secret room.

The door was untouched. Everything was quiet. From the fridge, he had taken Harriet's finger. It was cold. Damp.

Carefully, he pressed Harriet's fingertip against the turquoise little glass window. There was a small beep, and then he was prompted to enter a PIN code. He had seen Harriet use the four-digit code before. At the same time, he discovered that Harriet always used her left ring finger on the detection pad. With shaky hands, he typed in 1, 8, 7, and finally 8, Lise Meitner's birth year. It clicked, and the heavy security door began to move.

8 Jasmine Wakes Up

Jasmine Saunders woke up quietly and gently. Her eyes stuck in the damp darkness, but she could sense that she was in a long, narrow box, or was it a coffin? Warmth spread like flames through her cold body. What is warm, and what is cold? Her face was lit up by a large red button with the text EJECT. A cascade of heat spread through her body as she tried to move. Hard and cold, it rubbed and hurt. Strange tubes protruded from arms, legs, hands, and feet, everywhere. A persistent beeping came from somewhere near her feet, or was the sound above her head? Cool drops ran along her naked body, mixing with the water pools beside her.

Jasmine Saunders's real name was Ishani Sharma. She was born in Birholi, India. Her parents had died when she was only four years old, and Jasmine had grown up with her grandparents in a small house just outside the village. Both parents had worked spraying cotton plants. With insecticides. They never used any protective gear. They were promised that it was safe, by both the company and the authorities. The cause of death was never determined, but most suspected it was the toxins. They had coughed up blood for several weeks before finally falling asleep for good.

Much later, when Ishani was eighteen, a strange person visited. Billy Goldman Saunders, the man who invented the resealable soda and beer can. Actually, he didn't come up with the packaging himself but borrowed the idea from someone he called a friend. Anyway, Billy was now one of the richest people in the world and getting richer every day. Despite his immense wealth, he never shared his prosperity. He would rather scrap his Ferrari when he got tired of it than let anyone buy it. He absolutely didn't want to see anyone else driving his used car.

Despite his enormous wealth, Billy continued to expand his business. Cans were big, but plastic bottles were even bigger. A million plastic bottles were sold every minute worldwide. Billy knew that. But breaking into the plastic bottle industry with a new product was challenging. So Billy came up with a new product. A bottle made of corn and potatoes. Made of starch. A bioproduct. He called it bioplastic.

With good marketing, he managed to sell his new product. The key was to create a need among the people. The environmental movement was happy to help, without compensation. Scientists and professors worldwide produced research reports on the advantages of bioplastic, for a fee, of course. Newspapers gladly published these for free, which Billy laughed at every time it happened. This product cost a little more to produce, but consumers gladly paid this extra cost and more. Whether bioplastic improved the climate was highly doubtful, but it eased people's guilt about the environment. Bioplastic sold very well, anyway.

This meant that Billy earned even more on his bottle than if it had been made of regular plastic. The fact that he later used crude oil in his production meant that he made a lot of money. It was the same plastic as in all other bottles, but it had a green symbol and the text BIOPLAST.

Brilliant idea. You had to be smart if you wanted to become richer than the richest.

But there was one thing Billy couldn't buy with money: blood, red blood cells with a specific blood type. Only a few people in the world had Billy's type, PK43. In the event of an accident or emergency surgery, there would be no blood for him, he knew that. Even if he were to throw all his billions into it. So Billy arranged and paid for a large blood group investigation. It was very extensive, worldwide. He then found several people with PK43. Many were older. Some were children. He applied to adopt the children but was constantly rejected by the authorities. Despite his appeals, bribes, renegotiations, and even more bribes, he couldn't get any adoption approved.

He also found a young woman in India with this blood type. He promised a generous maintenance to the girl's grandparents and to start an investigation into the toxins that the girl's deceased parents had been forced to use in their work in the fields.

Billy then married Ishani shortly thereafter. Not because she was tall, intelligent, and beautiful, but to get a blood depot. The marriage ensured that there would always be a living body in the luxury villa, with blood and human spare parts. A guarantee. A reassurance for an anxious and frightened billionaire.

Ishani then called herself Jasmine, just like her grandmother always did. After the quick wedding ceremony, she was Jasmine Saunders.

A Ferrari goes very fast and requires an experienced driver. In a traffic accident, they were both seriously injured, and Billy ordered the doctors to take Jasmine's life because he needed her blood and organs for his own survival. The doctors refused even though they were all promised several million. However, he died on the operating table from his injuries, and Jasmine could instead be saved with organs from her late and very rich husband. Thus, almost half of her body was replaced, including her lung, liver, kidneys, one hip, and even her heart came from her late and very wealthy husband.

Unfortunately, Jasmine had complications with these implants. The problems were difficult to correct, and Jasmine chose to freeze herself in the hope that doctors in the future could fix it.

She wiggled her cold fingers and tried to lift one arm. A cascade of warmth pulsed all the way up to her head. The arm felt heavy and stiff. The whole body had to help lift the hand toward the button above her head. She had no idea what would happen, but she had realised that the only thing she could do was to press.

Click!

At first, nothing happened. Then a whirring sound started, the entire bed began to move. The red button disappeared upwards, and cold air streamed towards her damp thighs. The coolness then spread over her entire body. The bed stopped abruptly, and in the light of a few green emergency exit signs, she could sense that she was in the middle of a large room, many meters above the ground.

Hysterically, she tore off all the cables and tubes sticking out of her body. Despite the dizziness, she sat up with her feet dangling over the edge. The wall beside her was filled with metal hatches, all with large chrome handles. The green light gleamed on the dark metal.

Where am I? How did I end up here?

Underneath her, a clicking sound was heard, and one of the hatches opened. A prolonged swoosh, and a man came out lying on a bed. It was dark, but she could see that she didn't know him from before. The man was naked, just like her. Without looking around, he removed all the tubes protruding from his body.

Then he stood up, looked around, and then staggered over to some narrow cabinets on the other side of the room. Slowly, Jasmine adapted to the darkness and saw him retrieve something; it sparkled, a small flat box. The man swore and put on a white coat from the cabinet. In a crouching position, he walked along the walls of the room. Passed a closed door and something that looked like elevator doors. At each power outlet, he plugged in a connector, cursed, and then quickly pulled out the plug. Jasmine followed him with her eyes. It was clear that he had seen her, but the man didn't seem to care.

"Damn it, there's no power anywhere, completely powerless!" he muttered after walking around the room.

"And where is all the staff? There should be people here to help me!" The roar echoed in the empty room.

In his cabinet, the man had another gadget, one with a crank. After connecting his electronic gadgets, he quickly started cranking. Only then did he look up at Jasmine.

"Maybe you should jump down and put on something; it's chilly in here, and we don't seem to get any assistance," he said and then quickly looked down to see if his phone had started charging.

"I'm Mark, by the way, Mark Goldpeak, but you might recognise me as Macie-ducey?"

Jasmine looked astonished at the man, who also looked surprised since he expected some kind of reaction from the woman above. After all, he was well-known with over a hundred million followers on YouTube.

Mark Goldpeak, an English YouTuber, better known by the name Macie-ducey. He started by posting videos where he embarrassed himself, fell clumsily, and teased motorcycle gangs. No one cared about his video clips, except for a few toddlers who didn't know better.

On one occasion, he tried to do a simple trick with roller skates. Nothing extraordinary. But Mark fell badly. As usual, he also posted it on YouTube. This clip probably wouldn't have had any views either, except for the two-year-olds, if it hadn't been for the hockey World Cup the same evening. A well-known player fell in exactly the same way. Both clips became extremely popular, and after a few days, Macie-ducey had several million followers.

He followed this up by licking toilet seats in all the city's public toilets. When he filmed himself with open flaps the next day, the number of followers doubled.

A new record was set when he decided to freeze himself. Macie-ducey would go to the future. He was so blinded by the increasing number of followers that he didn't realise what he had gotten himself into.

What Mark didn't understand and never would understand was that the naked woman on the bed was frozen before YouTubers, TikTokers, apps, selfies, followers, influencers, and everything else that dominated his world. Now he felt a responsibility to his followers and tried to get his phone working as quickly as possible. What he didn't know was that he no longer had any followers at all. There was no mobile network at all. Not even any Internet.

9 The Secret Room

Samuel watched with excitement as the sturdy steel door silently slid open. The door was thick and heavy, with nine shiny bolts, as thick as scooter cylinders. The spotlights in the ceiling illuminated the room with a cold blue glow. In the large bookshelf on the side, there were notebooks and folders in blue and green. But what caught Samuel's eye was the peculiar machine on a small table in the middle of the room. It resembled a household appliance from the fifties, but instead of a mixing bowl, there was a small round glass container. It must be in there that Harriet saw what would happen in the future, he thought.

He dared not touch the device but continued to browse the shelf, captivated by two notebooks. "Everything is light," read one. Another book that caught his interest was described as "The Direction of Time, Forward and Backward?" He also flipped through the folders and found what he believed were drawings of the peculiar food processor.

Then Samuel heard the front door open. Oh no, is the lawyer already here? He grabbed more interesting notebooks, tucking a couple of folders under his arm. They looked important. And, of course, the drawings.

The light went out as he hastily left the room just as the sturdy door slid shut behind him. In the hall stood Lawyer Andrew Dayton with his two police officers, and Samuel backed into the kitchen. The refrigerator became the hiding place for everything he had grabbed. Harriet's finger he stuffed into a yogurt jar.

The three men approached him with determined steps.

"Everything that belongs to Harriet Hanson is to be confiscated and liquidated," explained the lawyer, holding a paper in front of Samuel's face. The fridge, thought Samuel, will they empty the fridge too? He couldn't think of anything to say, and the lawyer didn't expect anything either, having already passed him. Harriet's secret room was what interested him. The door was locked, and the lawyer had a long code written on paper. After several button presses and almost as many typos, he finally got the door open. He grinned with satisfaction.

Samuel curiously watched as the men entered. Could it be seen that he had just been there? Folders, books, and notes, everything was placed in moving boxes that the police carefully taped shut. They didn't care about the labels on the folders. With a haughty posture, Lawyer Dayton walked among the boxes, overseeing the work. It was clear that he was in the way of the police, but he didn't perceive it that way. On the contrary, he felt more that the police were in his way.

When the lawyer scrutinised the peculiar machine in the centre, Samuel couldn't keep quiet any longer.

"You're welcome to leave the sewing machine. I sew my own clothes."

With a superior smile, the man observed Samuel. Moments like these were what had made him want to become a lawyer in the first place—dreams that kept him going during those difficult study evenings. He tore off a tape roll from the nearest policeman. "This one is coming too!" Then he recklessly wrapped tape around the machine. Occasionally, he looked up to see Samuel's reaction. Pull out tape. Look at Samuel. Wind tape. Look at Samuel.

When they tried to lift the machine into a moving box, it didn't fit because of all the tape. The policeman who had to carry it to the car got stuck on a loose piece of tape and stumbled at the front door. Perhaps due to all the tape, the machine held, but the man hit his head badly and rested in the car.

The rest was carried out by the other policeman, and the two cars quickly filled with folders, files, and boxes. In the emptied room stood Lawyer Andrew Dayton.

"Everything that was in here is headed for destruction. Soon destroyed. No more! "He smiled because this would be even better. He would tell the young man at the door about the upcoming probate. A substantial collection of money.

"I want you to know that Miss Hanson had a fortune equivalent to eighteen million when she passed away"

"Oops, I knew she was wealthy, but not that much," replied Samuel.

"There is only one eligible relative." The lawyer tried to look serious.

Samuel thought of his childless aunt; she would never have been able to handle children, especially not young children. Unpredictable little creatures with all sorts of sudden needs like food, comfort, and diaper changes. "Well, of course," said Samuel. "She never had any children."

"You are the only relative I have found alive, and you are also the one she mentions in the will."

The lawyer began to walk towards the front door. A small smile appeared in the corner of his mouth as he turned to Samuel.

"Miss Hanson donated her entire fortune to various organisations in the last weeks of her life." He was eager for the next sentence he would get to say. "According to the aunt's will, you inherit nothing except the house! Eighteen million! Gone! Bye-bye!" Laughing, Lawyer Andrew Dayton walked towards the car. Life is wonderful!

"Can I keep Harriet's key to the house?" Samuel wondered.

"I'll put it in the mailbox," chirped the lawyer. "You'll also get the code to the big wardrobe. Maybe you can collect soda cans in there! Ha ha!"

10 Samuel Builds a Time Regulator

Excerpt from Professor Hanson's Notebook 1:

The present has always fascinated me. There is only one *now*. But what if we could control the speed of this single *now*? Then time could move slower or faster, just like when traveling at high speed or being near a black hole. However, we wouldn't notice anything, so what does it matter? But if we can change the speed, we should be able to stop it altogether or even reverse it. What happens if we run time backward? We probably wouldn't notice anything since everything resets exactly as it was when you move time forward again. You also don't experience anything when time goes backward because you are moving things out of memory, not into memory as when time goes forward. There's nothing to remember.

We might all have experienced this, that time went backward for a short while. When time turns right again, we get a feeling that we have experienced an event before, which we might have. Many call this *déjà vu.*

A random event somewhere in the Universe could temporarily change the direction of time. But I don't know how, where, or how often it happens. Then the Earth would reverse, rotate in the opposite direction, and move back to a place it had been before.

Excerpt from Professor Hanson's Notebook 2:

The direction and speed of time are controlled by something vast, which is simultaneously smaller than the smallest. It may sound peculiar, but I mean that time is a unit that fills the entire universe, but also something where the smallest particles fetch information about their time, speed, and direction. It's a unit that is immensely large, but particles exist only in a small part, in their own fragment. In this way, time goes in the same direction throughout the universe. Time may vary between atoms, depending on their speed and position, but the present is always the same for everyone.

If one could only access this vast unit that is time, one might be able to make it go in the other direction.

Excerpt from Professor Hanson's Notebook 3:

It's about creating a rapidly rotating plasma and blasting it with a pulsating laser. The free quarks don't know where to go for a short while, whether they are up or down. Then you make a pole shift that reverses time in the object. Instantly, this spreads in the basic unit that fills the entire universe. This pole shift makes time go backward everywhere, even in the most distant galaxy. This happens immediately, everywhere. After a certain period, time turns right again. Time and the universe have an original direction that it always falls back to.

Excerpt from Professor Hanson's Notebook 4:

The grandfather paradox does not occur when time goes backward. So theoretically, one could turn back time until your grandfather was young. Nothing would prevent you from killing him, except the moral aspect, of course. You wouldn't disappear or fade away. The timeline where you were born has not disappeared; it has existed but in the future. You were born in a different future than the one waiting for us now, one without your grandfather. Your father will not be born, but it doesn't affect you. Your father lived in a different future, one where you were born. A future that has existed but will not be recreated in the same way because you killed your own grandfather.

***

Harriet's notes were so enticing that Samuel skipped school for the next few days. He studied her drawings and planned to build a similar machine, a machine that could change the direction of time. He worked in Harriet's secret room and had modified the door sensor to now recognise his own ring finger for entry.

Some details of the machine needed modernisation. Harriet had also mentioned that in her notes, things she had thought of after completing her model. A couple of weeks later, the construction began. A transparent container, unaffected by the pulse, was placed in the centre. Harriet also had such a round container on the peculiar machine that the lawyer had now destroyed. The container worked by sending a contrasting pulse that prevented time from changing within a small area. This was to communicate to oneself what had happened.

This explained everything to Samuel. Harriet had experienced the events he thought were visions. She had reversed time and could therefore know what would happen. But the tumour? Why didn't she remove it at an earlier stage?

Late one afternoon, many weeks later, the device was completed. Earlier in the day, Samuel had attended a school lecture on the cosmos and mathematics. He had trouble concentrating on the topic because his thoughts had been on the secret room and the completed time regulator. During lunch, Lawyer Andrew Dayton called, wanting to schedule a meeting to finalise Miss Harriet Hanson's probate. Laughingly, the lawyer mentioned that Amnesty International had expressed their gratitude for the millions Miss Hanson had donated.

In the evening, it was finally time to test the machine. Samuel had locked himself in the room. The device was running, and with great anticipation, he pressed the button that would change the direction of time. Time would go backward, for how long he didn't know. He hadn't placed a note in the container; it was just a test. His hand trembled slightly as he pressed the start button.

Click!

On this day, Samuel had intended to go to school. The time regulator was almost ready to use, but he didn't feel ready to test it yet. Also, an intriguing lecture on mathematical puzzles in the cosmos sounded interesting. The lecture turned out to be very informative, initially. But Samuel didn't listen to everything. His thoughts had been on the time regulator, nearly completed in the small room at home. He felt like it had been finished for many days now, and Samuel decided that tonight would be the night. Now he knew it would work.

During the lunch break, Lawyer Andrew Dayton called and wanted to schedule a meeting regarding Miss Harriet Hanson's probate. They booked a meeting for the coming week. Samuel ended the call by asking how many millions Harriet had donated to Amnesty International. "That's classified information. I'm afraid I can't disclose that," the lawyer replied.

In the evening, Samuel locked himself in the small room with the machine he had been working on for the past few months. He had a strange feeling that he had already tested it. He hadn't written a note. He dismissed the thought and pressed the button that would change the direction of time.

Click!

Cosmos and the role of mathematics in exploring the universe were the topics of a school lecture that Samuel wanted to attend. He thought he recognised the subject and considered it might be a book he had read once. Perhaps a book with a similar title? The lecture was excellent even though his thoughts were often with the machine, now nearly completed in the small room at home. It felt like it had been ready for many days, and Samuel decided that tonight would be the night.

At lunch, he hung out with some friends in the cafeteria, which served meatballs that tasted like soy. He lost his appetite when Lawyer Andrew Dayton called to schedule a meeting. Something about transferring the house to him. In the evening, Samuel had locked himself in the little room. He looked at the button that would change the direction of time. The container was empty, and he hadn't written a note. It was just a test. Fascinating if this works, he thought, and pressed the button.

Click!

Cosmos and the mathematical puzzles were the topics of today's school lecture. Samuel found it interesting but felt he already knew everything about the subject. He chose to stay home. On his way home, he stopped at the grocery store and bought lunch. He looked at pre-cooked frozen meatballs but chose a can of ravioli instead. Lawyer Andrew Dayton called during lunch, booking a meeting about Miss Harriet Hanson's probate. Samuel then asked for a breakdown of where Harriet had donated all her money, to which the lawyer replied, "That's classified information. I absolutely can't disclose it to anyone."

Samuel had suspected as much but found it amusing to ask the question. In the evening, it was time to test the time regulator. Maybe he should write a note with the time and date to put in the small sphere. Otherwise, he might not notice if it really worked, he thought. He wrote the current time and today's date on a note, also drawing a small smiley. He put it in the container, the round sphere that would not be affected by the time shift. His hand trembled slightly as he moved his finger toward the button.

Click!

Samuel was doing the final touches when he noticed there was a note in the container on the machine. He leaned forward, wondering how it got there. There were some numbers on it, and Samuel picked it up. The numbers were time indications, and the date written was almost two days into the future. Samuel started counting and exclaimed, "Forty-two hours. The time on the note is forty-two hours in the future!"

He recognised his own handwriting and wondered what he had planned to do in the next few days. That's right, he thought, in two days, I was planning to test the machine for the first time. Forty-two hours; that's the time Harriet also mentioned in her notes. The time it takes for the direction of time to be restored, to turn forward after going backward for several hours.

Fantastic, what luck! Samuel became ecstatic because everything worked. Instead of attending the lecture on cosmos and mathematics, he chose to continue working to complete the machine. Now he knew it would work.

In the following weeks, he wrote texts about what had happened and sent the notes back in time. It was incredible! Samuel relived the days over and over again. Each time, the days were new to him, but with a short text about what would happen, an ordinary day became fantastic. Of course, he chose not to relive bad days.

He tried the lottery, aiming for a small win of one to one and a half thousand pounds. The highest win might attract too much attention. He did this just to see if it worked. When the week's lottery numbers were announced, he wrote down the winning numbers on a note. Sent it back forty-two hours in time. Two days before, he submitted the ticket but deliberately wrote one digit wrong.

Even though he knew he would win, it was exciting to watch the draw on TV. It was like watching a rerun where he knew which numbers would appear.

Now, Samuel was financially independent, and it would last for a lifetime.

11 The Probate

The probate at lawyer Andrew Dayton's office was something Samuel couldn't avoid, no matter how many times he restarted time. The peculiar thing was that the lawyer himself called and wanted to postpone the meeting by two weeks. Samuel was getting tired of lawyer Dayton, whom he now referred to as lawyer Nighton, and wanted to get everything over with as quickly as possible.

"No," Samuel had said. "The probate will be held as planned."

Samuel brought Harriet's yogurt-marinated finger that he had found in the fridge. Not because he planned to give it to the lawyer, but somehow, it felt right to have it at her probate.

It was an old house, sturdy and imposing, centrally located. The building had previously been a bank. Must have been in the 1800s, Samuel guessed as he entered through the heavy door. In the foyer, everything was stone and marble. The wide staircase curved up to the second floor, where lawyer Dayton had his office. Several lawyers sat here, all with fine glass doors engraved with names in the frosted glass.

"I have a meeting with lawyer Dayton," Samuel said to the young girl behind the desk on the second floor. She was reading a women's magazine and looked a bit annoyed that Samuel was interrupting her. She must have gotten the job because she was so attractive, was Samuel's first thought.

"What was your name?"

"Samuel Hanson. The lawyer is expecting me."

"Please sit down and wait." She nodded to a small sofa on the other side of the corridor. It was probably the cheapest piece of furniture in the whole house, Samuel thought as he sat down.

The law firm reminded him of a discussion he had with Harriet once, about lawyers. He had wondered why she disliked lawyers so much. Harriet had replied that lawyers revealed human shortcomings, the absolute worst sides of humanity.

"Why is that? They try to create justice, to make everyone follow the laws we've agreed upon," Samuel had asked.

Harriet had then told a story about two neighbours, two men in this case. The effect was more evident in men, she had explained. One morning, they found a carton of milk lying on the property line between their plots. They began arguing about whose milk it was. Both claimed to be the rightful owner of the milk. One argued that it was his milk because the colours of the carton matched so well with his house. The other because his dog liked to drink milk. Neither of the men really liked milk, but justice had to be served. It was important. They agreed on that.

They each hired a lawyer, and the costs escalated. It was no longer about the carton of milk; it was about neither of the men being able to live with the other getting the milk, and they themselves going without. The men would rather spend money equivalent to several thousand litres of milk on lawyers than simply buy a carton of milk and give it to the neighbour. It's this stupidity and selfishness that lawyers symbolise. If humans were intelligent and kind beings, we wouldn't need lawyers. Maybe not even police? We might even do without politicians!

A happy thought!

Lawyer Andrew Dayton came out into the corridor and went straight to the girl with the newspaper.

"This is going really well, Abigail. You're doing great."

When Samuel heard the lawyer's fawning, he guessed that the girl probably got the job because she was the daughter of some older and significant lawyer in the firm.

After twittering for the old man's daughter, Andrew Dayton turned to Samuel. "Oh, there you are too," he laughed. They greeted each other and then went into his office.

Floor-to-ceiling bookshelves in dark wood filled the room. Even the floor and ceiling were dark. A very large desk was placed in front of the tall windows, and the lawyer nodded to one of the chairs opposite. He himself sat in a broad office chair, much too large for the small man. He began by expressing his regret.

"I intended to postpone the meeting a few weeks because all the finances weren't settled." He seemed a bit downcast, Samuel thought. Not at all as unpleasant as he usually was.

"The money that Miss Hanson donated to Doctors Without Borders ended up in the wrong account."

"How could that happen?"

"It has been discovered that someone had written the wrong account number," the lawyer said, leaning back, but the chair's suspension was too strong, and he was immediately pushed forward. To avoid laughing, Samuel looked away. That's when he noticed a little dachshund sleeping in a basket beside the table.

"Harriet would never write the wrong account number," Samuel said. "She was a numbers specialist and could recite all her account numbers by heart."

"But now the account number was incorrect," the lawyer explained.

"So someone else wrote the number?"

"Yes, that's probably how it was."

"So, you made the transfer," Samuel pointed out.

The lawyer sighed.

"Yes, the professor had asked me to make the transfer, and it was me who wrote a digit wrong. I really regret it. But now the money ended up in the estate, and you will inherit the full amount."

The lawyer had hoped that the millions the client would inherit would overshadow his mistake. Silence him. Forget everything and not mention it to anyone, especially not within legal circles.

"But if Harriet wished for the money to go to Doctors Without Borders, then you should be able to correct it."

Idiot! The boy is getting the money instead of it going to some damn communist account. The boy should be happy, more than happy. Damn troublesome kid. The lawyer was even more angry at himself for making a mistake. Figures were not his thing, it had always been difficult. Math, oh hell.

"No, the money was returned, placed back in the estate, and you will inherit it."

"So, can we transfer the money now then?"

The lawyer could not in any way understand how a person could say no to so much money. He couldn't understand people at all. For him, right was as long as it was right under the law. How else would you know what is right and wrong? Damn people!

Many papers and even more signatures later, the two gentlemen finally completed the probate. Samuel ensured that the eight million were transferred to Doctors Without Borders. This time with the correct account number.

Samuel hoped he would never have to meet lawyer Andrew Dayton again. Never again.

When Samuel left the room, he threw Harriet's finger to the little dog in the basket. It happily munched on it, and somehow, Samuel's lie felt better now. After all, he had said it was a dog that had gobbled up Harriet's finger.

The girl at the reception was gone, and instead, a young man was sitting there.

"Where's the girl who was here earlier?"

"Whom do you mean, sir? I don't understand."

"I think her name was Abigail," Samuel explained.

"Oh, you mean lawyer Percy. She's in a meeting and then booked for the rest of the day. Do you want to schedule a time for another day?"

"I thought she worked here, at the reception."

"Oh no," the man laughed, showing his perfect white teeth. They were all perfectly even, as if he had bitten into a grinding wheel. "She filled in for me... um... because I needed to use the bathroom

As Samuel descended the wide staircase, he couldn't shake the thought of whether the guy got the job because he was so handsome or because his parents owned the law firm.

Sigh.

12 Otto von Mountbatten

YouTube enthusiast Mark Goldpeak, alias Macie-ducey, finally managed to get his phone working; at least, the screen started to glow. Jasmine climbed down using the large handles on the outer sides of the other pods. Her damp feet clung to the cold floor as she walked towards the cabinets to choose a white robe. "Freeze Yourself" was written in turquoise blue on the chest, accompanied by a small snowflake beside it, also in blue.

Mark stared at his phone the whole time, unable to comprehend why neither 4G, 5G, nor any other G appeared at the top of the screen. "No network available," it said, and there was no WIFI either. "It's not possible," he grunted, looking up at the ceiling, as if pleading to a higher power. "There must be Wi-Fi base stations here," he thought. Like a junkie without drugs or an alcoholic without liquor, Mark felt a big hole in his chest, empty in both body and soul. Obliterated and annihilated. "This can't be happening; it must work! It must!"

A new swooshing sound echoed, and both turned their gaze towards the wall with hatches. A young man sat up and smiled uncertainly while scanning the room. He cleared his throat and whispered, "Where are the guys?"

Otto von Mountbatten, 32 years old, was enduring his first bachelor party. After riding a limousine through the city and pouring several litres of champagne out of the windows, the whole gang ended up at the cryonics clinic. Through the well-off parents' credit cards, his friends managed to pay for Otto's freezing, the perfect joke. It cost a few thousand per person, but what did it matter? Money was meant to be spent. The plan was to thaw him just before the wedding, but it was forgotten. No one took responsibility for the reckless prank. The wedding was canceled, and Young Master Mountbatten never showed up. He was reported missing.

"Excuse me, but my friends played a prank on me; they're doing my bachelor party. Has my lordship, by any chance, seen them, or rather, heard them?" Mark now suspected that something was wrong with his phone because the date was completely off.

"No," Jasmine replied. "We're starting to believe that something has gone wrong here. Nothing is working. Both of us, like you, were just pushed out of our cryo pods." She looked at Mark. "Put away that gadget now, macki-docki; there are people who need our help in those boxes. We have to open them!"

They approached the hatches, while Otto freed himself from his cables, looking somewhat embarrassed.

"You'll find something to wear in the cabinets along the wall," Jasmine said. The handles on the wall were substantial, like large freezers in a slaughterhouse. A very small padlock was taped to one of the hatches, the kind you used to have on diaries. But neither of them paid much attention to it. Where should they start? Mark knocked on one of the hatches.

"Just open it," he said and pulled. With a faint hiss, the hatch opened, and the bed slid out. Parts of a model railroad were scattered on the mattress. Small locomotives, wagons, pieces of rails, and tiny German alpine houses with flowers under the windows. The person who seemed to have been there was gone. Mark looked around to make sure there was no conductor lurking on them. Then he closed the hatch.

"Maybe the person took the train to freezing and never arrived!"

No one laughed. At the next hatch, they heard a sound, and Mark immediately grabbed the large handle. The hatch slid towards them, and they peered behind it. A pair of feet emerged, pale white in colour. It was when they saw the legs that they recoiled. One leg was torn, chewed up. A piece of the shin was visible. Blood and water flowed over the edge. The smell burned in their noses. An angry growl came from the darkness. It didn't sound human.

As a young man, André Ichnek traveled to Brazil, the land of rainforests, the land of carnivals. It was initially intended as a gap year, a chance to relax from parents and studies, but after partying for a few months, he started working on a soybean plantation. Maybe he needed the money, but the reason was probably his passion for the plantation owner's daughter. She, Vanessa, the beautiful one. They met at a bar, and the next day, Vanessa promised him both a job and accommodation on the family's plantation outside the city. It was a captivating scene that greeted him on his inaugural workday. Expansive soybean fields extended as far as the eye could perceive—an astonishing sight of lush greenery stretching endlessly.

"Does your father own all this? He must be very wealthy."

"Yes, but not initially; the land was almost free. There used to be rainforest here that he had burned down."

"But soybeans? Who eats soybeans?"

"It's mostly used as animal feed. England buys a lot."

André worked his way up, both at work and within the family. He married in, and when Vanessa's father died, André Ichnek took over as the largest soy producer in the Amazon. The soy industry thrived for several decades. At its peak, they had sixteen combines across the fields.

But happiness was not enduring. Vanessa passed away due to a stroke. They never had children despite trying for many years.

As an older wealthy widower, soy ranch owner Ichnek got himself a Great Dane. The beloved dog, despite its size, was named "Chickpea".

They were often seen strolling along the fields at sunset. André was said never to laugh in the company of people; only the dog could make him happy. When Chickpea was four years old, she fell ill with bone cancer. All of Brazil's veterinarians were consulted, but the dog couldn't be saved. The only thing they could do was to freeze the dog and revive her when knowledge and technology allowed for a cure. Brazil's veterinarians declined; André had no choice but to freeze himself. He decided they would share the freezing compartment.

The dog began to bark and growl. Mark didn't hesitate and closed the hatch. "What are you doing?" exclaimed Jasmine. "It was a Great Dane. You can't just shut it."

"The man is dead, and the dog seems crazy; I'm not opening it again!"

"We can't leave it there. It will die of oxygen deprivation." Jasmine sounded desperate.

"At least it won't die of starvation," Otto said, who had also put on a white robe, albeit a bit too small.

"Then you'll have to euthanise it," suggested Jasmine, crossing her arms.

Otto began looking for something to euthanise a dog with. He found a medical cabinet on the wall that caught his interest. There was a bottle of chloroform. "We soak a cloth with this and throw it in; it should work." No cloth was found, but a white robe from the cabinet worked just as well. After soaking the garment in chloroform, Mark opened the hatch cautiously, and Otto poked the chloroform-soaked garment inside.

"Ugh, it stinks!"

Nothing happened. The dog continued to growl and bark.

"It's not working!" Mark began to bang on the hatch, and Jasmine stopped him.

"No, wait. That won't make it better."

A while later, it went silent, and whether the dog fell asleep or died, they never found out.

More hatches were opened, all with a red light shining on a pale motionless face. Not a sign of life.

"There's no point in opening the hatches. If anyone else survived, they'll push themselves out with the button, just like we did." Mark glanced towards the door under the emergency exit sign. "We need to get out of this morgue!"

Otto put his hand on one of the handles and knocked on the hatch.

"What are you doing?" Mark exclaimed.

"I'm just checking, one last time," Otto replied and opened the hatch. A bed slid out with small pale feet with pink nail polish, completely motionless.

"They're ice-cold," he said, wiggling the tiny toes. Jasmine turned away.

"Stop it; it's creepy."

Otto closed the hatch and also started walking towards the door. Jasmine had taken a few steps but stopped abruptly.

"Wait!" she shouted. "I hear something in here." She placed her hand on a hatch, and Otto approached quickly. Mark just shook his head.

"We have to open it," Jasmine said, and Otto gently pulled the handle. When the hatch opened, a short dog bark was heard. Otto prevented the bed from sliding out. Another short bark. Two barks. This wasn't a big dog, Otto thought.

"There are several dogs, very small," Jasmine exclaimed. "So cute."

They pulled the bed all the way out. Five Pekingese dogs jumped out. Their leashes came loose as they threw themselves onto the floor, yapping and hopping around Jasmine and Otto's legs. Woof!

"Stop it now," roared Mark, who had walked over to the elevator. "We have to get out of here."

No one expected the elevator light to turn on when Mark pressed the button. Instead, he opened the door, and they all emerged into a stairwell. In the dim light from the mobile, they could glimpse a rickety spiral staircase leading both upwards and downwards. "We have to get out." The dogs ran ahead of him as he put his hand on the handrail and took a few steps down the stairs.

13 CIA

After scoring a few small wins in the lottery, Samuel transitioned to selling and buying stocks. Somehow, it felt more honest. A lottery win consists of money from many people who have gambled and lost. Most are actually losers, often forgotten when it comes to gambling. No one wants to mention these losers, not the gambling companies, nor the players themselves. Everyone stays silent.

The idea was simple: if a stock was bullish, Samuel would write a note saying he would buy that stock. This way, he could purchase a large number of shares almost two days before it rose significantly. Similarly, if a stock plummeted, he sold it at the last moment. His capital grew rapidly. Easy. Samuel could now trade stocks just like the big corporate leaders. Simple as that.

One morning, as Samuel checked the time regulator, he found some newspaper clippings. They detailed four terrorist attacks in the USA: two hijacked passenger planes crashing into the Twin Towers of the World Trade Center in New York, another plane flying into the Pentagon in Washington, and a fourth plane demolishing the White House. Fortunately, George W. Bush wasn't in the building; he was visiting a school in Florida.

At first, Samuel couldn't believe it was true. It was too much to take in. It sounded like a terrible disaster movie, a real B-movie. But still, the newspapers looked real, and why would he deceive himself? Believe it or not, this is going to happen, he realised.

He tried to contact the CIA. On their website, he found a web form. After writing down the entire account and clicking Send, he felt he had to do more. He couldn't find a phone number, but through the number agency, he was connected to the CIA's tip line. There, he could inform them about the upcoming disaster. The woman who answered the call didn't react much to what Samuel was saying. Did she even listen?

Nevertheless, the next day turned into a tragedy. Two planes crashed into the World Trade Center, followed by one into the Pentagon. Finally, the terrorists managed to level the White House, just as it had been reported in the newspapers. "I warned the CIA, both online and on the phone! Why didn't they do anything? What went wrong?"

Somehow, he had to send the warning again, but with an addition that the CIA had to believe him, that they shouldn't think it's a joke. How could he prevent this catastrophe?

The contemplation took so much energy that he didn't notice the black van rolling into the parking lot in front of the house. Shortly after, the door flew open, and five black-clad individuals rushed into the building. With drawn weapons and crouched postures, they spread around the hall. They moved smoothly despite their bulletproof vests. On their backs, Samuel could read CIA. What are they doing here? Why are they coming?

When the CIA agents realised the very surprised man in the kitchen was unarmed, they pounced on him, holding him down to the floor.

"You're under arrest!"

Even though Samuel didn't resist, he was held firmly.

"What are you doing? You've got the wrong person!"

"Quiet, we know who you are! You speak when you're told!"

"But... I haven't done anything!"

"Terrorist scum!" The man with the long ponytail kicked him in the side.

"Get up!"

Terrorist attack, thought Samuel. They believe it's me. But how can I explain myself?

"I need to write a message to... um... the kids!"

"You don't have any kids," said the woman holding Samuel's hands tightly behind his back. He could hear the metallic sound of handcuffs.

"But... it's about the neighbour's kids, I'm supposed to babysit. They'll be worried if I'm not home when they come back from school."

The CIA leader wanted to leave the country with the apprehended terrorist as inconspicuously as possible. Even though the MI5 was always cooperative, unnecessary commotion was unwise.

"Fine, write it then."

Samuel took a notepad from the table and wrote, all the while wondering how he could place the note in the time regulator. The woman who held his hands read silently with an American accent.

Carl, Inez, and Arvid!

Be careful. There are other buns in the pantry! Coming soon!

/Samuel

"I'll just put it where they'll surely find it. It's best in the playroom," he said, nodding toward the secret room where he had left the door open earlier. He got the okay, and the revolvers followed him as he moved through the room. Quickly, he placed the note in the time regulator's container, on top of the clippings about the attacks.

Then he pressed the start button.

Click!

This morning was very peculiar for Samuel. In the time regulator were newspaper clippings about four terrorist attacks in the USA. There were pictures of fires in the World Trade Center; the buildings had collapsed entirely, to the ground. He could read about planes flying into the Pentagon and the White House. At first, Samuel couldn't believe it was true, but these were real clippings, the newspapers looked real. They were genuine. These events are going to happen, and he decided to stop them. There was also another note with strange names and about buns in the pantry, different buns. What does it mean? He recognised his own handwriting. But why had he written this?

Of course, he didn't find any buns in the pantry. He then focused on the other part of the text, the three names, and being careful. Carl, Inez, and Arvid, he didn't know anyone with those names? Who were they? He looked at the initials, C, I, and A. Could it be that CIA should be careful? If so, I would have written it in plain text, thought Samuel. I must have written this secretly. Under duress?

Could it be that he had already tried to influence this event? The only thing Samuel could think of was that he probably called the CIA and warned about the attacks, but no one took the warning seriously. But that meant he became the prime suspect for all the deeds. No one will believe me if I tell them what's in the newspapers. It's too unbelievable. But when it happens, I'll be blamed. CIA is quick to find a culprit, even if it's not the right one.

Samuel immediately started calling the airlines. On one of the clippings, he had written down all the flight numbers and now tried to book tickets. The two planes that were going to crash into the World Trade Center were fully booked. What about the plane crashing into the Pentagon?

Fully booked!

Airlines Flight 93, heading to San Francisco, had available seats, and as the coach of a Brazilian youth football team, he booked all thirteen open spots.

The young football team never made it onto the plane, even though the airline delayed the departure. The thirteen girls never showed up. The coach who booked the tickets couldn't be reached; the person seemed not to exist. The phone number the man provided went to an elderly lady in Wisconsin, who had played football once upon a time, but that was a long time ago. Somehow, the delay allowed the passengers to prevent the plane from reaching the White House. Upon hearing about the other disasters, they tried to prevent the hijackers from flying further. The plane then crashed in a field outside Shanksville, Pennsylvania.

Saving the White House went well; Samuel couldn't do more. Predicting the future can be very dangerous, and he must now ensure he isn't discovered. It would be a disaster if the invention fell into the wrong hands, and Samuel realised he had to remain anonymous.

14 Raw Meat with the Bone Intact

It was crucial to find a journalist who wrote well, yet the person shouldn't be too smart. I don't want this person to expose me, thought Samuel. After skimming through several newspapers, he settled on Isabella Hawke, a young woman who always insisted on having a picture of herself with every article. With her, one could read about the latest diet trend RMBI, Raw Meat with the Bone Intact. The concept was to eat raw meat and not just that, but to gnaw the raw meat off the bone. This supposedly released the right substances in both the brain and the digestive tract. There were also articles on homeopathy, also with a small picture of Isabella in the corner diluting a homeopathic remedy to purify water bodies.

Isabella Hawke would be perfect, thought Samuel.

After contacting her, they agreed to meet at a café near the train station. As preparation, Samuel knew certain events that would occur; he had already experienced the meeting once before. The entire sequence of events was written on a note that he had read many times that morning. She would be wearing a bright yellow hoodie and white pants. They chose an outdoor seating area, intending to sit at the far end. After talking for a while, she would order a latte and a large chocolate muffin. How this related to RMBI was something not written down, but it was good to know if one wanted to convince someone of being clairvoyant.

The crucial part was that he knew there would be some remarkable events. Two dogs would start fighting. One of the dog owners would try to separate them and, in the process, get tangled in the leash, falling into a puddle. Splash. After that, a woman in high heels, wearing a tight red dress, would have her oversized suitcase break right by their table.

"Hello, Isabella, please have a seat," Samuel pulled out her chair. "I wish to remain anonymous. You can call me Harry."

"Okay, that's fine," she replied, taking out a small notepad and a very short pencil.

"I haven't had lunch; maybe we should order something first?" said Isabella as she began to chew on the pencil stub.

"We'll wait a moment; I want to tell you briefly about myself. I am, in fact, a seer."

As a journalist, one must be critical, Isabella had learned at the Journalism School.

"How do I know you can really see into the future?" She sounded skeptical, but she already felt that this man was a prophet; she sensed it.

"May I borrow your notepad and pencil? I'll write down what you're going to order."

With a little giggle, she handed over the pencil and notepad. It felt like the man was about to crawl into her mind and dig around. So exciting.

In the notepad, Isabella had already written "Meeting with Harry, clairvoyant," and on the next line, Samuel wrote, "Coffee with milk and chocolate muffin."

"Now you can place your order."

"I want a latte and a chocolate muffin!" Samuel slid the notepad to the journalist, who read with wide eyes.

"Fantastic! Almost exactly what I said. A chocolate muffin – how did you know that? But the coffee was wrong!"

"Latte is coffee with milk," explained Samuel.

"Oh?"

After fetching her order, Samuel told Isabella about the upcoming events, the dogs' fight, and the woman with the large suitcase. Isabella marvelled as a small terrier started barking frantically shortly afterward. The retractable leash seemed to tangle for the female owner. The leash got longer and longer, no matter how much she pressed the button. The little dog zigzagged around an older man and his border collie. The woman's retractable leash got entangled around the man's knees, and he lost balance, sitting in a puddle. It all looked comical. Other café guests saw the incident and laughed quietly.

"Fantastic," whispered the journalist, then hesitated. "Could it be actors you've hired?"

"Yes, it's possible, but your order, I predicted that!"

Then the woman in the tight dress approached, making Isabella nearly choke on her muffin. The suitcase was large and didn't roll as the owner wished. It's challenging to maintain direction when trying to balance in high heels. As the woman passed their table, the suitcase slid over the curb and got stuck halfway into the street. Furious, the woman jerked it, and the suitcase flew open. Clothes spilled out, and small underwear blew away but were stopped by the small puddles along the street.

After helping gather the woman's wardrobe, Samuel sat back with the journalist.

"That wasn't acting, was it?" he said.

Isabella nodded and followed the woman in red into the station building. Now it was time for Samuel to make his demands.

"I will predict terrible accidents and other events. For example, plane crashes or buildings collapsing. You'll receive a message from me a day before. Then you can prevent the tragedy. It's crucial for me to remain anonymous."

Isabella nodded frantically.

***

The first thing Isabella learned was that a school bus would veer off the road outside Dumfries. The text message stated that the bus would roll down a steep hill. The driver wouldn't have the necessary license for such a large bus. Twelve out of the twenty-two children would perish. Many suffered severe injuries.

After reading the message, Isabella immediately deleted it. She was afraid the phone would emit a small puff of smoke if the text stayed.

"Hello! Is this McAllen Bus Company in Dumfries?"
"Yes, what can I help you with?"
"I'm Isabella Hawke, a journalist. I've learned that your bus drivers don't have the proper licenses."
"But what are you talking about? I can't believe that."
"Yes, it's true. Your bus drivers transport school children. Imagine if something were to happen, if the bus were to plunge into a ravine, and all the children die. What do you say about that?"
"All our drivers have licenses!"
"No, and they might drive off a cliff!"
"Is this a threat or something?"
"No, I mean, it could happen."
"I understand; accidents can happen. But don't worry, our drivers have extensive experience in driving buses. Do you have children who ride our buses to school?"
"What? No, I don't have any children! Why are you asking that?"
"You seem very worried that something might happen to the children."
"It's obvious something will happen!"
"Are you threatening us? I think I'll call the police!"
"No, not the police. I'm not threatening. I'm just telling you what might...could happen. And the driver must have the right license."
"Do you mean the correct authorisation?"
"Yes, exactly, kind of, yes, that's what I mean."
"Thank you for contacting us, and I promise that we will immediately check that all our drivers have the necessary qualifications to drive a school bus. You can rest assured; nothing will happen to the children."
"Uh, thanks!"

The company absolutely did not want any negative publicity and called for a meeting the next day with all employees. Those who were not qualified to drive a school bus were immediately assigned other tasks.
The accident never happened. All the children arrived at school unharmed.
But there were no headlines for Isabella Hawke. The newspaper didn't even want to write about some drivers at the bus company in Dumfries lacking the qualifications for a school bus.

"But think about the disaster that could have happened if the bus had gone off the road," Isabella tried to convince the news editor. "All the children could have died!"
"Well, nothing has happened now," replied the editor.
"But it could have rolled down a steep slope..."
"No, we won't write anything about the bus drivers in Dumfriės, no matter how unqualified they are!"

The same thing happened with the big fire in Sutton two weeks later. Isabella's mobile phone had alerted her to an upcoming conflagration—a burning row of houses. Two families, both incinerated. Three adults and five children. Two more children were sedated in the hospital due to severe burns. The fire had spread quickly because the houses had a common attic. It had started in one of the kitchens, and the fire investigation was sure that the fire was caused by burning frying oil.

A day before the fire, Isabella managed to get a full page in the local newspaper about how to extinguish burning frying oil. Here, she explained that one should never extinguish burning cooking fat or oil with water. Smother the fire with a lid or other non-flammable material, such as a fire blanket.

The big picture in the newspaper showed Isabella Hawke with a pot lid and a silly apron. Embarrassing. This was not the article she had hoped for when offered the chance to learn about tragic accidents and terrible disasters that would happen in the future.

There was no fire. The children got to enjoy their french fries, doughnuts, or whatever was being fried in the row house in Sutton.

***

"Plane Crash in CRAWLY. Explosion in the air. Bomb in suitcase. Heathrow Airport, destination Paris, flight BA571.

Samuel had waited until the last moment to learn as much as possible about the explosion. When the breaking news reported that it was a bomb in the luggage compartment, he sent the message to himself, forty-two hours earlier. When he found the note, he immediately sent a text to Isabella so she would have as much time as possible to prevent the impending disaster.

The first thing Miss Isabella Hawke did was contact Heathrow Airport. Flight BA571 was scheduled to take off in six hours, and swift action was crucial. As a journalist, Isabella could claim suspicion that a suitcase containing a bomb would be in the luggage compartment. She could refer to anonymous sources and other journalistic work. If Samuel had called, it would undoubtedly have been deemed a bomb threat.

High alert was in place when Isabella and her photographer arrived at Heathrow Airport. All luggage was scanned, and two bomb-sniffing dogs inspected all bags bound for Paris.

At the check-in for flight BA571, they closely followed the tough work of security personnel. When only thirty minutes remained, one of the dogs signalled. A short bark, and the dog refused to leave the bag, a black Samsonite.

Baggage handling at Heathrow Airport was immediately evacuated, and the police cordoned off the surrounding area. Bomb technicians assessed the situation, after which a bomb robot moved the bag to one of their bomb-proof vehicles. Then the bag was detonated in a secure location just outside Slough.

The bag's owner was easily apprehended. It was an elderly woman in a light green dress and a matching yellow scarf. The round glasses and striped hair made her look like a relic from the sixties. Peace and love, for real. The woman had no idea that her bag had caused this chaos. Isabella managed to reach the woman, who was quite irritated that her flight wasn't starting on time. Being taken aside by the police didn't improve matters.

"Irresponsible bastards. Damn cops! Why can't regular people move as they please?"

"But they're working for security here at the airport," Isabella suggested to calm the woman.

"But why pick on us? Now my plane is delayed. Why don't they lock up those Arabs right away!"

A policeman stepped in and announced that the woman would be arrested. The bomb squad had detonated her suitcase. Technicians had determined that the bag's contents equaled fifteen kilograms of explosives. They had found a timing mechanism intended to detonate the bomb sometime after takeoff. Everything was embedded in old clothes.

"But that wasn't my bag!"

"You checked in the bag two hours ago. We have cameras to confirm that."

The woman was shocked and seemed completely unaware of the contents of her luggage.

"I checked in the bag... for a friend."

"What's your friend's name, and where is that person now?"

It fell silent.

"We need to know this as soon as possible. It's very important that we can apprehend the person as quickly as possible."

The woman remained silent. Isabella was in the room and knew that she could be thrown out at any moment, but she couldn't stay quiet any longer.

"What did the person who gave you the bag look like?"

"There were two, kind of alike. Both had black beards and sunglasses."

"Can you describe their clothes?"

"Dark suits, I think they had black or dark ties. White shirts!"

"No friend, then?"

The policeman immediately slipped out and contacted his colleagues. Isabella was left alone with the woman. "But why did you check in the bag for them?"

"One man's wife had flown to Paris this morning but forgot her luggage. I was just supposed to check in the bag for her, and then she would meet me at the airport in Paris."

Didn't it seem suspicious to you?"

The woman hesitated for a moment before answering. "No?"
"Would you get paid?"
Isabella looked at the woman, whose gaze wandered around the room, the window, the door, the trash can...
"Yes, they offered me a small sum. As thanks. But it doesn't matter, I would have done it anyway. You should help your fellow human beings, right?"
"How much?"
The woman scrutinised all the objects in the room once again.
"You have to tell me how much!"
"Two hundred."
The policeman came in and stood by the door. The woman glared fearfully at the man in uniform.
"Thousand," the woman added hesitantly.

Isabella was satisfied; the headlines in the newspaper the next day told of her superb journalistic work. The front page showed a picture of her lying next to the photographer's large camera bag. The caption read: Isabella Hawke and the suitcase containing fifty kilograms of explosive. The bag was detonated shortly thereafter by the police bomb squad. In the newspaper, one could read further about the woman who had been deceived by the villains exploiting her naivety. The two men were never seen. The crime was never solved. For the woman with the round glasses, the trip to Paris was significantly delayed. Over a year."

***

"A month later, Isabella received another text message from Samuel. A bridge will collapse outside London. Queen Elizabeth II Bridge won't withstand the approaching storm. A combination of heavy traffic, strong winds, and cracks in the twenty-year-old concrete will cause parts of the bridge to end up in the water. Many people lost their lives as they drove over the edge in the darkness.

Five hours later, just over a day before the collapse, Isabella was on-site with her photographer. The wind had already picked up, and it was raining heavily. It was forecasted to blow even worse the next day.
After three hours of searching, a tired, wet, and irritated photographer took a taxi back to the hotel. He told the driver it would take hours for him to dry his long hair.

Isabella continued to search for flaws or damage in the bridge construction, but she eventually grew tired too. It was no longer possible to see in the darkness. The wind was strong, and the rain was pouring.

The next morning, she called the Department for Transport. She didn't have much hope that they would care about her comments. The bridge had cracks, but she had neither proof nor pictures. She didn't mention the latter.

To her surprise, the bridge was closed in the afternoon on the same day. Whether it was planned or not was something she never found out. There was no article either, just a note that Queen Elizabeth II Bridge would be closed for five weeks due to repair work. She had hoped her name would be mentioned in the text. When she pointed it out, it turned out the information was submitted by the Department for Transport.

Did they know the bridge was in poor condition? Had they forgotten to close the bridge? These were questions she would never get answers to.

It took two months before the next text message. Isabella had pushed aside the small messages she could receive about upcoming accidents. She was disappointed. They hadn't given her the publicity she had hoped for. Only small ridiculous notices. Often, it just felt silly since everything usually turned out fine.

This time, it was a ferry that had been traveling at too high speed and crashed into a pier. Casualties were reported because the ferry capsized in the deep water. Among other things, a tourist bus slid off and disappeared into the depths. Many passengers never made it out.

Isabella chose not to do any preparation. What would she gain by talking to the captain of the boat and asking him to drive slowly today? What headlines would it bring: Isabella Hawke saves ferry from sinking by urging captain to drive slowly?

No, never again, thought Isabella, and she called her photographer.

"Why should I film the boat?" wondered the photographer when the ferry was halfway across the strait. Isabella sighed.

"Just do as I say."

"This is ridiculous. The weather is nice, no wind. Nothing will happen here!"

The photographer started packing up his tripod, and Isabella pulled him by the ponytail.

"Look at the ferry. It's going way too fast!"

He looked up. "No, it looks completely okay. They usually drive that fast. Let's go back."

"No, you're going to film!" Isabella grabbed the camera strap.

"Leave it! There are better assignments than being here filming boats."

"You're going to do as I say. It's an order. Film the ferry now!"

"No, pointless!"

"Yes, you will film!"

"Nope."

With a loud crash, the ferry hit the dock. It creaked in the large trucks at the front. The brickwork of the dock popped into the water. A truck slid past the barrier in the bow and halfway into the water. The trucks behind rolled forward and to the side. The ferry dipped its bow and began to lean heavily. Water poured onto the deck, causing the cars to slide to the side and tilt the ferry even more. The camera quickly went up on the photographer's shoulder, and he immediately started filming.

The ferry twisted even more. Trucks and cars slid off and into the water to quickly sink into the depths. A fully loaded tourist bus rolled over the edge and into the dark water. People crowded in the doorways trying to get out but were hindered by the rushing water. Isabella saw frightened people pounding fists and shoes on the inside of the windows.

"Keep filming," Isabella shouted to the photographer as she walked toward a post with a lifebuoy. There were people in the water, and smaller boats approached to pick up the distressed. The photographer zoomed in and followed the bus as it disappeared into the depths. Most passengers never made it out.

Isabella waved to the photographer when the first motorboat with rescued people approached the dock. She threw the lifebuoy around a wet and frightened older woman. Unfortunately, the lady spoke only Swedish, and Isabella handed over her microphone to a man she thought looked English.

"How does it feel?"

Isabella pressed the microphone into the wet face.

"Have you lost a close relative? What were you thinking when the bus fell into the water?"

Frightened, the man tried to answer, and Isabella handed the lifebuoy, which the Swedish lady had over her shoulders. With a jerk, she snatched the wreath, and like a winner of the Vasa race, the man got it over his head.

Isabella finally got her headlines. Pictures of her appeared in all newspapers, and a long report was shown on TV. Everyone now knew who Isabella Hawke was. The excellent journalist. The one who was first on the scene when the car ferry sank. With a lifebuoy, she had rescued dying tourists from the water.

When Samuel saw the report on TV, he first wondered what had caused Isabella to fail to prevent the accident. Did something happen? What went wrong? Quite quickly, he realised that she hadn't tried to prevent the event at all.

It had been too long for him to stop his first message that he sent earlier. Unfortunately.

On the TV screen, an excited Isabella told about the dreadful accident.

Samuel could do nothing.

But a few more texts to Miss Hawke were out of the question."

15 The Salvager and His Family

On a stormy night in October, a passenger ship found itself in distress on the lake. The ship capsized in the powerful wind. No one knows exactly what happened, but the ship sank relatively quickly thereafter. An hour later, a helicopter with salvagers arrived at the accident site. They managed to rescue five people. Another nearby boat saved an additional fifteen individuals. Twenty-two people were never found, including five fathers with their teenage daughters. The girls had been on a horse riding camp in Poland with their fathers.

Samuel decided to try and do something and wrote a note to himself detailing the accident—everything he could find out, including times and positions. He would prevent this himself, without selfish journalists.

The day before, he had no way to stop the boat from departing; it had already left the harbour. Still, by making a few calls, he managed to summon another helicopter to be present during the upcoming rescue operation. Two ships altered their routes when Samuel revealed that the ship had a serious flaw.

When the accident occurred, they managed to rescue almost all the distressed individuals. One crew member did not survive. He had gotten trapped in a rowing machine in the ship's training room. Forensics couldn't determine if it happened before or after the capsizing.

Everything seemed to go smoothly, and Samuel managed to stay anonymous throughout the operation. Unfortunately, a helicopter ran into trouble on the way back and crashed into the sea just off the coast. No distress signal was sent, and the entire crew, including the winch operator, salvager, and the two pilots, perished.

A few days later, Samuel found a report about the young salvager on the crashed helicopter. He left behind a family with three children. The man was a hero in the town where they lived, having saved many lives during his career.

It was Samuel's fault that the helicopter participated in the rescue operation. If he hadn't called the maritime authority, the rescue team would have been on training in Dundee. Who knows how many people he and his team would have saved during their professional lives? Samuel felt guilt; he had saved twenty-two lives at the cost of four others. They were trained to help. Their job was to save other people.

Thanks to him, more people survived, but this rescue team could have saved even more in future disasters. What had he done? He wanted to turn back and redo everything. But there was no time for that.

But that wasn't enough. After the accident, it turned out that the men on the boat were not fathers, at least not to the young girls they called daughters. They had never been to any riding camp. The girls were bought and used as sex slaves. The girls had lived in the men's apartments, separately. They had gathered with each other and carried out gang rapes on their so-called daughters. They called these meetings riding camps.

It was these men that Samuel had saved from death.

Samuel cursed himself for what he had done. Nature had arranged a death penalty for these men, but why should Samuel change that? Now other people had to suffer. Whether they were the wrong people or not, one cannot know. Samuel had taken on the role of judge, and he felt that everything had gone wrong, terribly wrong.

The men's riding camp was discovered when one of the girls was taken to the emergency room because of injuries to her abdomen. A doctor became suspicious and found out the girl's origin. The girl later turned out to be thirteen years old.

This was too much for Samuel. If he had done nothing, the helicopter team would have survived because they would have been on another mission. The men would have perished along with the girls, the girls they called daughters. But what kind of life had he saved these girls for?

What have I done? Was this what Harriet had warned about? Why does everything get worse when I try to do right?"

***

St Mary's Church was a beautiful place. The large chestnut trees cast cool shadows over the freshly cut green grass. You could hear the city's hum and the chirping of birds. Otherwise, it was silent. No one else was visible; the cemetery seemed deserted from what Samuel could see.

Water dripped from the hose lying discarded on the gravel path by the water post. After gathering the hose, he turned the tap.

On the church tower, there was a golden cross. A peculiar symbol for Christianity, Samuel thought. Crucifixion was the death penalty of that time. What if Jesus had come later, in the 1500s, when they executed people by hanging? Then a noose would have adorned the top of St Mary's Church instead.

Lethal injections are a more modern method of executing people, prompting a syringe at the top of all England's churches. An embossed syringe in gold on all Bibles. How peculiar that would have looked. Not to mention the electric chair. If Jesus had appeared later, he would have sacrificed his life and been placed in the electric chair. Then a chair would have become a symbol of Christianity instead of the cross. Imagine wearing a little chair around your neck when confirming. Vampire movies would have been even more ridiculous when the attacked held up a small chair instead of a cross to ward off the blood-sucking zombies.

If Jesus had been executed in the 1900s, the top of St Mary's Church would have been adorned with a chair, a gilded chair.

The salvager's grave was not hard to find. There were significantly more flowers than at the other graves. Beautiful bouquets and wreaths in white and green. The ground was elevated, enhancing the feeling that a coffin lay down there, deep in the earth. The stone was carved in red granite, and the name was written with shiny gold letters.

"It's my fault," thought Samuel. "What have I done?" He got an unpleasant feeling in the pit of his stomach and wanted to smash everything. Restore everything... but that wouldn't be good either. How do you know what's best? I tried to do right.

A car stopped on the street outside the cemetery, but there was something Samuel didn't notice. Shortly after, three children came and stood beside Samuel. The children looked to be between five and ten years old. Together, they formed a circle around the grave. No one said anything; it was completely silent. The city's noise had ceased, not even the birds were chirping. The smallest, a girl, crouched down and placed a white rose in the grass.

"This is for you, daddy. I picked it myself."

Oh no, they are his children, thought Samuel. I can't say sorry because only I know it was all my fault. It would only get worse for them if I explained.

I can't handle this. Samuel turned around to go back to his car. Behind him stood a young woman, the children's mother, he guessed. She waved and smiled. Samuel waved back. For her, he was someone who wanted to show appreciation for her deceased husband. If she only knew, thought Samuel as he walked towards the car without looking around.

When he sat behind the wheel, he couldn't hold back the tears. He cried, banged his head on the steering wheel, and cursed himself.

Damn! Hell fucking shit!

What if he could have turned back time and prevented Hitler from coming to power? What if he could meet a young Hitler and influence him in some way? Stop his existence or encourage him to do good. Then neither Nazism nor the Third Reich would have existed, and thus, the Holocaust wouldn't have either. Millions of Jews would have survived. Everyone who died in the war. Maybe there wouldn't have been a Second World War? Then they would have prevented the persecution of vulnerable groups, mass executions of homosexuals, and sterilisation of the intellectually disabled. Hitler's political opponents and their families would have survived. What would all this have meant for the future of Europe?

It seems fantastic, but what if a new and even worse Hitler had come later and killed even more? Another dictator who had managed to keep control over Europe?

Then we would all be speaking German today.

Or all the books in your bookshelf would be in Russian. It might be completely empty, without books, because Stalin took over Europe and managed to retain power for a hundred years. We would all be part of a communist superpower and drive a Lada to work instead of a Land Rover.

16 The Tragic Awakening of Natalie Blom

Natalie Blom was a vegan; she found it peculiar to eat meat. The school cafeteria forced vegans to stand aside to get their lunch, labeled as special dietary needs. But Natalie often thought about how it would be if it were the other way around, if vegan food were always served, no meat or dairy products. In the cafeteria, vegetables, fruits, rice, pasta, and other delicious items would be served. Tasty stews with root vegetables and delightful sauces. Those who chose to eat meat would have to stand aside to get their special dietary needs.

Special dietary needs consisting of dead animals.

”We, the others, would stand and pick from all the vegetables and root vegetables laid out by the catering staff”, thought Natalie.
"The meat-eaters would stand at the kitchen entrance with their plates, waiting for someone to place a piece of a dead pig or a piece of a dead bird on their plate. On other days, they would wait to get a piece of a dead cow. Most of the time, they would get a piece of a hose filled with scraps from a dead pig.

Then maybe everyone would understand how sick it was to eat meat.

The most challenging part for Natalie was animal farming. The animals that humans kept imprisoned their entire lives, only to be slaughtered. Fine, sweet, innocent animals born in captivity, growing up in prison, often cramped and dark, only to be slaughtered. Perhaps she could consider eating game. An animal that had been free from birth and lived a good life in the wild. A life that the animal had chosen. A good life.

But Natalie didn't stand in any lines for vegans anymore.

It was a winter morning when it all came to a stop, not for the bus in this case, the one that passed the red light at high speed without stopping but for the little girl. The one who skipped across the street at the green light, looking forward to another day at school. This morning, she didn't arrive on time as usual. On this day, she didn't come to school at all. She didn't even cross the street. After a couple of meters into the crosswalk, she was hit by the bus, rolled under the front wheel, and got trapped by the rear wheel pair. With a crushed skull and a broken neck.

Blinking her eyes was her way of communicating after that.

Her room in the hospital was yellow. Mustard yellow. It wasn't a colour Natalie would have chosen, but she couldn't say anything, and no one had asked her what she thought about the room. The questions she got were about pain, hunger, thirst, and sleep. She blinked slowly to these questions, which meant yes.

Natalie was tube-fed, but not with vegan food. Her father had decided that she should be tube-fed with regular food, including meat and fish. This was because he had a firm belief that meat would make her healthy.

"She needs real food," he insisted. "Rice and beans won't make anyone healthy."

The father loved his daughter more than anything else. He couldn't bear to see her lying motionless. It was torture for him every day he visited her.

He decided that his daughter would be cryogenically frozen to be awakened in the future. Then the doctors could restore her life and mobility.

"We'll freeze you; it's not dangerous. We'll wake you up in the future, and the doctors can cure you. It will be great!" The father had already figured it all out.

Natalie blinked quickly, meaning no. Waking up in the future, without friends, was not something she wanted to experience. It was better to be paralysed with her family than to be able to walk alone in the future.

But her father wouldn't listen; he looked away. "It's the best we can do for you." He tried to convince himself that he had made the right decision. For him, it was better to tuck her away for an indefinite time.

He couldn't bear to see her suffer.

Natalie Blom woke up in the cryobox and immediately felt that she was alone. Nothing happened when she tried to move her arms. The legs were immobile. Paralysed, she lay in the darkness, wondering where everyone was. There used to be someone sitting next to the bed. Dad, mom, and little brother, where are you?

But it wasn't a bed she found herself in; it felt more like a dark, narrow box, or a coffin. Was she dead? And buried?

A large red button glowed above her, just a decimetre from her face.

EJECT.

She wondered what would happen if she could press it. Maybe the box would explode, and its walls would fly aside? It would become bright, and everyone would sit there at the edge of the bed?

Maybe it's a cannon, like at the circus, and I fly away and land on my feet? I stand up, and everyone applauds! But I don't have a helmet, thought Natalie. One of those colourful ones, with stripes and stars.

It was cold, damp, and lonely. Natalie was thirsty. If I close my eyes, maybe I'll wake up at home in bed.

She closed her eyes for a long time, hoping.

Natalie woke up to someone knocking. She was still in the dark box. A faint glow appeared at her feet, and she heard voices. Is that you, Mom? she wondered. Take me out, she wanted to shout, but she couldn't make a sound. She blinked intensely. It was her way of screaming.

Someone touched her. Tickled her toes.

"They're ice-cold," said a voice at her feet. Pull, thought Natalie, pull me out of here. Natalie felt someone continue to fiddle with her toes.

"Stop it, it's creepy!" It was a woman's voice. Then everything became dark and quiet again.

Only the glowing button remained.

EJECT.

17 THE INTELLIGENT ZEBRA

A nocturnal tsunami struck the east coast of Africa, claiming the lives of five Europeans, one of whom was of English descent. His grandmother was born in England, and at the age of five, she moved with her family to Belgium and later to Africa.

The tsunami made headlines in the newspapers. "Englishman perishes in the waves," read the headlines. The centre spread featured pictures of the man and the hotel where he worked. The staff was interviewed, sharing stories of how amiable the Englishman had been. A relative of the man recounted childhood memories of playing in Antwerp.

In another smaller report, details emerged about the small fishing village located three kilometres from the hotel. Over three hundred families lived there, relying on fishing and simple agriculture. The village had been situated on a promontory, and everything was washed away by the tidal wave. The buildings were completely destroyed and scattered along the coast. All fishing boats and equipment were ruined. Only sand and stones remained. Only a few from the village survived the tsunami. It was as if the village and its people had never existed.

One morning, Samuel found the torn articles about the devastation in the time regulator's container. "The catastrophe will be a reality the day after tomorrow if I don't do something," he thought. The decision was simple; he would personally travel down and warn the population about the impending tsunami.

The shrill song of cicadas filled the dark airport parking lot as Samuel hailed a taxi. He had plenty of time, knowing that the tsunami would strike the coast only the following night. "Hôtel Alliance, s'il vous plaît."

The warm air flowing through the windows as the taxi drove through the city provided relief despite the heat. The driver's name was Kendi Bankole, as Samuel could read on the ID card stuck to the instrument panel.

"I saw something strange as we descended for landing."

"Yes, flying is strange. I've never understood how it works," Kendi replied, keeping his eyes on the road.

"What do you mean?"

"I would never get into such a contraption. Trapped in a box high up in the air."

"But it's twenty-nine times safer to fly than to drive a car. So, you're more likely to die in your car than in an airplane."

The driver cast a brief glance at Samuel, as if to determine which idiot he was driving this time. "And you believe that?"

"Yes," Samuel hesitated, feeling that the discussion was heading in the wrong direction but couldn't leave the statistics.

"It's even more likely that you'll die at home than in the air. Flying is eighteen times safer than being at home!"

"I'm rarely home; I drive a taxi!"

"But your family is at home?"

"Yes, wife and six children, and they neither fly nor drive. What could happen to them?"

"A break-in, earthquake, or maybe a tsunami?"

Kendi Bankole continued driving without saying anything. Samuel wanted to change the subject, and now he had the chance.

"From the plane, I saw lots of animals. They were migrating, seemed to be fleeing from the coast." Samuel glanced at Kendi to see how he would react.

"Yes," the driver replied. "That happens if they are worried about something."

"They were in a line, elephants, rhinoceroses, and lots of buffaloes."

"It could be poachers," Kendi replied shortly.

"The animals left the coast, seemed to be moving towards the mountains."

"Then an earthquake is imminent," Kendi replied.

Samuel said nothing more. He hadn't seen any animals migrating, but he knew it was a sure sign of an impending earthquake. At Hotel Alliance, the driver contacted the communications centre. Samuel didn't understand what was being said, but Kendi Bankole spoke rapidly.

The man at the hotel reception appeared familiar to Samuel, triggering a recollection of the image of the drowned Englishman from the newspaper clippings. Samuel initiated a conversation about England, inquiring whether the man missed the fog and the dark, cold winters. The man's expression resembled a puzzled question mark; evidently, he didn't comprehend the reference. After a brief exchange, they reached the conclusion that the man believed his great-grandmother hailed from England. However, uncertainty lingered – was it England or perhaps Scotland?

"This man will drown tomorrow night," Samuel thought as he received the key to his room. "How can I save him? I can't go to bed without saying anything." After recounting the animals moving towards the mountains, Samuel ended by asking what the man would do if a large tidal wave struck the hotel and flooded the reception. Samuel expected no answer as he walked towards the elevator. The so-called England descendant followed him, horrified.

In the morning, Samuel made his way to the small village that would be affected. The simple houses stood close together, and on a bench in the small square, five older men sat in a row. They all smiled with toothless mouths as the young man joined them. The conversation ranged from the weather to young girls, but they also mentioned hearing that wild animals were moving away from the coast.

"It's a sign of an impending earthquake and tsunami," Samuel explained. "You should seek shelter inland."

But it was challenging to get them to leave their homes. Home is the safest place and where one naturally seeks refuge in danger. Samuel tried to be convincing.

"In a tsunami, the water will rise above the rooftops, and the currents will be so strong that no one can swim."

The men then went to their houses and told of the impending disaster. Slowly, the villagers began to understand the folly of hiding in their homes. They packed their most valuable possessions and prepared to leave the village.

In the evening, the entire village gathered on a hill a few kilometres from the coast. The rumour had spread during the day, resulting in the evacuation of the coastal part of the town as well. Everyone knew that the animals had moved away from the coast, and now they all waited for the impending earthquake.

Suddenly, it happened—earthquakes in the ground. The ground they sat on vibrated. Occasional anxious moans were heard in the darkness. A mother hushed and comforted her children.

After two minutes, it was over. It became completely silent. Everyone looked out over the sea, but everything was dark and still. The moon shone completely undisturbed over the sea, casting a long ribbon of light that sparkled towards the coast.

The younger children clung to their mothers.

"Mom, why are zebras striped, and why can't you ride them?"

The mother laughed; she had asked her own mother the same thing when she was little.

"I'll tell you about the intelligent zebra."

"The intelligent zebra?" The girl was not the only one surprised.

A long time ago, on a savanna far away, a herd of zebras lived. At that time, all zebras were white. No one knows exactly why they looked that way; perhaps they migrated from the north. Now they lived on the grassy plains, and the all-white zebras were a common sight on the vast savanna. There was also a watering hole where all the savanna's animals gathered to drink. The fresh grass did them good, and when they were thirsty, they could drink from the water collection.

One day, a zebra decided to place sticks around a piece of the savanna.

"This is my land; no other zebra can eat from this grass," he said. The other zebras found it strange behaviour, but the savanna was large, and it didn't matter much. There was plenty of grass elsewhere.

Everything had gone well if it weren't for another zebra also wanting land. It also set down sticks and firmly indicated that this piece of the savanna was hers. More zebras enviously glanced at the two zebras that were superior to others, and soon they, too, marked large areas. Soon the whole savanna was divided. One zebra had placed sticks around the watering hole.

When the zebras came to drink, they were told, "No, you can't have water here. You must bring me grass as compensation for drinking my water."

The zebras had to return to their staked-out land and graze extra to return to the watering hole with a load of grass on their backs. Only then could they quench their thirst. The zebra who owned the watering hole quickly had an abundance of grass, much more than he could eat himself. He ate and ate, became thick and fat. But there was still grass left. The grass that remained moulded and spoiled. This is not good, he thought, and after some thought, he came up with an idea. I must replace the grass with something that does not rot, does not spoil.

Across the plain, there was also a small mushroom, a black mushroom, that could be dried. It was poisonous, and the zebras called it The Black Poison. If everyone who wants water leaves a mushroom instead, and I can then exchange grass for the mushroom on another occasion, it would work.

All the zebras agreed to this. It was better because it was easier to carry a few mushrooms than a bunch of grass on their backs.

After a while, the zebra with the watering hole had an enormous amount of mushrooms, a huge pile. He had become even fatter because he could buy as much grass as he wanted, anytime. He didn't need to roam around and graze; he could lie down and eat his fill. This was brilliant. He had so many mushrooms that he also traded for small pieces of land from the other zebras. The poor zebras thought the mushrooms were more important than the land because they needed water to drink. Soon the entire savanna belonged to him, at least as far as the zebras were concerned. He couldn't control the other animal species; they came and went to the watering hole as they pleased. The zebras were now forced to pay to graze on the plain, but for this, they needed mushrooms, the black poison. They got it by carrying grass to the zebra, but also by performing other tasks. The rich zebra distributed mushrooms to all who worked for him. They had to dig ditches, plant trees, and beautify his favourite spot. Others stood guard at the watering hole. Some were forced to lick his fur and carry away his dung. Despite this, he was considered generous and helpful because without him, they would not get any water to drink or grass to eat.

But drought came, and the watering hole dried up. All zebras knew that there was another watering hole, far far away. According to hearsay, that hole had never dried up. The rich zebra quickly set off. He was indeed fat and unaccustomed to moving, but he could walk far without stopping. The other zebras had to stop and eat on the way. They realised it would take them several weeks to reach the water. They loaded the mushrooms, the black poison, on their backs as much as they could. Everyone had to carry, young and old. When they arrived, they would need all the mushrooms to be able to exchange for water and food.

The sun burned during their long journey, sweat ran along their backs. The black poison mixed with sweat and formed rivulets along the bodies of the struggling animals. When, after weeks of traveling, they approached the new watering hole, the mushrooms had run off, and the sun had burned the black poison into stripes on their white fur.

In the distance, everyone saw the rich zebra on a hill, but the ruler did not move when they approached to drink. They all managed to quench their thirst. The other animals of the savanna had come here to drink too. The next day they could also graze the dry grass and drink more of the fresh water. The rich zebra had chosen a hill with a good view of the water. There, he waited for the flock to bring mushrooms to him to get a drink. Here, he would stay; here, he would let them build a palace for him.

From his vantage point, he saw all the animals coming to drink—giraffes, wildebeests, elephants, and even occasional predators. There was also a species he had never seen before, a large herd of black-and-white-striped animals. What poor camouflage, he laughed; they can be seen very well. What foolish animals. But he didn't care anymore. He waited and waited, but his white herd of zebras never showed up.

The next morning, the zebras went out onto the plain to graze when one of the zebras stopped them all. She told them never to stake out a piece of land and say, "This is mine." The intelligent zebra went on to say that the land and water belong to everyone.

"We don't have to work for the white zebra; we can do well without the black poison. We are free. No one should ever dictate to us. Let the stripes we have acquired on our bodies forever remind us of this.

Therefore, my friend, all zebras are striped and impossible to use as riding animals."

The silence was total on the mountain; everyone, both children and adults, had listened to the woman's story. But the calm didn't last long before shouts and unrest were heard. A dark line appeared over the water, across the street. Everyone followed the dark line with their eyes as it slowly moved towards the coast. Closer and closer. Samuel looked around anxiously, hoping they had sought refuge far enough up the mountain. The wave gained speed as it approached. The wave grew higher and higher. Now they heard the roar as it struck the shore. Over the fishing village, it surged and then hit the city. The light went out in the houses closest to the water. A car alarm honked for a while, then lost its tone and finally fell completely silent.

Then everything went dark, even along the roads. Everyone sat silent, listening to the frightening sounds. Some closed their eyes and silently prayed. The water never reached the mountain where they had sought shelter.

The night was long with waiting. Some of the villagers wanted to go back to see if the houses had survived, but Samuel explained that it could still be dangerous. It's better to wait until tomorrow when all the water has receded.

The city had not suffered much damage from the tsunami. All the large buildings on the shore, most hotels, had survived. In the commotion that arose, a young Norwegian woman had been trampled. She was not mentioned in the first tsunami; it should have been in the newspaper clippings Samuel had.

What have I done now? I save some, and someone else dies?

When the sun began to rise in the sky, they all went down to the village, or rather to the place where the village had been. Sand and stones were all that remained. Everything was gone, their crops were gone, the soil was washed away. Where there had been houses before, there were now only puddles. In despair, some women sat down and cried. The men walked around, kicking among the stones as if trying to find something of value. What were they going to do now?

Some children shouted and pointed inland. A black Russian luxury car had stopped where the road ended. A man in a dark suit got out and surveyed the beach. Everyone fell silent and turned their gaze to Samuel.

When Samuel started walking towards the car, someone clapped their hands. More joined in and then cheered. Some started singing. Samuel was a hero and would get to meet the president. Finally, he had succeeded, he thought as he walked towards the car. Many were saved, and there was no suspicion that he knew everything in advance. He couldn't be blamed for causing a tsunami.

When the back door opened, he saw the liquor cabinet in lacquered hardwood. It smelled of old smoke. It doesn't matter, thought Samuel as he sank into the soft leather seat. The villagers formed a procession on the side of the road as the car slowly swayed away. With a small press of the gold-plated button, he lowered the side window and could hear the people singing. Finally, finally, I have succeeded!

The president's palace was a stately building, with tall columns connecting the grand entrance. The Russian car stopped, and Samuel was greeted by bowing staff who showed him up the wide staircase. After being searched, he was placed in a room with gold-trimmed paneling. The dark leather armchairs in the middle of the room were worn and frayed. Heavy paintings depicting inflated personalities hung on the walls.

After a long while, the president entered the room. One of the paintings probably depicted him, thought Samuel, but he couldn't guess which. They looked very alike; maybe they were all related?

The big man sat down in one of the chairs, and Samuel did the same. What would happen now? Samuel was a hero, he knew that. Would he receive a medal? Maybe be painted and hung on one of the walls in this room?

"What the hell have you done, you little shit?" the president began.

Samuel looked around. Where am I? What is the man saying? Is this really the president?

"I saw the wild animals," Samuel replied. "They left the coast?"

The president leaned forward towards Samuel.

"And now several thousand people are without land, without homes, and without work. Fishing boats are destroyed, the land has been washed away. They need houses, jobs, food, and schools for their children. Who will pay for this?"

The man leaned back, and the leather creaked as he waited for Samuel's answer.
"I... I don't know?"
"Exactly!" The man leaned forward again. "And then one should not come here with visions."
"But... but I saved their lives."
"You little idiot!"
It fell silent. Samuel was speechless; he didn't know what to say. Dreams shattered as the president began to scold him. Who will take care of the survivors? No homes. The land they used was gone. The boats were destroyed. Had he not warned them, they would all have perished, and then they would not have been a burden to the president and his regime. This president has too little of everything. Too few raw materials. Few industries. Not many tourists. Too little in his head. No heart. The only thing that matched his ego was the size of his palace.
"I can buy materials for new homes and boats," Samuel replied. After all, he had plenty of money.
The president fell silent. This was not the answer he had expected. What had he really expected? Bringing the man here was mostly a way to vent his aggression.
"But then you leave the country! You will never be able to come here again; I'll make sure of that."
"But the villagers need electricity, water, and sewage. Only the municipality can arrange that for them."
After a deep breath, the president stood up.
"If you build homes, I can probably arrange water and sewage," he laughed. "Now get out of here and never come back!"

The luxury car was nowhere to be seen when Samuel left the building. By bus, he went to the city's building stores. There, he bought tools, lumber, roofing sheets, nails, and a lot more. He bought all the appliances they had and arranged delivery within a couple of weeks. Everything would be unloaded at the coast, near the place where the village had been. Initially, he had thought of distributing money to everyone who had lived in the village, but he was dissuaded by a Swedish aid worker for Sida. Instead, everyone should help rebuild the village.

A few days later, Samuel visited the site to see how the construction had started. All the lumber lay untouched. Some construction workers and supervisors he had hired sat playing cards. The tools and machines were nowhere to be seen. He went to some women who had laid out some planks in a square on the ground.
They hadn't been able to do anything because the tools were gone. The men were gone. It turned out that during the night, the men had taken everything and gone to the city. At first, Samuel thought they had taken other jobs, but the next day he got the explanation. Everything they had taken, they had sold. Some had drunk up the money. Others had checked into luxury hotels. Many had spent the money on prostitutes. Two of the men had flown to Cairo and back; it had been their dream, to fly. But the wives forgave them,

the whole village forgave them. They got applause and hugs when they returned a few days later, tired and worn-out heroes. Samuel then bought new machines and tools but made sure that the women took care of them.

The president had talked about them being unemployed, and Samuel considered organising education for everyone in the village, women, and men. Then there would also be a need for preschool for the children and nursing homes for the elderly. But is this the right way to live? Would it be a better life for the people in the village? Is my upbringing the best for everyone? Samuel thought of the Norwegian woman, the one who would have been alive if he hadn't acted. These people would have died if I hadn't done anything, but then the president would have been satisfied. But what could I have done?

A very desperate Samuel walked slowly back to the hotel. It can't be easy to be a god, to have so many lives on your conscience, thought Samuel.

All of Earth's different gods have affected a lot with their influence, and long after they appeared to us. Jesus healed people; he even raised people from the dead. Those people themselves may have influenced the afterworld. But Jesus' mere existence has affected a lot more, and far beyond when he walked on Earth. All the churches built over two thousand years, all these missionaries spreading God's word further. Priests and forgiveness. A lot has happened in the name of God, not to mention the Inquisition. Things would have been different if Jesus hadn't shown up. The whole Earth might have looked different. Maybe we would have avoided all wars, or maybe we would have had even worse wars. Who knows? Nobody knows!

This applies to all Earth's gods. They have all had and have a very great impact on us humans and earthly life. One really hopes they know what they're doing; one easily gets the feeling that all the gods threw in the towel a long time ago.

18 Diesel Engines

On the next floor, they found yet another large room. It was dark, and nothing happened when the YouTube geek pressed all the switches.

"Still no power," he sighed.

In the light from emergency exit signs, they could see some display cabinets and tall desks.

"This is not a freezer room like the other one," Otto noted.

There were a couple of computers, and their dark screens looked like black square holes in the dark room. Folders and papers were scattered on the floor. The light from Mark's mobile reflected in the glass cabinets, making it difficult to see.

"This must have been some kind of laboratory."

Further into the room, two large sofas stood in the middle, almost like a living room, or a hotel lobby.

"But where is the entrance? How the hell do we get out?"

Then shouts were heard from the floor above.

"More people awake? Guys?" Otto immediately turned around. "I'll go back and help them."

In the light of his mobile, Mark continued searching and ended up in front of a cabinet with lying bottles. A wine cooler with wine.

"No food, unfortunately, but we can have a glass of wine," he said and opened the cooler.

"We need food and water, not wine," commented Jasmine, sinking into a leather sofa. Her gaze fixated on the carpet under the table; the yellow-green rug she had seen before. The sofas, the carpet, the table, she had been here before, she remembered.

"Check out the wine!" Mark yelled. "The bottle is from 2035! What a lousy joke!" He tried to connect with his followers again. Out of sheer habit, he always tried to comment or film what he was doing when he encountered something. He even wrote when he didn't encounter anything, but now it was especially important. In the past hour, so much had happened that Macie-ducey was completely excited.

"Must have WiFi and the Internet," he mumbled. "Must get it out." To calm himself, he took a selfie with the wine with the peculiar year. When he searched further, he found that all the wines had years far into the future, 2027, 2032, 2038.

Otto came back with five people. A little disappointed that it wasn't his buddies he heard upstairs. The newcomers looked around nervously in their white coats.

"What have you found here?" Otto asked when he saw Mark at the wine cabinet. Mark showed them the peculiar wine bottles while Jasmine greeted the newcomers, four older women and a middle-aged man. She couldn't remember seeing any of them before.

"Are these your dogs?" she asked. The man had spasms and had difficulty speaking. Everyone looked like question marks and shook their heads.

"You have just become owners of a little dog, a cute little Pekingese." Jasmine pointed to the dogs yapping around the newcomers.

"We have all been frozen, even the little dogs. There's no staff here, nothing to eat or drink. No electricity for that matter. We're trying to get out of the building to get help." Jasmine started walking towards the door to the staircase.

"Come, there's nothing here. We have to get out! Out of here!"

"I'm going first." Mark took a wine bottle under his arm and squeezed past. The Pekingese squeezed past him in turn.

"You should have your animals on a leash!" Jasmine said to the five question marks. "You can maybe find some strings in some of the office drawers in here."

The stairs continued another floor, and they all thought it was the bottom floor. Finally, they would find an exit, get out of this horrible building.

But the joy was short-lived; it looked more like a basement. No windows, warm and humid. In the middle of the room stood a diesel engine. An emergency power generator. Heat radiated from the hissing valves, like a crouched animal, a dragon that could rise and breathe fire over them at any moment. The horror made them all form a ring at a safe distance around the green monster.

Beyond it was a huge tank, filling half the room, like a wall of metal. Mark knocked on the cistern with his wine bottle. No one mistook the hollow sound.

"I want a picture of this." Mark quickly climbed the narrow ladder leading to the low space on top of the tank. The hatch on the top was closed.

"If we fill it with diesel, we can start the engine. And get power in the house!" he yelled.

"We should get out," Jasmine suggested.

"There is no way out," Otto replied. "But electricity would be good; then maybe we can get the elevator to work or call for help."

There was a bang in the tank when Mark opened the hatch. "There's some fuel at the bottom!" His yell echoed in the empty container. "But it doesn't reach up to the fuel pipe."

Then it fell silent. No one said anything. They just looked at each other, at the engine, and at Mark up there under the ceiling.

The man with spasms started gesturing. His hands moved around as if pouring something.

Otto shook his head. "Idiot, anyone can understand that we should fill it with diesel. But we have no diesel!" He said the last part slowly and articulately.

The man didn't care but pointed shakily at Mark and the wine bottle.

"How dumb can you be?" Otto kicked the diesel engine. "You can't run the engine on wine!"

The shaky hands moved up and down, at different levels. One of the women had just finished tying the leash for her dog. "He means that diesel floats on top of the wine."

Only then did Mark understand what it was about and slammed the bottle against the edge of the tank. The gurgling sound was amplified in the large tank. It quickly ran out. "We need more. Fetch more bottles!"

The dogs tried to run after Otto when he rushed towards the stairs but were stopped by the new owners who pulled on their homemade leashes.

Quickly, Otto returned with more bottles, and Jasmine helped send them up to Mark. The wine poured into the tank as the man with spasms went to something that looked like a control unit. He tried a few buttons, but nothing happened. He pumped a few levers and pressed some buttons again. Everything remained silent.

Suddenly, it started to sound. A starter motor. With a whining sound, the engine started. Slowly, it revved up. Small lights lit up on the control panel, and the numbers on the display increased faster and faster. 10, 20, 30, 50...!

The lights in the ceiling began to shine; in a short while, the room was flooded with light.

"Yahoo!" Mark shouted from the top of the tank. "Soon I'll have WiFi so I can reach my followers! They missed me, and they LOVE me!"

19 Gangsters

Disasters, wars, school shootings, terrorist actions, and children falling into wells. What could Samuel do? He couldn't save everyone, and was he the one to decide who should live and who should die?

Samuel decides to stop saving the world, to stop playing God. He shouldn't be the one determining who should live and who should die. It could go wrong, far, far into the future. A life saved today could cause mass deaths tomorrow. In a thousand years.

Samuel had placed the time regulator on the kitchen table to tinker with it. A small handheld computer would be integrated for better control during a time shift. The kitchen was a more pleasant place to sit and work, better light, and sometimes he could gaze at something outside the window, at a distance, which was soothing for the eyes.

A black Mercedes had stopped on the street, and Samuel looked absentmindedly at it. It wasn't so strange, but when four men in dark suits stepped out, he began to sense trouble. Four grown men don't usually ride together. Like oversized meerkats, they scanned the street, then approached the house. The house where Samuel lived.

"They're coming here," thought Samuel, ducking under the table. "The door is locked, I'm not home."

Three knocks on the door, then silence. Samuel waited, hoping to hear the sound of car doors closing. Instead, three powerful thuds hit the door, and in shock, he banged his head against the underside of the table. Then there was a crash, and suddenly, the four men were in the hallway. Two of them stormed into the kitchen, lifting Samuel and forcing him back onto the chair he had just left. Powerful fists dug deep into Samuel's shoulders. Casually, the other men approached the kitchen, one short and stout, the other slim and bony.

Absentmindedly, the slim man looked around, as if on an apartment tour, then sat on a backward-facing chair in front of Samuel. The stout one did the same. His black polo shirt pushed up his chin, making his small mouth protrude, and his closely set eyes stared wearily at Samuel.

"Samuel Hanson, we know you can see into the future," the man smiled arrogantly.

That's not possible, thought Samuel. How can they know?

The men calmly observed Samuel. When they ask questions, people usually answer. They knew how to get the answers they wanted.

"No," said Samuel. "If I could, I would have known you were coming and called the police before you arrived."

No one seemed to understand what Samuel had just said. The man in the polo shirt nodded to the men holding Samuel. With a jerk, Samuel flew up in the air, and the other man hit him hard in the stomach.

"I said we know you can see into the future. We want to know how it's done!"

They're going to beat me to a pulp, thought Samuel. I need to do something. But what?

The man with the fist seemed eager to use his hands again.

"I... have a... time... machine." Samuel struggled to speak, his lungs felt small, and breathing became short. "With it, I can... travel in time." He pointed to the machine in the middle of the table with an open hand.

Everyone stared at the strange device on the kitchen table.

"Can we see into the future with that?" asked the polo shirt, looking at the container as if it were a crystal ball.

"I don't just see the future, I travel there!" Samuel declared.

"You're bluffing. No one fits in that machine!" said the man with the fists, raising his thick arm again.

"No, not like that. Everyone who places their hands on the machine travels with it."

"The container, what's it for?" smirked the slim man.

What should Samuel say now? All time-travel movies he could recall popped into his mind. Back to the Future, Time Bandits, Midnight in Paris, Twelve Monkeys, Terminator.

"That's where you put metal objects. You can't take things made of metal with you when you time travel."

"Metal objects?"

The man should know what metal is, thought Samuel. How stupid can you be?

"Yes, for example, coins, or a screwdriver, or whatever you'd like to bring."

Polo shirt fell silent for a while, then pulled out a pistol. "We're taking this with us," he said. "Open it!"

Samuel opened the container, and the man placed the gun inside. It fit perfectly.

"I want to go to 2012, nine years into the future," said Polo shirt. "The rest of you stay here and guard. You come with me and operate the machine."

He nodded toward Samuel, who carefully took the handheld computer. "Any specific time?"

"October 7th, 8:00 AM. It's my sixtieth birthday, and I want to see what presents I'll get!" The man laughed triumphantly, looking at the others who wouldn't be joining the trip.

08:00, October 7, 2012

With shaky hands, Samuel held the handheld computer for everyone to see what he had written. The man placed his hands on top of the container with the weapon. He looked like an oversized child about to go on a carousel for the first time. Samuel placed his left hand on the machine. He would have liked to write a note and explain what had happened, but he realised there was no opportunity for that. The date he had written meant nothing; Samuel knew time would be rolled back forty-two hours, that's all that would happen, to a moment before these gangsters invaded his house. The giant baby grinned, trying to hide his nervousness.

"Then we're traveling!" Click!

The shopping bag from Currys PC World contained a small, latest-model handheld computer. It would be integrated into the regulator for better control and documentation. But first, Samuel needed to review his and Harriet's notes, just to be safe. It wasn't clear how the implementation should be carried out.

But with his finger on the scanner, the door to the secret room slid open. With the codes he had received from the lawyer, Samuel programmed the mechanism to respond to his own finger. The lawyer's dog had eaten Harriet's finger.

At regular intervals, Samuel checked on the machine in the secret room. Sometimes there could be a note or a newspaper clipping from the future, something that told him what would happen in the next two days. Now, there was no note, but the container wasn't empty either; something else was there, something dark. Samuel cautiously approached.

In the container lay something mysterious; it looked like a weapon.

It's a weapon, thought Samuel, a black pistol. Has someone else been here? Is there someone hiding in the room? It's not possible.

After staring at the object for a long time, he realised he must have placed it there himself. But how, and why?

Samuel had never owned a gun, never held a weapon. Of course, he had shot an air rifle many years ago, at a friend's place. But this? This looked dangerous. Carefully, he lifted the pistol, to avoid ruining any fingerprints and to avoid leaving his own. What should he do? A firearm? What did this mean? On the side of the handle, he found a serial number. Perhaps they could trace whose weapon it was?

But how do you do that?

With the weapon in his inner pocket, Samuel went to the newspaper where the journalist worked, Isabella Hawke, the one who had filmed the sinking boat instead of preventing the accident.

"Hello!"

Isabella looked up from the computer, observing the man standing in front of her with surprise. The man had his hand inside his jacket, as if he were about to take something out, something he wanted to show. She certainly recognised him. She remembered the ferry disaster, which she deeply regretted, but also the mocking pictures where, in a kitchen, she demonstrated how to extinguish burning oil with a pot lid. This was the man who could see into the future.

"Hello," she answered hesitantly. It was barely audible amid all the sounds in the open office landscape. "You must recognise me, H... Harry, the seer?"

"Of course! And I know who you are, Samuel Hanson, my brother has had your mom as a teacher."

"That's true, but I'm not here to talk about any impending disaster, unfortunately. I would need help with something. If you have time?"

The recent assignments Isabella had weren't particularly exciting. Now she was writing about some frogs that had died in a ditch in Sweden. How fun is that? Dead frogs don't make headlines. Isabella found wild animals difficult to understand. How do they survive when no one feeds them? I mean... there's no animal caretaker or farmer to give them food. I don't understand how wild animals can survive. Who takes care of them? Who takes them to the vet when they get sick? Insemination... how can they reproduce themselves, it's completely incomprehensible?

The chief editor had frowned when she heard her request to write about the dilemma of wild animals and told her to further investigate the dead frogs instead.

But with the help of this seer, new opportunities opened up. She might learn about some terrible accident that would happen in the future? She reluctantly smiled at Samuel and answered quickly.

"Sure, what is it?"

"I would like to know more about this."

Samuel crouched down to the desk. He retrieved the gun from the inner pocket and observed the journalist's reaction as he pulled it out and placed it on her paper-filled desk.

"I need to know where this came from."

Isabella looked at the weapon for a short while. She then took a firm grip on the barrel and stood up.

"I know someone who can find out. Wait here!"

In a moment, she was gone, and Samuel passed the time by studying everyone working in the office. He saw a few at the coffee machine and contemplated going there when Isabella returned.

"Let me show you. The weapon belongs to Dragan Shovodovic, an infamous small-time gangster in Ilford."

She placed the gun on the table and hurried away again. Samuel carefully put the weapon back in his inner pocket when Isabella returned with a printout.

"This is what he looks like. Do you know him?"

The picture showed a man with a round face, around fifty, with closely set eyes.

"No, I've never seen him."

"His accomplice is named Boris, Boris Milosevic."

Isabella tossed out another picture of a bald man with a narrow face, very narrow.

"You can get Dragan's address." Isabella quickly typed on the keyboard before rushing off again. The line at the coffee machine consisted of only one person, but that was not an option because Isabella was quickly back.

"Here's the address."

Samuel looked at the note, then at the picture, and felt the weapon against his chest in the inner pocket. He couldn't understand any of this. What kind of man had managed to place his weapon in my time regulator, in the secret room with a steel door and nine locks? Or did I put it there myself? But then I should have written a note? Perhaps I was forced? Threatened, with a gun? With this pistol? Samuel was finally interrupted in his contemplation by an impatient journalist.

"Do you know something that will happen in the future, something exciting?" She hoped to learn something really macabre. On the note next to Dragan's address, she began writing some numbers.

"Here's my new mobile number if you figure something out."

"Okay, I promise to get in touch. Thanks a lot!"

Just outside the entrance to the newspaper stood a dark car parked. Samuel wondered how he would get to the address he had received when he saw the man in the back seat staring straight at him.

The man was Dragan Shovodovic.

It was unmistakable. Samuel became completely paralysed and just stared as all the doors of the car opened. Out stepped Dragan and three men in suits. They began walking straight towards Samuel. Dragan was short and round, wearing a black polo shirt. On both sides of him walked two black-clad brutes. Behind them was a tall, slender man in dark grey, wearing a suit that was way too small. That must be his accomplice Boris, thought Samuel.

He didn't dare move and thought about Dragan's weapon lying in his inner pocket. They know who I am. Do they know I have their weapon in my pocket?

Without a change of expression, the two brutes scanned the street. Then their gaze fell on him. Now it's over, thought Samuel.

But the four men walked past him and into the building behind him. What happened? They stared at the entrance, not at him. None of them recognised him; they didn't care at all about the frightened man staring at them as they approached. They were used to people looking terrified at them. But what were they after? At the newspaper office? He couldn't do anything but follow them into the building.

In the reception, Samuel heard them asking for Isabella Hawke. The young boy at the reception pointed to Isabella's place, after which the four men approached the young journalist. It wasn't possible to hear what was said, but shortly after, Isabella stood up. She was pale, walking stiffly towards the door with the four men close behind. Samuel ran ahead and out onto the street. When the four men came out, they went to the dark car, placed Isabella in the back seat, and drove away. Outside the newspaper, there were some vacant taxi cars, and Samuel jumped into the one in the front.

"Follow the black Merc!"

"Like in the movies?" the driver responded with a smile.

"Exactly, but not too close. We must not be detected."

They followed the black Mercedes to an industrial area. The car drove into an abandoned property, a large building in corrugated iron. One could imagine that the facility had once been painted green, or maybe blue? The taxi stopped on the street outside.

"Should I drive in?"

"No," said Samuel. "You'll get double if you wait while I go in." ”

Sure, no problem. Just pay up front."

Samuel paid the man and kept glancing at the courtyard to see what was happening. The Merc had stopped in front of a large gate, also made of corrugated iron. The car turned out to be empty, and Samuel crept towards the entrance. The gate was so skewed that even if it was closed, Samuel could slip in without opening it too much.

Here, there was a scent of chaos and old tools, oil, and rubber. The darkness made the smells more pronounced. Samuel was about to step on a worn-out tire. Quickly, he adjusted to the faint light seeping in through the gaps in the ceiling and walls. A bit inside, the four men were gathered. Three of them had taken off their shirts. In the middle, sitting on a chair, was Isabella, tied up. Terrified. Opposite her sat Dragan.

"You knew there was a bomb on the plane to Paris. How could you know that?" Isabella looked despairingly at the three men standing closest. As a journalist, she had chosen to be a celebrity. In every article, she always had a picture of herself, a picture where she was both tough and stylish. The photograph was also included in the articles she found on other sites and news agencies. The image was important to her; it was her signature. A symbol, a logo. It might seem strange with a picture of a person when we read an article about something completely different, but as a journalist, you have to market yourself hard to stay on top.

Now it wasn't the small picture that got her picked up by these men. Her name was on all the articles about the bomb. Everyone knew it was the young reporter Hawke who stopped the plane that was supposed to explode on its way to Paris.

A fist struck forcefully right into the solar plexus. Isabella lost her breath and bent over. The other man pulled her up by the hair.

"How did you know about the bomb?" Dragan spoke slowly and articulately.

Isabella stared at the men. She couldn't understand what she had gotten herself into. She couldn't comprehend that they could do this to her. It's not possible. This isn't true. She began to breathe again.

With the pistol that Samuel had in his pocket, he could shoot them all. Four quick shots, and then rescue the girl from the building. But he couldn't complete that thought. He had never used a firearm before. Never fired a shot. Much less pointed a weapon at another person. It was completely unthinkable. This wasn't a cheap detective novel; this was real.

On a couple of chairs hung the men's clothes. Samuel crept closer. His gaze was drawn to a grey jacket, and he guessed it belonged to the slender one Isabella called Boris. With great caution, Samuel placed the pistol in the inner pocket of the grey garment. The note with Isabella's mobile number also slid down. When he glanced at Isabella, to his horror, he saw that she was staring straight at him.

Boris smacked her across the cheek. "What are you staring at?" Samuel quickly ducked behind the chair when the slender man peered into the darkness. "There's nothing there. No one can save you now." Another blow to the stomach. "Crko da Bog da! Who knew about the bomb!?" Isabella received several blows while Samuel searched for something to write on. A dirty piece of metal would do, and he wrote "Boris" with his finger in the dust.

The sun penetrated through the roof in a few places, and Samuel sneaked to one of those spots. Isabella's wandering gaze went up to the ceiling, but sometimes also on Samuel.

"Sssamu…," she tried to utter. Samuel held up the sign in the light so Isabella could see. The metal cast a sun cat right in her face, and he saw her reading. Then came another blow to the face.

"Schamu…? Who is that? Is it the one who told about the bomb?"

"Bor…" Another blow, right over the mouth. Say it, thought Samuel, say it. ”Booris!” said Isabella. Boris lunged at her and took a stranglehold.

"You're lying, damn bitch, I'm going to kill you!" He released one hand and pulled out a stiletto knife from his pocket.

"You won't!" Dragan grabbed the man's arm firmly. The two men stood like statues. The girl hung with her head in the chair but seemed to be okay. One of the gorillas went and started rummaging through Boris's clothes.

"Dragan! Your pistol is here! Boris took it." The gorilla held up the weapon for everyone to see. Dragan tightened his grip on the slender man. The man with the pistol continued to search the grey jacket.

"A note, with your address and…it looks like a phone number, and it's not yours."

"Call!" Dragan ordered. The man struggled with his large fingers on his mobile. After a short while, a ringtone was heard. It came from Isabella's handbag.

"What we're going to do now is not suitable for young women to see!" said Dragan, and the three men dragged Boris further into the room.

"She's lying!" he shouted. "I'm going to…!" Then the first blow came, and after that, it wasn't possible to hear what the slender man was trying to convince his comrades of.

The stiletto lay on the floor, and Samuel could quickly cut Isabella loose from the chair. What had he done? It was his fault the girl had been hurt. The girl seemed okay and could stand up.

"Can you walk?" Samuel asked. Isabella nodded, blood spattering from her nose. They sneaked toward the gate, stepped over old tires, and squeezed out. Samuel took Isabella's hand as they ran across the courtyard. The taxi was still there, and the engine started as they threw themselves into the back seat.

"Drive! Drive back! Just drive!" shouted Samuel. With a screech, the car set off. The gate remained unmoved, and Samuel heaved a sigh of relief. After driving a bit, the two had calmed down.

"Maybe it's best not to make a big deal out of this?"

Isabella cried, wiping away some blood from the corner of her mouth with her shirt.

"Shouldn't I report them to the police?" She had trouble speaking, and Samuel examined the swelling on her neck, two large red marks. The face was bloody, and one eye couldn't be opened.

"Then they won't stop, and you'll have Dragan after you for the rest of your life. They think they've found the culprit. They're not interested in you anymore."

The girl nodded.

"However, maybe you can find a way to get them for something else."

The tough reporter had shrunk; all that was left was a frightened person. But then a glow returned to the open eye.

"They were the ones who planted the bomb in the plane! Someone on that plane would have been liqui....they wanted to get rid of someone!"

"The police might be able to get a tip?"

"Yes, and they don't need to know from whom."

"Drive to the hospital," Samuel said to the driver. "We have someone who needs patching up."

20 The Mass Murderer

A small handheld device was now built into the time regulator. With it, Samuel had better control over what happened during a time jump. The container remained as before. Written notes and newspapers were still the best way to convey what would happen.

During his daily check of the machine one morning, he found a daily newspaper. It had headlines about a passenger plane with a hundred and twenty passengers that had disappeared without a trace over the Atlantic. On the morning of March 8, 2004, a Boeing 737 took off from Heathrow Airport heading to Los Angeles. Shortly afterward, the plane disappeared completely from the radar.

It was still March 7, and Samuel had over a day to investigate what would happen to the plane. This was not a natural disaster, or...? Out of pure curiosity, he had to find out what had happened. But how?

The airport was the best place to start the inquiry.

When he arrived at Heathrow Airport, he realised he didn't have access to the airplanes. He booked a flight, the one with the ill-fated flight to Los Angeles, the plane he knew would disappear. The booking went smoothly. But then... what to do?

After reading all the displays at the airport, Samuel started looking at people who seemed suspicious. They were everywhere. Everyone had peculiar behaviour. Why is the old lady pacing back and forth by the window? Those beer-drinking guys laugh artificially and seem to have no luggage at all. The father of the little girl seems completely lost, rolling a stack of luggage in various shapes and sizes. Is one allowed to travel like that just because they have a child?

An hour before departure, he couldn't accomplish anything. The plane was parked outside the gate. It looks fine, he thought, and smirked to himself. What did he know about airplanes? Nothing. What could he do? Go to check-in and say the plane is going to disappear? Not possible. It's best to board and see if anything seems wrong during takeoff. Then he can point it out and stop the flight.

Boarding, Samuel played nervous.

"Is it safe that you perform all the checks before takeoff?"

The flight attendant tried to calm Samuel, primarily to keep him quieter so he wouldn't worry the other passengers.

"Yes, we perform all the checks as required. Where is your seat?"
"Can I have a look into the cockpit now, before takeoff?"
"Unfortunately, sir, that's not possible. But maybe later during the flight."
The hostess sighed quietly about these overgrown children and guided Samuel further down the aisle.
"I thought there was a cable hanging from one wing. Can you check if something is broken?"
"Now, let's take it easy. I'll follow you."
When Samuel got to his seat in the fifth row, he pointed out of the window.
"I see that a plate is loose. I want to get off!"
"No, sir, you must calm down now. Everything will be fine."
The purser quickly arrived and urged Samuel to be quieter; he scared the other passengers.

Samuel decided, after all, to go along.

Just as they were about to close the front door, a mechanic jumped aboard. He wore a dark overall and a bright green vest. The flight attendant argued with the man for a long time, making it clear he couldn't come on board. Then he looked at his wristwatch and closed the door after all. The man with the vest took a seat at an available place in the third row. Could this be something causing the disappearance? But what should Samuel do now? Something had to be done. He stood up.
"Who was that?" he shouted loudly. The passengers in front of him glared and hushed him.
"Sit down, for heaven's sake, we're about to take off!"
The man next to Samuel grabbed his shirt and pulled him down in the chair. "Quiet, for heaven's sake! If we miss this slot, it could be hours before we take off."

The cabin crew no longer cared about the nervous passenger and fastened themselves into their seats.
When the plane took off, and the seatbelt light went out, Samuel went to the front restroom. An odour of sweat and old urine entered his nose as he passed the mysterious man. The overall was dirty, oily; he looked like he was sleeping. When Samuel returned to his seat, he sat up straight, but not too much; he didn't want the urine smell again. It was essential to keep an eye on the man with the vest.

When the cabin crew later prepared the carts for the first round, the pilot was talking to them. The door to the cockpit was open. The man with the vest moved. He stood up. With quick steps, he moved forward. Samuel tried to rush forward but had difficulty passing the man sitting in front of him; his legs were stretched out, and the man was deeply asleep. When Samuel looked up, the pilot and mechanic disappeared into the cockpit. The door closed.

The plane continued flying for an hour. Everything was calm. Nothing happened. The mechanic remained in the cockpit. Maybe they knew each other, old buddies. Samuel tried to calm himself with that thought. Then there was a bang at the back, and the plane made a sharp turn. The plane sank rapidly. Seatbelt signs lit up, and an ear-deafening noise filled the cabin. Samuel put his hands over his head. What was happening? Is this the cause of the plane's disappearance? No, what should I do now? So stupid to go along!

Oxygen masks sprang out from their slots in the ceiling. People screamed, reaching for the masks. The plane tilted heavily and looked broken with all the hatches and masks hanging from the ceiling. Help! Do something!

The flight attendants had their own oxygen masks as they fought their way down the aisle to help passengers put on their masks. Samuel pressed his oxygen mask over his mouth and tightened the strap behind his head. The plane had stopped tilting, but there was a strange sound at the back of the plane. Something was loose. It clicked in the loudspeaker, and everyone expected the pilot to tell them what had happened.

After a long pause, a sluggish voice began speaking.

"I've been working hard all week... only slept three hours in the last five days. Must check that the planes are in good condition before they take off."

This was not a pilot speaking.

"...and I found a fault today. The rear door had small damages, couldn't close properly. But I still gave the green light to start. I had to; I had no choice. Don't know what happened. He he, strange!"

It was silent in the cabin except for some crying at the back. "It's important that the planes take off on time."

It must be more important that they're whole than taking off on time, thought Samuel. The voice in the speaker continued.

"The rear door didn't hold. But you can rest assured; no one will have to hear about this mistake."

There was a click in the loudspeaker. What did he mean? The door to the cockpit opened, and the man with the green vest stood there with a small axe in his hand. He had an oxygen mask on and a tube on his side. The pilots sat in their seats in the cockpit. The co-pilot's head hung motionless to the side. The first pilot's seat couldn't be seen.

The flight attendant stood with her back to the man and didn't have a chance to turn around before she felt the axe in the back of her head. She fell flat in the aisle. The man ripped the oxygen masks from the front passengers. A man stood up and tried to stop him. He got the axe straight in the chest and fell over the people who had just lost their masks.

A flight attendant with a gas mask rushed forward. When he was a couple of meters away, he hesitated. What should he do? He tried to say something, but no one heard anything behind his gas mask. The man with the axe took a step over the flight attendant lying in the aisle and slammed the axe into the throat of the flight attendant. More gas masks were torn apart as the man swung his axe wildly. Several men stood up, and Samuel did the same. We have to stop this madman!

After taking a deep breath, Samuel ripped off his mask and pushed forward with some other terrified men. A young guy looked terrified and seemed to prefer running the other way. Even though they were several people, only one person at a time approached the man with the axe. Two men ahead of Samuel fell, and he stepped over them to move forward. Breathing was rapid. Now he was close. Samuel barely had time to see when the axe swung straight toward his neck. Smack! It sounded throughout his body. Samuel placed his hand against the wound and felt everything getting warm. The warmth spread over his shoulder and chest as he slowly sank to the floor. Strange people with yellow beaks followed him with big eyes. The plane tilted heavily, and he closed his eyes. How quiet it became? Where did everyone go? Slowly, he sank into a warm bath, full of soft pillows. Then everything went black.

21 Henry Freeman

Henry Freeman was the man who started early in manufacturing and selling simple coolers and refrigeration systems. His company, Henry Freeman Fridge Ltd, known as HFL, grew rapidly and became one of the largest companies in England. They sold and manufactured refrigerators and freezers for both domestic and industrial use. In recent times, the company also developed air conditioning systems, both for home use and industry. Despite his age of over seventy-five, Henry could do nothing but make money and continued to do so. He was known as Mister Freezeman, with his silver streak. HFL Ltd had thousands of employees worldwide.

For a long time, environmentally harmful substances were used, and Henry resisted the transition to environmentally friendly refrigerants. It increased the manufacturing cost, and he simply would earn less money.

"The environmental movement's demands will lead to significant layoffs," he preached in the media. "We cannot allow this. How can we compete with other countries when faced with such absurd environmental requirements?"

He paid researchers and professors; it was an easy way to approve his hazardous substances. He spent large sums on lobbyists, both in England and the EU. Politicians were easy to influence; you just had to know how to do it. The environmental movement was more challenging; they were getting stronger, requiring different methods to influence them. The most challenging part was public awareness, where he could only rely on journalists. But journalists were easy to handle. If they had something to write about, they wrote, regardless of whether it was true or false. For example, he got a young journalist to drink diluted refrigerant on TV to show how harmless it was. Propane. Ammonia. Toxic stuff. But Miss Hawke didn't even want payment; she genuinely believed she would be cooled down. The liquid would keep her cool, even if it was mostly just water.

In the end, Henry was forced to give in and produce a trial series with environmentally friendly refrigerants. There were some expensive modifications in the manufacturing process. In the end, the costs were only eight percent higher. These environmentally labeled devices sold very well despite him raising the price by over thirty-five percent. Mister Freezeman earned even more money.

Shortly afterward, the state subsidised environmentally labeled coolers by twenty percent, allowing him to raise the price another thirty percent. What a brilliant business. State money straight into his pocket. English politicians sometimes didn't even need bribes, thought Mister Freezeman as he started his air conditioning in the luxury villa in Knightsbridge.

Henry Junior Freeman, Mister Freezeman's obnoxious son, called Hey-Ji, eagerly wanted to take over the company. He thought his father was too old, senile, and stingy with money. Besides, the old man was too cautious with money. Hey-Ji wanted a larger and more luxurious boat. As for the car, he wanted to trade the old Porsche for a brand-new Lamborghini Murciélago. For over twenty years, he had hoped the old man would die. Finally, he decided to take matters into his own hands.

The house they lived in was large, very large. Henry Freezeman himself naturally had the largest bedroom. The built-in bookshelves in Canadian bird's-eye maple were filled with unread books. The wall-to-wall carpet was purple with small threads of real gold, sparkling at night in the light from the large crystal chandelier. The duvet on the large bed was made of double-folded silk. Henry liked to sleep cool. Very cool. The room, of course, had the best air conditioning ever constructed. The air conditioning adjusted the exact temperature in just a few seconds. It could be programmed in every conceivable way. A week, a month, several years. It could be set to lower the temperature by 0.3 degrees at 13:43 on July 4, 2098. The humidity was adjusted with decimal precision. Everything was controlled by a large remote control. With a colour display.

One evening, before bedtime, Hey-Ji sneaked into the bedroom and programmed an increase in humidity to one hundred percent. It would happen at three in the morning. Shortly afterward, the temperature would drop to minus sixty degrees. But only for an hour. Then the temperature and humidity would return to normal. He then took out the batteries from the remote control and replaced them with some old, completely worn-out ones. For good measure, he made sure there were no extra batteries anywhere in the room.

When Papa Henry fell asleep, Hey-Ji locked the door from the outside. Later, it turned out that he didn't need to.

At three o'clock, it became humid. Very wet.

Then cold. Damn cold.

Early in the morning, Hey-Ji sneaked into his father's room. To his surprise, his father still lay in bed and seemed to be sleeping as if nothing had happened. Had it not worked? Had he programmed it wrong? That's when he saw his father's horrified face. A white grimace, his eyes staring at the ceiling. He was dead. The red silk duvet lay plastered around his body. Like a wet plastic film. The remote control was on his chest, and the son gently picked it up, replaced the batteries, and checked what had happened during the night. Everything matched; humidity and cold had hit at the planned times.

He deleted the night's history for safety and placed the control back on his father's stomach.

Hey-Ji grinned broadly as he sneaked out of the room to sleep in his own room. Very satisfied.

The autopsy report showed that Henry Freeman froze to death. For unknown reasons, the air conditioning had kicked in and lowered the temperature significantly during the night. The damp duvet had frozen around his body in an instant. Mister Freezeman froze to death, unable to move.

That an air conditioner from HFL Ltd could malfunction, causing someone to freeze to death in their sleep, was a bad start for Henry Junior, who took over the company. Sales plummeted, and he had to lay off many people. That he simultaneously bought new cars was something the newspapers liked to write about, and he ended up on the front page in his newly purchased sports car.

HE FIRED THREE THOUSAND WITH A TEXT MESSAGE!

That the car cost over a million didn't help. The company was in crisis, and Hey-Ji sought new markets for his products. One idea was to freeze people, so-called cryonics. It would bring in quick money, and he could charge a lot. Perhaps he could use his father's exit in marketing?

Henry Junior Freeman, CEO and Chairman of the Board of HFL Ltd, now had the largest bedroom and always kept extra batteries hidden in the room.

22 A Strange Restart

A beeping sound emanated from the secret room, and Samuel placed his finger on the display to unlock it. It was a new sound he had never heard before. The door opened. The sound became louder, but it was hard to pinpoint its origin. The lights on the ceiling turned on, and he stepped inside.

It turned out to be the small handheld computer that was beeping, and he covered the tiny speaker with his hand as he searched for the volume button. Restart. The display blinked. A reset had been performed. Something must have gone wrong, but what?

This was a new feature he had designed for the machine. It worked in a way that if Samuel planned to do something that could go wrong, the machine would initiate a reset if he didn't return in time. However, he couldn't find out what had actually happened, only that something had gone awry in the future.

The next day, the headlines on the machine were alarming. A passenger plane was missing. It had disappeared from radar screens while over the Atlantic. The plane was en route to Los Angeles with one hundred twenty people on board. Many passengers were from Scotland, Ireland, and England. A few hours after takeoff, the plane vanished from radar. Samuel began planning what he could do to prevent the accident when he remembered the automatic restart that the time regulator had executed. I must have done something that led to me not doing well, he thought. Something happened, but what? Perhaps I didn't make it back home? Did I board the plane and disappear, maybe perish over the ocean? How eerie.

On Saturday, Samuel contemplated what he could do to prevent the plane from taking off. His first thought was to go to Heathrow Airport, but the eerie restart made him extra cautious. Not Heathrow Airport. Something creepy might happen. I could bomb-threaten the plane, thought Samuel. Without second thoughts, he went to the phone booth at 7-Eleven and called Heathrow Airport, speaking with a dark, altered voice. "There's a bomb on the plane to Los Angeles." Then he quickly hung up the phone and made sure no one saw him as he exited the booth. Perhaps the takeoff would be delayed? Some passengers wouldn't board? The course of events should change if the plane were threatened. There was a small risk he would be blamed, that someone saw him, but he was willing to take that risk. Now Samuel could do nothing but wait.

The next day, Samuel monitored the flight on Heathrow Airport's website and saw that the takeoff was delayed by over two hours. That's good, he thought, hoping. The arrival time in Los Angeles matched well, just over two hours later than scheduled. In the evening, the plane landed at Los Angeles International Airport, and Samuel could breathe a sigh of relief. Everything had gone as planned. The plane arrived, albeit slightly delayed.

When Samuel woke up the next day, he was content. Everything had gone well, and he could toss the newspapers into the trash. The event described had never happened. The plane and the one hundred twenty passengers were safe. In the evening, Samuel turned on the TV to watch the news. He felt fine. It felt good that everything succeeded, and he wanted to make sure nothing serious had happened. "A plane with two hundred seventy people on board has disappeared over the South China Sea!" The newsreader tried to look serious, but the satisfaction of presenting a real headline was still evident. This is precisely why he chose this profession after all. Similar events occur when a well-known English musician or actor dies. It's as if the entire media world rejoices. Finally, they get new viewers, and there's material for new reports, exciting interviews, and special programs. Relatives and friends queue up to be interviewed, a much-anticipated publicity, essential for many, and it's also free. There will be extra airtime and moments of silence. Hello and cheer. Now it became fun to work. It's macabre to see their enjoyment, thought Samuel, trying to focus on what was being said. "A plane from Heathrow Airport en route to Kuala Lumpur disappeared from radar systems overnight. According to Vietnamese authorities, the plane crashed into the sea off southwestern Vietnam.

No, it can't be true! I saved one plane, but now this happened instead? Would this have happened anyway?

"Now traces of oil and debris have been found in the sea, and it is suspected that the crash site has been located." The newsreader smiled a little and then continued, almost a bit proudly.

"On surveillance footage from Heathrow Airport, a mechanic is seen boarding the plane just before takeoff. The police are doubtful about whether this is related to the crash."

No, what have I done? Or have I? You idiot! Don't do anything. Don't do anything at all! It will only go wrong! Wrong, wrong, wrong!

23 LIGHT IN THE DARKNESS

Despite Otto's persistent presses on the elevator button, no elevator appeared.

"The elevator is still out," he shouted to overcome the rumbling diesel engine. "We'll have to take the stairs. Come on!"

Light flooded as they entered the cluttered lab. However, it wasn't the mess and light that astonished them; it was the view. Everyone recognises London, a city adorned with magnificent architecture, gentle hills, and a meandering river that gracefully extends to the horizon. Below, cars form orderly queues while a flock of doves playfully weaves through the urban landscape. The evening sun casts its golden rays upon the River Thames, creating a mesmerising glisten. In the midst of the city's ambient sounds, a distant signal horn pierces the air, adding to the utterly fantastic atmosphere. They all had a strange feeling of having been transported from the basement to a hundred meters up in just a few seconds.

"I've been here before, during the freezing process," Jasmine pointed out. The others nodded. They had all woken up here and spent brief moments in this room.

"There's something not right," Otto approached the large glass openings. His eyes shifted sideways as he neared the windows. The buildings started tilting, and the ground seemed to rise. He almost lost his balance.

"These aren't windows. These are large screens. We're still in the catacombs!"

"You're joking," said Mark. "I can see that it's real!"

As they moved around the room, the perspective changed, and they all walked forward to get a better view. When they approached the windows, the technology could no longer visualize the London view. The images crashed, and they all realised they were still in the basement.

"Turn this crap off!" Mark uttered, heading towards a just-booted computer. After confirming that there was no internet and the screens couldn't be turned off, he started walking towards the stairwell.

"We won't find anything here. Come on, let's move on, upwards!"

Otto had already pressed the elevator button several times and shook his head. In a procession, they all moved silently up the stairs.

The freezing room where they had all woken up was empty; no one wanted to go in there again, not even to glance inside. On the floor above, there was a similar freezing room. A juice mixer spun in the ceiling, and each compartment had a red light flashing in time with the alarm. Honk, honk, honk. None of the hatches had opened, and blood-mixed water ran along the wall, seeping from the over a hundred freezer compartments. Otto chased the dogs out as they had begun to drink from the floor.

"Disgusting. Close it. We can't do anything here."

On the next floor, a similar signal sounded, and Mark slowly opened the door. He peeked in. His face glowed red in time with the juice mixer. Disgusting red water came over the threshold. Mark shook his head and quickly closed the door.

"Disgusting, we must continue upwards!"

On the next floor, there was a large room with a high ceiling. Up at the top, a skylight, elongated, with real light, daylight. Half of the window was dark, seemed to be covered with sand or soil. Some of the window panes were broken, and sand had fallen onto the round tables in the middle of the room. On the side was a bar counter and bar stools. A fridge hummed next to it as Otto approached the water tap behind the bar counter.

"Dry. There's no water here either."

"And no internet either," Mark sighed, putting his phone in his pocket.

In the fridge, Jasmine found plastic-wrapped chocolate balls and slim cans of Ginger Ale. Finally, they could get something in their stomachs. The sand on the chairs was easy to brush off, and they sat down. The plastic around the grey-brown treats was fragile and easy to tear open, but the filling put up much more resistance. The chocolate balls turned out to be dry and hard.

The newly minted dog owners introduced themselves as Eve, Mae, Edith, and Lily. The man also said something, but Jasmine didn't catch what.

"There's still no way out here," Mark concluded, dropping his chocolate ball on the floor, where it pulverised. The door to the stairwell beckoned, and he walked there with determined steps.

The hard chocolate balls dissolved in the mouth if you took a sip of Ginger Ale at the same time. It tasted like McDonald's, they agreed, and laughed. They could finally breathe out; maybe everything would work out after all? Soon they would get help. One of the elderly ladies, Eve, vomited on her dog. With wagging tails, the other dogs licked up the chocolate soda mixture.

After a while, Mark came back.

"There's a door one floor up, but it won't open!" He tore the plastic off a chocolate ball and put the whole thing in his mouth. It was dry. Very dry. A humming sound indicated that he had more to say. After chewing for a long time, he could continue talking.

"The door seems to lead out, but it's impossible to open."

Everyone sat silently, chewing and drinking. Their gazes moved up to the ceiling. It had started to get dark.

24 The Golden Hamster

"What does a hamster cost?"

It wasn't the price that mattered to Samuel, but it was a pleasant way to start the conversation at the pet store.

The man behind the large wooden counter wore a colourful apron and adjusted a jar of fish food. The table was filled with items: dog treats, cat toys, dog chocolate, bags of dog food. There was even a bowl with a small turtle. Everything a customer might need was on display. Items hung from the ceiling – dog leashes, bells, and plastic snakes.

The man answered loudly, almost in falsetto, so that even the twelve-year-old boys on the other side of the store, tapping on the glass of the zebrafish tank, could hear.

"There are different breeds of hamsters. Which one did my lord have in mind?"

Maybe the man had been a teacher, Samuel thought. They tended to speak so that everyone in the classroom could hear, no matter who they were talking to. Perhaps he couldn't handle the teaching profession and chose a quieter workplace? How one could find a place with squawking parrots, forty-eight bubbling water pumps, rabbits kicking, whimpering puppies, kids running between rows of aquariums while adults asked stupid questions, quieter was beyond Samuel.

"What breeds are there?"

"Oh, there are many," the man said, hanging both hands on the small area cleared on the counter. He pushed forward his hips, tilted his head, and only now looked Samuel in the eyes. "We sell golden hamsters and dwarf hamsters."

"Golden hamster will do. I'll take one!" Samuel replied quickly.

"But shouldn't you look at them first?" The apron-wearing man sounded disappointed.

"Yes, of course."

"And you asked about the price."

"Yes, that too."

"Follow me," the man said, and Samuel did not take the outstretched hand.

Since Samuel had only shown interest in hamsters, the apron stopped talking in the shrill voice. He no longer swayed his hips as they walked toward the cash register. Samuel had decided on a golden hamster. The animal didn't cost much, a fraction of the total, because he also bought a cage, bedding, a few toys, a wheel, vitamins, a water bottle, and a food bowl. Also food, of course.

Once home with the hamster, Samuel decided to wait a few days before placing the little animal in the time regulator. He wanted to get to know her first.

The hamster was named Andromeda, and Samuel had her on the kitchen table for a week. Sometimes Andromeda was allowed to run free on the table. The tiny legs moved incredibly fast, Samuel thought, having never had a pet during his childhood. He began to like the little creature. Andromeda was going to be the world's first time traveler, he had decided.

The plan was to place Andromeda in the time regulator in two days, on Sunday afternoon at four. If he did that, Andromeda would arrive two days earlier, forty-two hours earlier.

On Friday, two days earlier, at ten, Samuel opened the secret room to meet the world's first time traveler. Never had the door opened so slowly. Samuel squeezed in. This was the first time he was at the time regulator directly after a time jump. On previous occasions, he had discovered notes and newspaper clippings at random times, often much later.

When he entered the room, steam rose from the machine as the lights came on. Cold mist flowed down over the table and onto the floor. Samuel hoped she was okay and gently placed his hand on the container. It was cold. Ice cold.

The cage was still there. It lay where it should. The water bottle was shattered, glass everywhere. The metal tube, from which Andromeda used to drink, was stuck in a large block of ice. Andromeda? Samuel thought as he took off the lid of the cage. She was nowhere to be seen. Gone? Missing? Where could she have gone? He poked in the bedding and found a rock-hard lump. A fur-covered stone?

Andromeda was the world's first time traveler, but she didn't survive the journey; she froze to death during the forty-two hours she was confined in the container.

***

"Are you buying another hamster?" The apron-wearing man was surprised that Samuel would buy another pet just a week later. The pink scarf was wrapped several times around his neck. He apologised with a cough.

"Slept on an ice block in a very cold room. Should have dressed warmer."

"Yes, it's the cold season now," Samuel replied, wondering if there were times without colds.

"You don't own a snake, do you? If so, you won't get any pets from me!" The man began to walk towards the rodent section.

At first, Samuel didn't understand what snakes had to do with Andromeda, but after a while, he realised that the man was referring to live food for snakes.

"No, not at all. I just want another golden hamster."

"Unfortunately, the golden hamsters are sold out!"

"But... I don't have a snake. I'm going to buy another one... for my niece."

"There was an article in the business news this week, a tip that it's time to hoard gold." The man had stopped in the aquarium aisle; the luminous glass boxes with fish extended up to the ceiling. "The next day, I sold all the golden hamsters I had, thirty of them. People are quite crazy."

A loud sneeze made the entire aisle shake, and Samuel feared that all the water containers would fall on them.

The scarf moved on and stopped at some small cages. The man blew his nose, wiped himself with a small handkerchief on both sides of his slightly red nose. "I have Chinese dwarf hamsters."

***

The new hamster was named Jintao.

Initially, Samuel had thought of arranging a small gas heater for him but became uncertain whether there would be oxygen in the container for such a long time. Placing Andromeda in the container forty-two hours backward before knowing what could happen was unplanned and foolish. Idiotic animal cruelty, nothing else. Samuel felt ashamed and was still sad about missing Andromeda.

Before Jintao could time travel, tests had to be conducted. A thermometer, a camera, and gauges for both oxygen and carbon dioxide levels were connected to the handheld computer already placed at the container. A small tea light was lit in the centre. Then the entire package was sent back in time.

Two days earlier, Samuel could observe that it was always dark outside the glass container, pitch black. Even pictures taken with a flash showed that the room couldn't be illuminated from the inside. Apparently, nothing could be seen in a room when time and, consequently, light moved backward.

The little tea light should have significantly warmed the container, but cooling caused the temperature to drop ten degrees during the time the light burned. When it went out, the temperature dropped to minus fifty degrees. The thermometer couldn't detect more. Poor Andromeda, confined in total darkness and extreme cold until she couldn't survive any longer. She burrowed into the bedding to keep warm, but it wasn't enough. Samuel also realised that oxygen in the container was not affected by the light burning; there was oxygen all the time. Thus, Andromeda's death was not caused by lack of oxygen. It was the cold; she froze to death, alive. The container probably wasn't completely airtight, and there must have been a gas exchange with the surroundings during the backward time.

Two days later, Jintao, with his cage, was placed in the container. The cage was insulated, and at the bottom were battery-powered hand warmers. They were connected to start at different times. This was because Jintao needed heat for forty-two hours. He also got a lamp that would light up during the day. The whole cage was wrapped in a blanket for safety. It became cramped, very cramped. Lucky for Jintao that he was a dwarf hamster.

Shortly after Samuel finished the first temperature test, Jintao appeared. He was the first living being to survive a time travel. He turned out to be completely okay. The warmers had started as planned, and the temperature had stayed around twenty degrees, and the lamp had lit up during the day. Everything had worked. Samuel didn't think Jintao would notice any difference in life. He probably wouldn't realise that the next two days were a replay, that he had experienced them before.

A new feature was added: the handheld computer could be set to start the machine again after forty-two backward hours, exactly when time was about to turn in the right direction. This meant that Samuel could now send objects back eighty-four hours in time, three and a half days. Objects could be sent even further back, but Samuel was unsure if the battery would last that long. There was no way to supply power from the outside. With its power source, he could reverse time for a year or maybe even more. The machine would have to be modified first so that the sphere included the machine itself. Otherwise, it would be dismantled when time was reversed over a long period before it was constructed.

Imagine living a year with a yearbook always available. Every morning you read your diary, knowing what would happen. Talk about being a know-it-all at work.

Samuel no longer saved the world. Natural disasters and accidents were left untouched. He wasn't the one to decide who should live and who should die. If he happened to experience something bad, he reversed time, but only then, just like his aunt Harriet had done. It was important not to influence the outside world too much with these time shifts.

Sometimes Samuel found it challenging to resist. One day, he found a newspaper clipping about a parent who had run over their own child. The man hadn't noticed that his youngest child, a fifteen-month-old boy, had crawled behind the car when he left for work in the morning. Samuel had written a time, date, and an address on the edge of the newspaper. The tragic accident was to happen tomorrow morning. This must be one of the worst things one can experience, thought Samuel, and understood why he had sent the clipping to himself. This should not happen.

Early in the morning, Samuel got off the bus in the neighbourhood where the accident would occur; he was the only passenger. It's not common to travel to a residential area in the morning; most people leave when the sun is rising. A few people were waiting for their bus on the other side of the street. They looked a little curiously at him. Maybe everyone knows everyone here, thought Samuel.

It was not a problem to find the address he had noted earlier. He watched from across the street. There were people in the kitchen, and a white Volvo was parked in the driveway. There were fifteen minutes left until the man would take his child's life, and Samuel took a walk to a nearby playground. Everything was quiet here, but you could see traces of the activity that had taken place the day before. The calm before the storm, thought Samuel. He will prevent a very tragic accident, and if he fails, chaos will soon erupt in the entire neighbourhood. The residential area would forever be associated with the tragic accident. Maybe people will avoid the area, not want to live here in the future? A child dies; many will cry, but perhaps most because the value of their property has plummeted.

When he returned to the villa, he stood on the other side of the street and watched. Some children had come out into the yard and were chasing each other. They were too big to be fifteen months old, thought Samuel. But he wasn't entirely sure.

Three minutes left. A little boy also came out, just learned to walk. He had a ball that he threw in front of him and then picked up. Everything happened with great joy. A man came out and hugged the older children. The little boy received a kiss on the head, after which the man's phone rang. He answered with a loud voice and walked toward the car. Apparently, a colleague. The little boy continued to play with the ball while the man got into the car and started the engine.

"This looks like it's going well; maybe I don't need to intervene," thought Samuel. But the man didn't drive away immediately; he continued talking on the phone. The little boy threw the ball, and it rolled behind the car.

Now it's happening, thought Samuel, and ran across the street. The white taillights lit up, and Samuel saw how the man squeezed the phone against his ear with one shoulder. The car rolled slowly towards the child, who crawled behind the rear tire. In the last second, Samuel lifted the child and banged on the rear window of the car. Sudden stop. The frightened child began to cry, and Samuel put the boy on the lawn. The side window went down as the man tried to end the call.

"Excuse me, I have to end this now. We'll talk when I get to work. Kiss!" The man stuck his head out.

"What the hell are you doing?"

"It might be good to look around before backing up."

"You're deliberately blocking my driveway! This is my property! Move! Get lost!"

The man's wife came out of the house and met the crying child. "But little Boris, did the mean man scare you?"

"Stay on the sidewalk in the future!" the man in the car yelled as Samuel stepped aside and onto the sidewalk. The car reversed sloppily onto the street. The tires screeched as the man drove away. Samuel followed the white car with his eyes. When it disappeared around the corner, he checked on the little boy.

"Get lost! You leave the children alone!" the woman at the house screamed. "If I see you again, I'll call the police!"

Now let's hope little Boris doesn't turn into a new Hitler, rapist, or shoot everyone on the schoolyard as a teenager, thought Samuel as he walked back to the bus stop. If I had really saved the child without reversing time first, it would feel better. But now there was an alternative future, one that I chose not to follow. How did this affect the future? The child, who now got to live on? What will it lead to? Perhaps the family would have had even more children if the boy had died, children who are not born now. This child will grow up and take someone else's partner. Future relationships that never happen. Their children, in turn, did not get a chance here on Earth. And their children, in turn. Thousands of lives that were supposed to happen, but I prevented them. I have changed a lot that may have been meant to happen.

"What have I really done?

It became a very anxious bus ride home, filled with troubling thoughts.

I must stop playing God!"

25 The Great Time Bubble

The experiments with hamsters were a way to ensure that living beings could withstand the strains of the time regulator. Samuel had plans for a large container, so large that he could fit into it. Then, really strange things would happen. Imagine going back two days, experiencing the same days again. Not just writing down what happened, but truly reliving everything, exactly as before.

You walk down the street and meet exactly the same people, the same cars passing by. A bird chirps at exactly the same second as last time. Trains are exactly as delayed as they were the day before. You know what people will say to you, at least from what you can remember. How strange it must be to talk to a person when you've already had the conversation once before, exactly the same. It would be exciting to try.

But... after the experiments with Andromeda and Jintao, Samuel realised that it would be difficult to place himself in the regulator, if possible at all. He would have to spend almost two days in a closed container. This means he needs food, water, and of course, a toilet. It's going to be cold, damn cold. Heat must be supplied. What would he occupy himself with? How big does the container need to be? If one would want to go back for a longer time, a week, or a month. Then it would have to be as big as a caravan. According to both Samuel's and Harriet's calculations, it wouldn't work. The container cannot have a diameter larger than two meters to function. The professor had written that in his notes.

Samuel thought about Andromeda, how she froze to death. Poor animal. I wish I could bring her back to life, thought Samuel, and got an idea.

If you plan a freezing, lying frozen all the time, then thawed out, brought back to life again? Then you don't have to pass the time, and you also don't need that much space. No food or toilet is needed. It seems to be really cold when time goes backward anyway. Good idea, it might work.

Samuel began to read about cryonics, a way to store bodies in a frozen state. He found that the temperature must be lower than minus fifty degrees, which shouldn't be a problem. The challenging part would be restoring the person to normal temperature and good health. He found an institution in Michigan, the Cryonics Institute, which was at the forefront of technology. He was in contact with researchers there, and after six months of rigorous study, he believed he had enough knowledge about cryonics. It might be possible to freeze himself and turn back time a year to then relive the past year.

Exciting! It would be fantastic if it works!

26 A Very Good Deal

Two British researchers had been studying cryonics for fifteen years. Their technology was completely superior and based on a substance that replaced the water in the body, in individual cells—a water that did not change its structure at different temperatures. Both of the largest companies in cryonics, Alcor Life Extension Foundation in Arizona, and Cryonic Institute in Michigan, were very interested in buying the technology. Negotiations had been ongoing for a long time, but the one who eventually succeeded in making a deal was Hey-Ji, Mister Freezeman's son. He had been working for a long time to start a cryonics company and had often been in contact with the two researchers. One of his arguments was that the technology would stay in the UK. The deal made big headlines in the media, and when a specially commissioned science program on TV was aired, Hey-Ji was, of course, a guest in the studio.

"Think of all the job opportunities this will generate!" Hey-Ji tried to look determined on the TV screen.

"For me, it's important that the UK is at the forefront of new technology!" The program was about where our research funds go, but for Hey-Ji, it was an attempt to improve his company's bad reputation after his father's accident with an air conditioner gone haywire.

"Henry Freeman Fridge Ltd freezes the technology in the UK," the company leader finally said in front of millions of viewers. "Our country will become a world leader in cryonics!" The deal, the biggest in the UK in ten years, was completed because Hey-Ji paid the highest, plain and simple.

The two researchers shortly thereafter resigned from their jobs at the university in Oxford and moved to the Bahamas.

Samuel had also been in contact with the researchers. Not to buy the technology but to use it in his time regulator. Shortly after the deal was concluded, he got a job at HFL. His tasks were to support the continued development of the technology, which suited Samuel perfectly. Now he could follow the process and see if it could be modified and adapted to his time regulator.

The UK labor job market did not get as many jobs as promised by Hey-Ji, who kept the company as small as possible. Sometimes it seemed like he wasn't interested in developing the technology at all. Research costs money, whether the technology works wasn't so important. Hey-Ji was most interested in selling freezer spaces in his converted bunkers, consisting of old military barracks that he had bought cheaply from the state, very cheaply. He had promised several hundred new jobs for each bunker he got. If you can even call it a purchase when you only pay one pound?

At Freeze Yourself, as the cryonics company was now called, if you had a few million, you could purchase a personal freezer unit. You could opt to be cryogenically frozen for a specified or unspecified duration.The technology worked well, and they managed to revive seventy percent of the experimental pigs that had been frozen. Samuel was not satisfied with those numbers and worked hard on the safety of the freezing process, and of course, the thawing. The numbers had to improve. Hey-Ji used the statistics in his way, claiming that a hundred percent of the animal experiments in the last month had succeeded. It wasn't a lie since they had only thawed one pig that month, and it had gone well. Samuel disliked this manipulation of statistics, but he had no say in the company; he was just an employee.

Many hoped that the awakening of the frozen would work in the future when it really mattered. It could be a real possibility since progress is moving fast forward. For Samuel, it was nothing to think about; for him, everything had to work one hundred percent today. Automating the thawing process was also important, and Samuel managed to ensure that the facilities would operate during power outages, long outages. The bunker outside Oxford had a very large fuel supply, which meant that the facility would be operational for several years if the power was cut.

Hey-Ji wanted to exploit this forced improvement in marketing. "Even if the world ends, we'll keep our customers frozen!" But Samuel managed to convince him that it was a bad idea.

The shortage of staff at Freeze Yourself meant that Samuel was constantly given other tasks. He often ended up in the reception where he provided information to customers interested in being frozen. Sometimes he had to show freezer boxes to close relatives. Which, in itself, wasn't so troublesome because it was the same box shown to all visitors, but it was a cumbersome and uncomfortable ceremony. It took time and didn't feel good when the relatives cried, placed their hands on the freezer box, and felt the frozen person's presence. Some thought they heard the person's voice, despite the fact that the frozen relative was stored in a bunker far outside the city. Several miles away.

***

The unnecessarily wealthy widow had a pack of dogs. The small Pekinese dogs were reaching the age, and she couldn't bear the thought of living without them in the near future.

"They will soon turn twelve," shouted the widow Angela with a shrill voice as she made her entrance at the Freeze Yourself office one morning. The widow wore a shiny green-

speckled dress that she filled out nicely, and the numerous necklaces consisted of differently coloured wooden beads. Her thin hair was grey, on the verge of bluish-purple.
"I am soon turning seventy-eight, and I will outlive my little darlings... or... terrible thought, I won't be able to live without them!"
"Unfortunately," said Samuel. "We only freeze humans here at Freeze Yourself. However, we use animals in our experiments, but it's not something I can recommend."

The small animals ran in their excitement around her legs, barking and whining. The leashes tangled in all her necklaces as she lifted one of the dogs.
"Oh, look at little Chewbacca, isn't he cute?!" She squeezed Chewbacca under her arm and lifted another dog.
"This is Darth." She kissed Darth on the mouth, and the dog immediately licked its nose. With a loving gaze, she looked at the other dogs on the floor.
"That's Leia and Luke. The smallest one there is Harrison Ford." With a jerk, she lifted the bust and the two dogs she had in her arms. With a determined look, the wealthy widow looked at Samuel behind the counter.
"I want to freeze them and bring them out when I've grown old! Is that understood?" Angela was used to getting her way.
"As I said," said Samuel. "Unfortunately, we cannot accept your dogs."
Hey-Ji had heard Angela's shrill voice in his office and now stood in the background, listening to the conversation. The dogs on the floor started barking at him as he approached.
"Wait, I think there might be a possibility!" Hey-Ji had never thought about freezing pets before but saw an opportunity to earn a few extra million here. He had heard about the woman and knew that it wasn't just the bust that was extravagant.

Angela was forced to pay for a freezing compartment for each dog. It was the only way to carry out the freezing in a hundred percent secure way, Hey-Ji explained. Additionally, she would pay an extra pet handling fee, both before and after freezing.
"It will be costly because we usually don't freeze dogs."

When the contracts were signed and the money transferred, Hey-Ji began fantasising about what he would do with all the millions. Very pleased, he put down the pen and looked at Angela, who struggled to hold back tears.
"You can request the dogs to be awakened whenever you want. Just let us know twenty-four hours in advance."
"You are wonderful," the old lady sniffled.
"Then the little animals will come running and lick you in the ear."
"You are too kind. But am I supposed to leave my darlings to the unpleasant man behind the counter? Ugh! I won't do that!"
"Of course not. They will come with me, into my office."

After a big session of kissing and licking, Hey-Ji led the dogs into his office. Angela cried as she walked toward the taxi; she was both happy and sad at the same time.

Shortly after, Hey-Ji handed the bundle of leashes to Samuel.
"You arrange freezing for the animals immediately."
"But I don't think we have five compartments ready for freezing."
"No, idiot, put the disgusting animals in one and the same compartment. It should work fine."

***

One morning, Samuel found an orange in the container of his time regulator. He couldn't comprehend it. An orange? He thought of the occasion when there had been a gun. How eerie and how badly it could have turned out. But an orange? Why had he sent an orange to himself? It couldn't be that he was forced to put it there, like when the gun was there? Samuel looked around, as if it was a prank.
He picked up the orange, rolled it in his hand, and smelled it. It seemed to be a whole and fine orange. A bit mushy, perhaps, cold, a small crack in the peel, but a completely ordinary fruit. He decided to take it to work. Took a napkin from the napkin box, a green-blue napkin. The old package was half-empty, and he wondered when he had last had guests. When did I buy this package? He couldn't recall opening it. The package had an orange price tag, the kind used in the past, 20-30 years ago. Strange!

At Freeze Yourself's office, Samuel had a desk, and he placed the orange on his desk, with the napkin on top. He stared at the creation for a long time and still couldn't understand the presence of the orange. Why did I send myself a fruit?

Amelia, Freeze Yourself's young receptionist, was on parental leave today, which meant Samuel would again work in reception. A line had formed outside; some had apparently been waiting for a while. The crowd consisted mostly of relatives who wanted to see the freezing box where their family member lay, much like when people visit the cemetery and talk to their relatives' gravestones. The more freezings there were, the more relatives came to visit. Hey-Ji wanted to introduce a fee, but Samuel persuaded him to refrain.
A woman inconspicuously entered and sat in the waiting room. An hour later, when Samuel had shown the freezing box to several guests, she was still there. She was very beautiful, nut-brown skin, tall, perhaps a model, Samuel thought. Large floral dress, hair tied up. It was hard to look away from her.
She had left the armchairs by the window and now sat at the coffee table, in the middle. With great surprise, Samuel saw her take out an orange.
An orange!

Without thinking, Samuel went to get his fruit. He placed the napkin on the table and sat opposite the woman. She was lightly made up, an oddly slanted face, eyes a bit uneven, but still beautiful, very beautiful.

"Hello, I'm Samuel. Can I help you with something?" Customers usually stood in line and approached him to ask questions. This was a bit odd.

The woman looked up.

"Hello, excuse me, but I'm not in a hurry. I can wait with my freezing." She smiled. The most beautiful smile Samuel had ever seen.

"No problem. There's plenty of time." Samuel started peeling his orange.

"You're unusually young to undergo freezing?"

"Sorry, I should have introduced myself. My name is Jasmine Saunders."

The name sounded familiar to Samuel. A bit of orange juice splashed on the table as he divided his orange. The napkin came in handy.

"I recognise the name?"

"My husband was billionaire Billy Saunders. You might know him?"

"Sure, Billy Goldman, the one who manufactured cans for all soda brands worldwide. Yes, I know him, who doesn't? He crashed his car, didn't he?" Samuel grabbed his napkin. "Oh, sorry, that might have been harsh."

"It's okay. There's probably no one on this side of the galaxy who misses him."

They laughed together and had a good time at the table all day. There were some interruptions because Samuel had to show the freezing box to some guests. But as soon as he had time, he sat down with Jasmine. They talked and laughed.

In the evening, he invited her to dinner. A nice and cozy romantic dinner. Then they stayed up all night just talking about everything. But it wasn't just laughter and joy, as Samuel learned that Jasmine had been through a lot. About life in India, about her parents, and the wealthy husband. There was also a time with suicidal thoughts.

"I wanted to take my own life, but I didn't want anyone else to deal with it, take care of the remains. If I hanged myself, someone would have to take the body down from the hook in the ceiling. What an unpleasant task that must be. The same if I took an overdose of sleeping pills, someone or some people would find the body in bed, maybe it would lie there for a long time and rot. No, I don't want to go through that."

Samuel sat silently and listened; he thought it was good for Jasmine to talk about this.

"Imagine jumping off a bridge; then divers would have to drag the body. It would probably be better to jump from a high cliff in Norway. But what if you land wrong, on an inaccessible ledge? Climbers would then have to make a very risky climb to find and retrieve the body."

It was hard for Samuel to stay silent.

"But it wouldn't be better to land at the bottom of the valley either. Yuck, to pick up all the meat slush."

They both laughed, laughed at death. A way to get over the nasty thoughts.

"I wanted to go to the hospital and lie down on an empty bed. If someone from the staff asked, I would say I'm waiting for death. But then the problem was dying. How do you die best in a hospital? Even if it's the place where most people die, it's difficult to do it on purpose. If you take an overdose of sleeping pills, they'll quickly pump your stomach. Hanging is not an option either. You'd be discovered before you suffocate. The hospital is not the best place if you want to die on purpose. The best idea I had was to jump into a crematorium at once, direct cremation. Then there wouldn't be much for the relatives to take care of. No fire or hospital staff would have to work extra over the body."

"Unfortunately, the authorities do not offer this fast cremation option," Samuel remarked. "In a steel mill, there are, of course, hot vats with molten steel that you could jump into. That would be quick."

This made Jasmine think. "But what happens to the steel afterward? Does it have to be poured away? Because you can't sell steel that consists of one percent human? Even if you did it in secret, I couldn't live with the thought that the milk truck's tank at the school cafeteria contains a small part of a human body, my body."

Samuel couldn't help but laugh. "No, it would be tough to live with that."

"Ha ha, it would be about pouring away the steel, maybe pouring it directly into the grave. Yuck, no, it would be unnecessarily costly and troublesome."

The silence that followed made them both serious. Death requires reflection; it's not something one should laugh at, Jasmine thought.

"That's when I decided to freeze my body."

A previous traffic accident had left Jasmine's body full of spare parts. It didn't endure much. The hope was that in the future, doctors could fix her up. Samuel nodded.

"And luckily for that, I got to meet you!"

The laughter returned and continued until the sun came up.

The following day, Samuel placed an orange and a napkin in the time regulator. He smiled when he thought that he would find the orange in the container forty-two hours earlier and get to experience these wonderful days all over again. Jasmine and Samuel had many weeks together. For Samuel, it became more than just a few weeks as he relived many of the days. Perhaps the best and most delightful days of his life.

27 John G Brookstream and His Friends

"I want to be cryopreserved!" The tall man looked down at Amelia, who was sitting at the reception of Freeze Yourself today. She was young, perhaps too young to make a serious impression on customers, but their CEO, Hey-Ji, liked her. Her false eyelashes were too big, as was her neckline. She liked to put her ponytail over her left shoulder so she could wrap her finger in the split ends. The black skirt was tight and short. That's how Hey-Ji wanted her to dress. Whether it was for the customers or for her own sake, no one knew. Anyway, the man with the light curly hair wasn't particularly affected by her attire, at least not by her body.

When John G Brookstream approached fifty, he inherited a significant amount from his childless aunt. Johnny loved trains. The Märklin railway in the basement could finally become as big as he had dreamed. All the walls were knocked out, and the railway now filled the entire basement floor. Here, Johnny could sit in his conductor's cap and just smell the locomotives and carriages.

But there was plenty of money left. He donated a large part to AIDS research and for combating the disease in Africa. The remaining part he intended to use to freeze himself in the hope that a cure would be found in the future. At least, that's what he told his friends. John G Brookstream had been suffering from AIDS for a long time and knew he would die within six months.

Actually, he didn't have any hope that AIDS would ever be cured, but it felt easier to leave his friends with cryopreservation than to lose his life entirely, to leave them for good. Above all, it would feel better for his friends, and they meant the most to Johnny.

Johnny's farewell party started with everyone receiving a train ticket to Kiruna. His friends were asked to bring clothes for a couple of days. Nothing festive, just something comfortable. A recommendation was to bring extra socks and an extra sweater, the reason for which was not explained. A toothbrush was a must.

When the group arrived in Kiruna, a bus was waiting.
"Chill out, you're almost frosty enough!" was a scrolling text on the display above the driver. The bus was strangely quiet. Not everyone knew everyone, and the few who knew each other spoke quietly to each other. If Johnny had been on the bus, he would have been surprised; were these really his cheerful friends?

But the awkward silence didn't last long. After twenty minutes, they arrived at the ice hotel in Jukkasjärvi. At the entrance stood a cheerful and proud John G Brookstream, everyone's happy Johnny. He was wearing a yellow-white sheepskin coat, a military coat from the 50s, so large that two more could have fit under his arms.

"Welcome to the ice hotel! Now it's party time! But first, you need to choose your rooms!"

The entire facility was booked for the party, and the room distribution went quickly. Many chose heated rooms.

"Cowards," laughed Johnny, who himself would sleep in a room without heating, on a bed of ice. The ice-cold guy.

The party started in the bar, which was also carved out of ice blocks. The drinks were served in glasses made of ice. Johnny welcomed everyone and told them about his illness. At the end of his speech, he announced that he would freeze himself.

"This way, you won't have to say goodbye to me yet; we'll meet in the future," he said, raising his glass.

"I'm freezing myself, and I don't want anyone to feel under the ice at my farewell party."

Here, bleak roe was served on ice. Elk with smoked eggs and spruce shoots, also on ice. Reindeer fillet was served with a sauce made of mosquito larvae and lichen. Dessert consisted of cold crowberries with ice cream. Of course, there was ice in all the drinks. What a wonderful party it turned out to be. Johnny wanted to leave his friends with joy and happiness; that was his greatest wish.

That wish was fulfilled. With interest.

Everyone felt as if their friend Johnny was going away for a while. One beautiful day, he would reappear, and they would all get to hug his broad chest, run their hands through his curly hair.

No one shed any tears; everyone laughed and toasted when he left them later in the evening, never to return.

"Sure," chirped Amelia with her wonderful girlish voice. "If you want to book a session, would you like to meet one of our advisors?"

"I want to know how it works first," muttered Johnny.

First, we will conduct a medical examination and perform diagnostics. It's free of charge," Angelica giggled. It was thrilling to use a more sophisticated vocabulary at times. She felt a sense of distinction. However, it became a bit daunting when customers responded with complex words; it got too challenging when they spoke rapidly, using intricate language.

"We do this to ensure that the person is suitable as a cryonaut." The girl pointed to a picture of a happy couple in white morning robes.

"Hm, okay, then what? How does the process itself work?"

"Well, first, the cryonaut receives a special water, like, to be drunk for a month. This is to replace the water in the body with cryonics water. This water prevents the cells in the body from freezing during cryopreservation. After this month, the solid food must also be composed of cryonics water. But then, of course, you'll be admitted here to Freeze Yourself."

Amelia stood up and showed off the fine premises, just as she had been taught. It was Hey-Ji who had shown her how to turn her body slowly and hold her hand high. She had been instructed several times.

"We do this to ensure that all food is cryonics-produced."

"So all the water in my body should be replaced?" Johnny sounded a bit hesitant. Was this possible?

"Not all water. It's enough that seventy percent is exchanged. It works a bit like the windshield washer fluid in a car." Amelia put her fingertips to her mouth. "But I'm not allowed to say that. Not allowed!"

"So, this takes another month?"

"Yes, but you are lodged in our fine facilities during that time."

"How much does all this cost?"

Amelia folded the brochure and pushed it forward to the customer.

"Prices vary depending on how long the customer wants to travel as a cryonaut. Our advisors can discuss the exact price with you when you meet them."

"Roughly?"

"One option is to be a cryonaut for a specific period. Then the cost is between three and ten million. A shorter time is more economical. Of course. Cheaper."

"What else is there to choose from?"

"You can also let external conditions affect the time you are cryopreserved, such as something happening in the world, a technological breakthrough, a curable disease."

"None of these fit for me. I don't want to meet any advisors; I want to talk to your boss right away."

John G Brookstream had decided how he wanted to do it.

Later, Johnny agreed with the owner Hey-Ji to be registered as cryopreserved but not actually frozen. He paid for the entire process and was also forced to pay the business owner a hefty sum to carry out this fake cryopreservation. He would leave parts of his beloved Märklin railway in the freezing compartment but move on to another place.

John G Brookstream went abroad, to a place where they took care of his body in an alternative way, without leaving any traces.

"I want to see my husband!" The woman had just passed through the doors of Freeze Yourself, and she screamed with a shrill voice.

"I must see my husband!" The bags under her makeup-free eyes indicated that the woman hadn't slept much in the last few days. The wrinkled white shirt was partially tucked into the tight jeans as she walked barefoot ahead of the queue with the family from Hinkley Point. They stepped back politely. Adrian, radiation-damaged, could wait with his visit.

Amelia at the reception desk responded as usual.

"It takes a moment to retrieve the cryonaut capsule. Which social security number is it?"

"I don't want to clap any damn freezer box! I need to see his face. I want to see that he's really here!" The woman began to cry.

Samuel left his office and offered to help. This seemed to be too difficult for the young girl to handle. As Samuel approached the woman, she had her hands on her face.

"Come, let's sit down over here," Samuel said calmly.

The woman looked up in fright.

"Go away, don't come near!" She pushed Samuel away but immediately regretted it and apologised.

"I need to see my husband. He's stalking me. Spying on me, even though he's frozen here!"

"It shouldn't be a problem. Come into my office, and we'll sort this out."

After some hesitation, the woman followed into the office. When she sat down, and Samuel closed the door, she calmed down.

"Whom does it concern?" Samuel wondered.

"Professor Anthony Deerhaven, the multi-billionaire."

"How much money the person has doesn't matter here. But I need to ask for your identification."

The identification was correct, Lily Deerhaven, this was Anthony Deerhaven's wife. The man Freeze Yourself froze over two years ago.

"According to what I can see on the computer screen, he is frozen here. What makes you think otherwise?"

The deep breath indicated that she would finally get to talk about her husband.

"Anthony is a wonderful man, but he's incredibly jealous, insanely jealous. If I talk to a man for a few minutes at an event, that man usually loses his job just a few days later, no matter where he worked. If I smile at a shop assistant, Anthony buys the store a week later, puts it into bankruptcy, fires all employees. I have often not been able to go out."

"That sounds awful."
"But Anthony is very kind, deep down. I love him. He only hits me when I've been foolish and disobedient."
"But that's not good, is it?"
"But he doesn't mean it. He's just so incredibly jealous."
"But what makes you think he's no longer cryopreserved?"
"When Anthony received the news of his incurable illness and decided to freeze himself, I hoped that this persecution would end. But it doesn't. It continues. He still stalks me!"
The woman may not be entirely healthy, thought Samuel. She imagines all this. In any case, she must be allowed to see her cryopreserved husband.
"We will arrange for you to see your husband. But he is not here... at the moment... but we can take my car."

For the last stretch to Bunker B13, they had to walk on foot. It was possible to drive all the way, but the only parking space available was reserved for transports. In the car, Lily had become worried again. She was afraid Samuel would be the next victim, just because they had been seen together. It was enough. He could also be in danger.
"What makes you think something would happen to me?" Samuel wondered.
"I've had several men after Anthony was cryopreserved. All have disappeared or been harmed."
"Disappeared?"
"Yes, Spencer, the first man I met. He got a very good job offer in China shortly after we met. He traveled away, and no one has heard from him since."
"But maybe he got a very good job?"
"I don't think so. He is reported missing by The British Embassy Beijing. Then I met Stuart, very nice and sympathetic. After the first night together, he was forced to go to the US for work. Then he was also gone. Disappeared."
That's what some men do; they don't want committed relationships, Samuel thought silently to himself. But how do you explain that to her?
"He might not... have wanted a deeper relationship?"
"Even his employer missed him. It later turned out that they hadn't sent him away. No one knows who did."
"That was strange."
"Then I met Silas, a young guy. He left the morning after. He got a job in Thailand and disappeared. No one has heard from him since. I decided not to meet anyone at all. I lived alone for a long time."
"If someone offers me a good job in Australia, I should decline," Samuel laughed, but Lily didn't listen.
"But I became very fond of Sebastian, wonderful Seb. I asked him early in our acquaintance, and he hadn't applied for a job abroad. He told me he didn't apply for jobs and never traveled for work."
"Smart."
"He was robbed and murdered outside his home shortly after our first date."

Bunker B13 was a discreet building, well camouflaged. All that was visible were a few windows embedded in the rock and a green metal door on the side.

In the first room, the staff sat in white coats, having coffee, chocolate balls were popular. It smelled like coffee. Samuel cheerfully greeted them and then called for the elevator.

Lily was astonished when they entered the room with all the freezing compartments. She hadn't expected this. That there were so many. And so big.

"There are several floors," Samuel explained. He went to a specific compartment and placed his hand on the handle.

"He won't look nice. Grey, frosty, full of nasty tubes. I can only show him for a short time. The temperature must be kept constant."

Lily nodded.

There was a click as Samuel pulled the handle. Out came the bed with the billionaire Anthony Deerhaven. Cold vapour ran on the sides, and it immediately became cold around their feet. Lily looked stunned at the man on the bed.

"Professor Deerhaven, is it him?" Samuel asked.

"Yes, that's him. Thank you!"

"Shall I close him in again?"

Lily nodded.

"Close it properly! Thank you!"

There were no job offers for Samuel, and he was not robbed or murdered. But after a few days, a unmarked police car came to Samuel's home. Three police officers got out, one was in plain clothes. The man in a suit had a search warrant and asked Samuel to unlock the car. After looking around in the car, the man stuck his hand under the front seat and pulled out a bag of white powder. The man tasted the white powder.

"Samuel Hanson, you are arrested and must come to the station. Right away."

A bag of drugs, thought Samuel. How could it end up there? I've never done drugs, never had anything to do with narcotics?

"I just need to fix something in there first," he replied.

The man nodded to the two police officers to follow. "

"Getting my toothbrush," Samuel said and walked towards the secret room. Unlocked and stepped in.

The two policemen stood in the doorway and marvelled at the strange little room where the arrested man kept his toothbrush. Samuel wrote on a small note.

Thursday, 2:30 PM. Police here. Drugs planted in the car, under the driver's seat.

He quickly stuffed the note into the container and pressed the button. Click!

A day after Samuel was at Bunker B13 with Mrs. Deerhaven, he finds the note in the machine. She was right; someone is trying to harm him for being with her. Now he had a different agenda than the other men in her acquaintance, but still, she traveled in his car. He dropped her off at her residence. Apparently, that was enough. Someone must have seen them together.

But who? It can't be Mr. Deerhaven. He's cryopreserved!

There's only one thing to do, Samuel thought. I have to spy on my own house, see who will plant drugs in my car.

After renting a car, Samuel parked it on the street, opposite his residence. The car was a Mazda 2, sandwiches were prepared, and he had placed a thermos of coffee between the front seats.

He waited. It got dark, nothing happened. The coffee kept him awake, but it was still challenging to keep an eye on the street and the car on the other side. His eyelids became heavy, and his gaze wavered. Suddenly, Samuel noticed the man, a person in dark clothes sneaking around his car parked in the driveway. In the glow of the streetlight, he could see that it was a young man. Should Samuel rush forward, or what should he do? Everything happened quickly; after just a few seconds, the driver's door was open, and the man leaned into the car, then silently closed the car door. The person quickly disappeared down the street.

Who was that? I have to follow, thought Samuel and jumped out of the Mazda.

A block away, the person got into a car, an older Ford Pinto. The car immediately drove off, towards Botley Rd. Samuel ran as fast as he could back to his rental car.

Full speed ahead. Two minutes later, he caught up with the car, and then it was no problem to follow it; one taillight was missing.

The old Ford pulled into a large parking lot adjacent to a high-rise area. Samuel parked on the street. When the man disappeared through a gate, Samuel wasn't far behind. The gate was not locked, and he heard the man climbing the stairs. Silently, Samuel tried to close the gate and then quietly approached the staircase. The man glimpsed under short moments as he struggled up the stairs. On the fourth floor, the man disappeared completely from view, to the left. With long silent steps, Samuel followed, he heard a door being unlocked and opened. With a bang, the door fell shut just as Samuel reached the floor. Then it was quiet.

The door said Peter Downslope. No Advertising, please.

The next morning, Samuel called Jasmine. They were spending more and more time together, and this was a good opportunity to be together. After picking up Lily, they all went in the rental car to the apartment belonging to Peter Downslope. Mrs. Deerhaven did not know the man and could not recall her husband ever mentioning the name or visiting the residential area.

They rang the bell.

The man who opened was the same person Samuel had followed the night before, Peter Downslope. After assuring him that they were not from the police, they were let in. Jasmine almost slipped on advertising from ASDA and Sainsbury's just inside the door. It smelled sour, probably from one of the trash bags along the floor in the hallway. In the kitchen, the dishes had crept over to the kitchen table after filling up the entire sink. Jasmine grimaced at all the cigarette butts floating in many of the glasses. Peter Downslope sat in the old sofa in the living room. The grey sweatpants were sticky, but the faded Iron Maiden shirt looked quite fresh.

"I know nothing about any Deerhaven. Never heard the name," the man assured and lit a cigarette.

Lily then told him about her husband, about the cryopreservation, and the mysterious disappearances her boyfriends had suffered.

"My husband is unable to do anything. I have to find out who is helping him!"

"I don't know," replied Peter and blew smoke carelessly into the visitors' faces. "I got the job via email. At first, I thought it was spam, but there was an address mentioned here in Oxford. I went there, a warehouse, with a door code. I think it was called Boxer Self Storage."

"That's my husband's company... or... it's part of his conglomerate," Lily added.

"The code I got worked. Inside, there were lots of compartments, all with codes. In the compartment I got the code to, there was a bag of drugs and five hundred quid."

"Was there anything else?" Samuel wondered. "A note or something?"

"No, after that, I got an email telling me what to do with the bag. I arranged it, and today I'm picking up five thousand more. In another compartment."

"Did you also contact the police?"

"No way, not the cops!"

"Can we see that email?"

"Sure!"

After forwarding the email to Samuel's inbox, they left Mr. Downslope in his apartment. He looked satisfied. Boxer Self Storage awaited him, and then the racecourse.

Who tipped off the police? Who sent the email? Neither Samuel, Jasmine, nor Lily had any idea how to trace an email.

"But I know someone who might be able to, a journalist should know this stuff, her name is Isabella Hawke," exclaimed Samuel. Together, they drove in the rental car to the newspaper office.

Indeed. Isabella's colleagues found loads of hidden information in the email. The message had come from China, and before that, Japan. It had passed through South Africa, spent an hour in Grimsby, and originally sent from an address on Islington in London. An apartment belonging to Razvan Albu.

"Never heard the name before," Lily assured.

"No, we haven't found anything about him either," said Isabella.

"Interesting," muttered Samuel, who was in completely different thoughts. "But I have to leave now. The police will be visiting me in a little while. They're conducting a search."

Isabella reacted immediately and looked curiously at Samuel.

"It's okay. They won't find... oh, damn it."

He glanced briefly at his wristwatch.

"I have to leave now, right away. That damn bag is still in my car at home!"

The police found no drugs in Samuel's car. Just before they arrived, Samuel had thrown the white bag into the rental car he had parked on the other side of the street.

***

The elevator was small and cramped. If you were a bit round in the stomach, it would be difficult to fit more than two people, thought Samuel as he pushed aside the grate at the elevator door on the fifth floor. Jasmine was with him; they were spending more and more time together. They both stood in front of Razvan Albu's apartment door, an old double door with frosted glass panes. So, this is where the man who sends emails around the world so that a tired metalhead can collect money in a compartment lives.

No one answered when they rang the bell. It was quiet inside.

Samuel and Jasmine decided to take turns observing the building and the apartment. They had to find this Razvan; he was their only lead. After driving around the block fifteen times, they found a parking spot from where they could keep an eye on the entrance.

On the second day, they learned who lived in the building, who came and went. It made surveillance easier. Samuel wondered how many elderly ladies lived in the building. They all looked the same, but the shopping cart they struggled to push up the first flight of stairs was of different make.

On the third day, nothing. Who is this Razvan? Maybe he lives abroad? But he emailed young Mr. Downslope quite recently. Where did he go after that? Samuel thought as he sipped his coffee. It's not a cheap apartment he has; it must have cost over a million, for sure.

In the evening, all the apartments were lit. In some rooms, a cold blue glow blinked. The ladies are watching TV, thought Samuel, adjusting the blanket over his knees. Razvan's apartment was still dark.

On the fourth day, the same people came and went again. The warm coffee caused the car windows to fog up, and Samuel wiped a small opening with his sweater sleeve.

In the evening of the fifth day, a young girl with a suitcase arrived. The long green cardigan looked worn but not dirty. The hair was dark, loose; the girl didn't look older than fifteen, definitely a teenager, thought Samuel. The suitcase, on the other hand, was old, one without wheels. After walking back and forth, passing the gate several times, she looked up at the building's façade and then confidently walked through the entrance.

Samuel threw himself out of the car and hurried across the street. The elevator was already going up when he entered the stairwell. With a pounding heart and quick steps, he followed the elevator up through the building.

The elevator stopped on the fifth floor. The elevator stopped on the fifth floor. A few steps down, Samuel could see the girl ringing the doorbell to Razvan's apartment. After ringing five times, the girl sat down on the floor, next to her suitcase. She sighed.

"Are you looking for Razvan?" Samuel asked, approaching the girl.

"Yes," the girl answered without changing her expression.

"Do you have nowhere to stay?"

"I'm waiting for Razvan."

"I am too. He hasn't been here for a week."

"So, he's alive?" the girl asked, looking happy for a brief moment. Then the sadness came over her again.

"I don't know," Samuel replied. "I've never met him."

"I have, when he was alive. Razvan was my older brother. He's dead and buried back home in Romania. For several years now."

"But who are you waiting for then? I thought you were waiting for Razvan?"

"Dad sent me. This is Razvan's apartment, registered under his social security number. But my brother died poor. This Razvan is rich, very rich. He has accounts with a lot of money in many countries."

"But you don't know who he is?"

"No, I don't."

"I think the person living here has nothing to do with your brother. Someone bought his identity."

"Bought his identity?"

"Yes, if you have a lot of money, it's not uncommon."

"Do you have any papers about him?"

"Yes, here is his passport, death certificate, and some other documents." The girl showed, everything neatly arranged in a plastic folder.

"I'm Samuel. What's your name?"

"Flora."

"I think we should go to the police, Flora."

"No, not the police!"

"The police are there to help."

"Are you joking?"

"You can stay with a friend of mine, and I'll take your papers to the police. Then we can find out who's living in your brother's apartment. Does that sound okay?"
Flora hesitated, then nodded quietly.

After dropping off Flora with Jasmine, Samuel immediately went to the police station. There was a long account of the Deerhaven couple, strange persecutions, and missing persons. The missing men were well known to the police, and they promptly arranged a search at Razvan Albu's place.

When the police broke into the apartment, they found only computers and servers. A data centre. Otherwise, the apartment was empty. There were monitors monitoring the Deerhaven couple's home. The street and some other places were visible on the screens. There was a lot of advertising in the hallway. The refrigerator was turned off. It seemed like no one had been in the apartment for several years. The police officers seemed very satisfied.
"We will investigate the digital equipment here and get back to you as soon as we know something. We suspected something fishy was going on here, but we didn't have any evidence before. You deserve great thanks!"

A few weeks later, Samuel found out what was on the computers. A highly advanced AI that monitored Mrs. Deerhaven 24/7. The entire system was likely programmed by Professor Deerhaven himself. Using facial recognition, the program could find people near Lily. It created its own emails, even called people and had real conversations. Money and other items stored in advance at Boxer Self Storage had been distributed according to an agreement. The program had even transferred large sums to accounts, both in England and in other countries. There was suspicion that this was payment for information, but it was also suspected that there was compensation for making people disappear.
Razvan Albu was an identity that Anthony Deerhaven had bought to keep his AI running while he himself was cryopreserved. The program was very sophisticated. None of the police's computer experts had ever seen anything like it.

This computer scheme later became a gold mine for Britain's lawyers. For one thousand pounds per hour, they dissected Anthony Deerhaven's activities for several months. What a wonderful scheme, a cryopreserved man who turns out to be guilty and convicted of conspiracy to murder. If he is awakened, he will die due to his illness. Thus, he cannot be revived. At least not at the moment. But how can he be punished as cryopreserved? The police lawyers finally concluded that the cryopreserved man should be kept in prison.
"But cryopreservation is very advanced," Samuel tried to explain when he was called in as a cryonics expert during a meeting.
"Oh, anyone can handle a freezer!"
"No, it's much more than a freezer. Large parts of the prison have to be rebuilt!"
"We will look into it!"

"But the convicted person can't escape, can't move, he's cryopreserved!" Samuel fought hard for the lawyers to understand, but... maybe they didn't want to understand?

Negotiations continued for several more months, and even more millions in costs. In the end, it was decided that a padlock should be placed on Deerhaven's cryobox.
"I can arrange that," replied Samuel, smiling to himself.

But the lawyers' association did not give up with this, and the meeting rooms at the law firm were filled with eager discussions.
"But what happens when the crimes become statute-barred?"
"Should a convicted criminal be given the opportunity to freeze himself during his sentence?"
"Thawed out like a free man?"
"There are rumours that the Liberal Democrats want all criminals to be offered that opportunity."
"At the state's expense."
"Are you kidding?"
"But isn't it a dumb idea? To freeze all criminals?"
"Idiot, then we'll be out of jobs!"

***

The cryopreservation process begins with the individual to be frozen, known as cryonauts, replacing their water intake with cryonics water. The patient is affected by this water, feeling tired and worn out. Then, in a state of sleep, the patient is moved to the bunker where they will be stored. The few occasions when the patient is awake are spent in a room in the basement. Large screens cover the walls, giving the feeling of being high in a skyscraper, sometimes on a farm in the countryside. This is to calm anxious cryonauts. No one ever finds out that they are lying and resting deeply, several meters underground.

"I feel nauseous!"
Jasmine didn't want to gaze at the view over London any longer. Samuel had his arm around her and sneakily stole glances at the panoramic images over the Thames.
"I'd rather die than eat that watery lentil soup again."
"Here, have some water."
Jasmine took a sip of cryonics water. The taste was exactly the same as regular water, but Jasmine grimaced.
"My beloved Jasmine, it will be fine."
"But I will miss you. We have had such a wonderful time together. Why didn't we meet earlier in life? I love you!"
"And I love you."

The leather sofa in the bunker was soft and comfortable, but with cryonics fluid in her bloodstream, it was hard for Jasmine to sit still. Samuel held his arms around her and kissed her on the forehead.

"Imagine if we had met before you got sick?"

"It would have been difficult. I lived in India then, with my grandparents."

"Where in India?"

"The village is called Birholi; we lived a little outside. It was similar to here, more people but fewer cars and not such large houses."

"What if I had come to get you instead of that rich guy?"

"That would have been wonderful."

"Maybe we can meet later?" It was a thought Samuel had had since they first met. To freeze himself together with her.

"What do you mean?" Jasmine lifted her gaze.

"I might freeze myself too. Maybe we can wake up together in the future? And then, doctors can make you healthy?"

"What a wonderful thought!"

29 REF. NO: 362 - ALAN PEMBERTON

"We have to find a way out," Otto said, struggling to swallow the dry pieces of his chocolate ball.

"I still think we can find a solution through the computers," Jasmine suggested. "Maybe we can open the door with their help? I'll go there again."

As she approached the door, the man with tics stood up to follow her. He handed over his leash to Eve, the one with the vomit-covered dog.

There must have been a break-in, Jasmine thought when they stepped into the illuminated office again. There were broken folders and torn papers everywhere. Strangely, the thieves hadn't taken more wine bottles. The computers were still there, and the screensavers displayed images of insects and sunsets. The tic-man started tapping on a keyboard, quickly finding surveillance footage of the rooms. On one of the videos, they saw people working at the desks, some leaving, others entering. All of them wore white coats. Occasionally, a few people sat on the sofas. The most recent video showed a man in a linen shirt and shorts entering and pulling folders and other items from the cabinets.

"What is he looking for?" wondered Jasmine. They watched as the man shoved some papers into a bag along with a few wine bottles. Then the man started walking toward the door.

"Freeze the frame there!" Jasmine shouted. "Can you zoom in?"

The tic-man grunted. As the face became larger, Jasmine saw that it was Hey-Ji, the cryonics billionaire, the man who built several cryopreservation facilities worldwide.

"Are there more videos?"

The man shook his head even more intensely. "This...was...the latest."

"What's the timestamp of the video?"

The man zoomed in on the date.

20/08/2040 18.44

Jasmine read aloud, "The twentieth of August, the year two thousand forty."

"What's today's date? What year is it?"

With a shaky finger, the man pointed to the bottom of the screen.

13/11/2050 18.15

Jasmine read aloud again, "November thirteenth, two thousand fifty!"

They both fell silent. The labels on the wine bottles were correct. They had all been awakened almost fifty years into the future. The last time someone was here was ten years ago. They had both suspected this but didn't want to believe it was true. Now they knew for sure—they had all woken up in the year two thousand fifty, and there was no one here to help them.

"Do you find anything else? How to open the outer door?"

The man searched through the files on the hard drive. He opened a file with a plan of all the boxes in the cryo room. There were many names, significantly more than those currently moving around the house. With a certain pride, he highlighted a name, No: 362 - Alan Pemberton, and tapped his chest. Jasmine smiled and placed her finger on her name when she, with horror, saw the name on the cryo chamber next to hers.

There stood Samuel Hanson.

30 A Synthetic Owl

It was a long time since I got to see an owl. It had been a while since seeing any bird at all, thought Samuel, as he lit a candle in his boarded-up house.

Outside, it was dark, black clouds covering the sky. That's how it had been for the past few years. It was hard to determine if it was day or night. For several months, there had been silence outside the house. No people, no shouts. Not even a car had been heard. Even if someone had been there, he wouldn't have been able to see it since all the windows were sealed. It had been weeks since he last stepped outside the house.

A live owl is a fantastic creature. Imagine creating an artificial one, a mechanical robot, and comparing it to a real owl. The owl-bot would surely be able to fly, and its feathers would be masterfully crafted, perfect in their imitation. Its calls would be exactly like the original. No one could distinguish it from a real owl at a distance. The built-in batteries would keep it running for several days, and it would autonomously seek out the charging station well in advance.

Samuel remembered a peculiar machine that could transform a vole into energy. Naturally, the prototype couldn't capture the small creature by itself. It couldn't move at all, let alone fly, as the device was as big as a dishwasher. The process involved placing a vole in a container—naturally, a deceased one—and then the machine supplied power to a light bulb for an entire day. It would be amusing to witness the dishwasher attempting to catch the rodent, a task effortlessly accomplished by a real owl.

But researchers continue to work on their replicas. The latest owl-bots even had feathers that regenerated if the bird were to lose one. Perfect engineering.

One might think it's a masterpiece!

But... it's still pathetically ludicrous compared to a real bird. An owl takes care of itself entirely, finds food and water, needs no charging station. Naturally, it stays clean, wounds heal on their own. Adaptation to the environment is unbeatable. The most amazing thing is that it creates copies of itself that are even better suited to survive. It raises and teaches its offspring, effectively programming its own copies. All of this is done without attending university for eight years. There are no engineers involved in updates and other modifications. No one checking the charging station, ensuring it works properly and isn't filled with debris. The charger isn't needed at all. Evaluations and analyses are handled by the owl itself, without education and computers. The owl manages most conditions, rain, cold, and heat. Moreover, it is biodegradable. All its parts are automatically recycled; you don't need to take it to any collection point when it's done. No mining for rare chemicals is needed, and it leaves no challenging waste. On the contrary, it contributes nutrients to other plants and animals.

Absolutely fantastic when you think about it.

Incredibly amazing.

An owl is the ultimate masterpiece. The owl-bot is ridiculous in comparison. Pathetic. All it demonstrates is how skilled designers we have, or at least they want to believe so.

31 The Desolate Landscape

It can't be true, thought Jasmine as she rushed up the stairs. It mustn't be true. If Samuel was in the box next to mine, he should have woken up, must have woken up. Otherwise? Didn't the thawing mechanism work for him? Many had died in the freezer boxes, Jasmine had seen it. Only eight were alive, and there were several hundred freezer compartments in just the room where she woke up. Everyone else was dead. What if Samuel is in the box? Dead?

The box was placed high, and Jasmine climbed on some handles to reach it. There was no sound from inside. With a firm grip, she grabbed the handle of the box. What if he's in there? He must be alive; he can't be dead, she thought. Her hands shook, and her heart pounded as she tearfully pulled open the hatch. The bunk slowly slid out.

It was empty.

Anxious but with a certain expectation, she looked around. Had Samuel already woken up; is he here? Where is he? When she calmed down, she realised he had never been placed in the freezer compartment. The cushion was untouched, the protective plastic was still there. Everything was clean, no traces of ice or water. But where is he? she thought. I needed him now. Samuel, dear, beloved Samuel. After a while, she realised what year it was, that Samuel should be very old now, if he were even alive.

Alan followed her in silence as she tearfully walked back up the stairs. Jasmine counted the steps, one, two, three, a small tear fell on the fifth. She watched the drop land on the red grate and then disappear into the depths. Alan pushed past her, and she stopped to look upward into the dark concrete shaft.

"Samuel, where are you?"

She ran her hand along the unpainted concrete as she continued up to the others with heavy steps.

The light from above was no longer visible. It was dark outside, pitch black. Mark and Otto lay on the floor. They were sleeping. So were the dogs that had curled up beside them. On the tables lay the four ladies with some chair cushions as pillows. Alan and Jasmine did the same.

Tomorrow they would get out. They would leave this bunker forever.

When the dawn light seeped in from the ceiling, they attacked the sturdy door. It wasn't locked, but something seemed to be blocking it on the other side; it couldn't be budged. It seemed like the only way out was through the skylight in the break room.

They stacked several tables on top of each other, but there were still a couple of meters left to the skylight. The broom Otto used just reached to poke through the glass. Mark also climbed up, holding his phone up to the windows to catch the faint signals from a potential base station. But no, not the slightest bar of signal made itself known.

With the help of some extension cords, Jasmine managed to tie something resembling a rope ladder, with hooks to place their feet in. The plan was for someone to climb up and out, then try to open the door from the outside. Perhaps remove whatever was in the way.

A leg from one of the bar stools served as an anchor for the rope ladder. Otto threw it first, up towards the window without glass. The idea was to throw it through the opening and then get the leg to stand horizontally. Each time he missed, the stick and the ladder fell to the floor, and they helped to send it up again. Glass and sand rained down on them after each attempt. When the leg was across, Otto tried to place a foot in one of the loops. He swung out from the table, immediately lost his grip, thudded into the top table, and then fell awkwardly to the floor.

Bruised, he stood up and looked sourly at the ceiling.

"I'll try," said Mark and climbed onto the tables. He placed his foot in the loop, made sure the heel stopped right in the loop. With one foot still balancing on the table, he balanced on the rope ladder. When he stopped swaying, he placed the free foot higher and managed to get a little closer to the window. Jasmine climbed up and grabbed the lower part of the rope ladder. It was easier to climb when the ladder didn't swing too much.

When Mark stretched, he could reach the window, and with support from Jasmine's shoulder, he managed to squeeze through the opening.

Then he disappeared. There was no sound. Jasmine tried to see where he had gone. Could he leave us hanging? Just like that? The others looked disappointedly up at Jasmine and at the skylight in the ceiling.

A long while later, Mark, alias Macie-ducey, stuck his head through the opening. One of the older ladies then recognised him from YouTube. "But it's him! The handsome boy from the Internet!"

"It's very strange! I can see the cellphone tower on the horizon, but still, I have no signal." Then he turned to Edith and smiled. It felt a bit like a thumbs up. A very small thumbs up.

"The door, Mark, you have to open the door!" yelled Otto and Jasmine.

"I got it!" he replied and disappeared again. Otto and Jasmine rushed to the door to help from the inside.

The steel door appeared to be built to withstand a nuclear bomb. Otto slammed into it with his shoulder. Nothing happened. After a while, a scraping sound was heard above, outside. Mark used a chair leg to try to push away all the soil covering the door.

In the small opening created, earth cascaded down, and Jasmine widened the gap with her hand. As the light streamed in through the crack, they all pressed on the door to help. Sand and soil fell in, and the dust tickled their throats. Otto fetched the other legs from the bar stool, and when the gap became large enough, they all began to scrape the soil from the inside. The soil was tightly packed. The dust created curtains of light sandy colours as it entered through the opening, moving up and down. As the pile of sand and soil grew inside the door, the gap also became larger.

When the opening was big enough, they crawled up and out. First Otto, then Alan and the four ladies in line. Jasmine sent the dogs out and then crawled out herself; she was the last. They left behind many hundreds of thawed bodies. People who didn't get the start-up they needed. All unknown. Forever forgotten. Their relatives and friends had long been dead.

Outside, the sky was covered with dark clouds. A warm breeze met them, considerably warmer than inside the building. If one could call this a building. The only things visible were half a door and the break room's skylight, small glass slots embedded in the rock; the rest was rock, soil, and sand. They had all been in a bunker, and if one didn't know that there was an underground structure here, it would never be discovered. The road leading up to the site had been covered with soil and sand.

"If I had a connection, I would have called a taxi!" Mark lowered the hand with his mobile, which he had held up, and looked disappointed at the screen.
"Or an ambulance," Otto replied.
"Maybe I should try calling 9-1-1?"
"Shouldn't that be the first thing you do?"
"No, why?"
"Do you seriously believe that only the cellphone tower is out of order?" Otto laughed. "Don't you understand that something more has happened than just our bunker losing power?"
"Stop it!" Jasmine interjected. "We can't do anything more than start walking. Come on, let's follow the road!"

It was an open landscape that met them. Fallen trees, burnt logs everywhere. A forest fire, or several, had swept through some time ago. The vegetation had not recovered. The ground was dry, burnt, and dead. After walking along the road for a few kilometres, they reached a larger road. Coarse wheel tracks were visible over the mounds of soil that partially covered the asphalt.
"Which way should we go?" Jasmine stood in the middle of the road, scanning. "Where is the nearest town?"
"Downwards. We follow the road downwards," said Edith and jerked the leash so her dog did a somersault in the air. "That's where the dogs want to go."

The others nodded silently. What had really happened? Why were there no people? Where were they? Slowly, it began to dawn on them that it wasn't just their freezer facility that had been affected; the forest was destroyed, everything was destroyed, perhaps the whole world?

In silence, they continued walking, pondering what awaited them when they reached a town.

The air was dry and warm. The older ladies, who were already sick before freezing, found it difficult to walk. Alan stumbled often. Slowly, they moved forward with faltering steps in a desolate world. It began to get dark, and they decided to stop. Otto threw himself into a ditch with sand.

"We can sleep here!"

The air was still humid, the sand warm; there was no risk of freezing. It felt more like a tropical night. Tired, hungry, and thirsty, they lay down in the pit.

"Don't we need someone on guard?" Eve asked anxiously, looking along the road. It was difficult to see anything because it had become dark, really dark.

"Guard? Against whom?" Otto replied.

"I can stand guard," said Mark, sitting on the roadside. The screen on his mobile was black. The battery was dead, and he took out his crank.

Despite all the anxious thoughts, the others quickly fell asleep. After cranking for a long time, Mark looked disappointed at the screen, scrolled back and forth among his apps, and then crawled into the sand. Even though he was tired, sleep did not come immediately. Everything was quiet. He closed his eyes, opened them; everything was black. Or wasn't it? Hadn't the sky and clouds become a bit brighter?

Mark stared upward; the sky brightened, grey, purple, there was something. The dark clouds were increasingly illuminated, but there was no sound. A light accelerated towards their location. Mark could hear his own breathing becoming more rapid. He stood up, holding his mobile tightly. He was too excited to think, to wake the others. With a loud bang, the light struck in the direction they had left earlier in the day. Then the black night returned, and it became quiet again.

"Help! What was that?"

"I'm blind!" someone shouted in the darkness.

"Calm down," Mark explained. "It was a comet or something that hit the forest. Now it's calm."

The sky was dark again; the only things visible were small points of light on the ground, slowly fading away. Not a sound was heard; everything was quiet, except for the heavy breathing of those who couldn't fall back asleep.

The next day, they continued along the road. Sometimes the drifts were so high that they had to walk around them, sometimes they were directed off the road, on the side. A flock of crows and vultures had started to follow them from a distance. In the afternoon, they could see some buildings in the distance. Water, rest, perhaps food? Someone who could help them and maybe someone who could tell them what had happened?

As they approached the houses, their hope diminished. It was a small village, only a few houses. All abandoned. Broken windows, smashed doors. Garbage everywhere. Some of the houses were burned. There wasn't a soul here, and no one had been here for many years. In the middle of the road stood a burned-out bus. It seemed to have driven into a pile of soil and come to a stop. Otto noticed that there were bullet holes in the side of the bus but said nothing to the others.

"We can't go on," said Mae, staring at a brick villa whose outdoor pool was filled with debris. On top lay something they guessed was a horse carcass.

The door stood wide open, and most of the windows were shattered.

"We go in," Jasmine suggested. "We can maybe stay in the house tonight."

They opened drawers and cabinets in the kitchen, pulling out boxes and empty cans. Someone had been in the house before them and emptied it of all edible items long ago. In the pantry, they found a few small bottles of water – mango-passion and pear-ginger. Despite the unpleasant taste, they managed to quench their thirst. The dogs also drank, albeit hesitantly.

Jasmine called from a room with several mattresses laid out on the floor, "We can rest here!" There were also some pillows and a table. They all threw themselves down on the floor. Through a broken window, Otto looked out at the other houses in the village.

"Let's go see if we can find something to eat in the other houses," he suggested. No one responded, so Otto and Mark went off together.

Late at night, they returned. Empty-handed.

After sleeping for a few hours, a scratching sound was heard under the floor. Mice, they thought at first, but it sounded larger. Rats? Even larger, more like dogs. The sounds got closer, now coming from the bedroom, near the door. Mark took out his mobile phone, and in the glow of the screen, they all saw the hefty rat, as big as a badger. It ran along the wall, and another one entered the room. Another. More rats ran in and scurried under their covers, between the mattresses.

"Ouch!" Mark roared. "It bit me on the foot!" It flashed, and everyone saw with horror the large creatures filling the room. With backward-bent heads, the rats showed their large yellow front teeth, thick as fingers. They behaved more like dogs, but instead of barking, they hissed. The Pekinese dogs had tucked their tails between their legs and huddled in a corner. The older ladies lay huddled together; none of them dared to look up.

"Stand up!" Jasmine took command. "Put the mattress in front of you." Together, everyone stood up, causing the rats to start following the walls. Using the mattresses as plows, they tried to chase the giant rats out of the room. The animals hissed and spat but were reluctantly pushed towards the door. Their tails held the creatures high, almost reaching the ceiling, and at the doorway, the rats turned around to once again show their teeth.

"There's no door!" Otto shouted and tore away a tail that had wound itself around his neck. "The table," Mark shouted. "We can use the table!" The large piece of furniture kept the animals out, and panting, Otto sat down on one of the mattresses, exhaling. Now everyone wanted to see Mark's foot, but instead, they saw a picture of the rat he claimed had bitten him.

"Look, how ugly it is, the Macie-ducey rat!" He couldn't show any wounds. The rest of the night, they all lay staring at the ceiling. The dogs slept. The scratching sound continued all night.

In the morning, Alan and Eve took the five Pekinese dogs out for a short walk – just so the dogs could relieve themselves. Not a trace was seen of the rats that had terrorised them during the night. It was hard to determine if the sun had risen, but it wasn't pitch black anymore. Otto and Jasmine tried to get water from a well they found in the neighbouring yard.

They all heard a car approaching in the distance. Alan and Eve immediately turned and hurried back to the house. A grey pickup truck appeared. It was driving fast along the road, and a bearded man with a machine gun stood on the flatbed. Alan and Eve started to run, but the car caught up and pulled in front of them. The man on the flatbed waved his weapon. The dirty military jacket was way too big, and a black cap shaded his eyes. He spoke loudly, as if on a theatre stage. "Well, what do we have here? How cute. The old couple is out walking their dogs?" The raucous laughter could be heard from afar. Alan had trouble standing still and waved his arms eagerly. The man on the flatbed looked up at the dark clouds covering the sky.

"We saw a glow in the night. Do you know where?" Eve shook her head. Alan seemed to point in all directions.

"Stand still when I'm talking!" the man with the cap shouted, pointing the gun straight at the elderly man's face. The waving only intensified. Alan began to have difficulty standing.

"Stop!" the man shouted. "I said stop!"

The shot that followed went straight through Alan's head. All ticks and twitches ceased, and he fell relaxed to the ground. Eve became paralysed but managed to gather all the dog leashes. The man who fired the fatal shot jumped down right in front of her.

"Who wants to get it on with an old lady?" he laughed and grabbed her hair to show her face to the men sitting in the driver's seat. The hair came off, and the man got a large clump in his hand that stuck to his sweaty palms.

"Damn, that's disgusting. You're sick, woman!" With a slight push, he pushed Eve and grabbed all the dog leashes. When he got on the flatbed, he lifted the leashes so the animals hung along the side of the car.

"We'll put these on the grill tonight!" he laughed. "Drive, guys, there's nothing more to get here. We have no use for old people and the sick! No one wants to eat old meat!" The dogs were thrown onto the flatbed. Gravel sprayed in all directions as the car skidded away. Everyone thought it was over when the car drove off, but the man fired a few shots

in Eve's direction, who still stood paralysed next to Alan. One shot hit her in the arm, and she spun around. The man on the flatbed howled with joy.
"I'll be back!" The next shot hit her between the shoulder blades. Slowly, she collapsed over Alan and lay lifeless.

In the meantime, the others had stood inside the house and observed the scenario. They could do nothing. No weapons. None of them had ever used a weapon. What kind of world had they landed in? Otto ran towards the lifeless bodies lying on the road. Silently, the others followed him with their eyes as he knelt beside the two friends. His hand gently touched their faces, and he shook his head slowly.

Horrified, they all sought refuge in the house. What had happened to the world? They couldn't stay, but where could they go?
"We still have to move towards the city. It's the only place where we might get help," Otto said, looking questioningly at the elderly ladies.
Mae and Edith had advanced cancer, and Lily had a back injury that made walking difficult. They simply didn't have the strength. The house they had spent the night in was a better and safer place for them than the road and the city. If the man with the pickup showed up, they needed to quickly seek shelter. The rats were not a problem; they knew how to fend them off.
"We'll come to you as soon as we find help," Jasmine promised, who herself was very tired. Her joints ached, but she didn't give up, not now, not when they were so close.
"We're going to the hospital and will come back with an ambulance." Otto tried to sound as encouraging and credible as possible but wasn't at all sure they would find any ambulance or a functioning hospital when they arrived.
After dragging the two bodies into a garage and covering them with a tarp, the three began their trek towards the city and the hospital. Now they had to be vigilant.
Dark clouds moved low across the sky. Crows cawed, and vultures had reclaimed their place, sailing after them in circles. Nothing was visible from the nightly fires.
"Damn vultures, they give away our location!" Mark waved a fist at the birds, but they were so used to seeing his hand raised that they didn't care. Jasmine tried to avoid thinking about what the rats would do with the bodies they left in the garage.

In the afternoon, they approached a city, everyone guessed it was Oxford, but no one could say for sure. Not a single person was in sight. Not a soul. Many apartment buildings were burned, with shattered windows. Some crows flew away as they approached something lying by the side of the road, something with clothes. No one wanted to go forward and see what it was. Abandoned cars stood on the streets. Some had crashed, others were left in the middle of the road; when the power ran out, people simply abandoned their cars. Despite all the garbage and waste, Jasmine began to recognise the surroundings.
"I have a friend who lives nearby." She felt confident that they were approaching the area where Samuel had his house. "I want to go there and look."

Otto peered into the back seat of a car just to find it empty.

"Good, I think we all should go there. I don't believe there's any functioning hospital left."

"Maybe we can find out what happened there." Jasmine tried to read the street signs to figure out where they were.

"I'm in," said Mark, who took a selfie in front of a burnt-out car with doors angled straight up. He sighed and followed the others. "I experience so many cool things, but I can't share them. No one gets to see what I do!"

As Jasmine approached Samuel's house, she was dismayed. Only now did she begin to realise what had happened. This was a place she had experienced before, before the devastation. The idyll in the area around Samuel's house was easy to remember; it wasn't long ago that she was there. The beautiful park. The greenery in the trees. Children cycling and playing. Now everything was gone or destroyed. The trees were dead, standing like pillars among destroyed cars and burnt-out houses. Samuel's house was barricaded with nailed windows, a car had driven halfway into the yard and burned. It was completely silent except for some magpies cawing about their arrival. The front door was open, as if someone had left the house hastily and couldn't bother to close it. Jasmine wanted to go in immediately and look. Perhaps there was some evidence that revealed what had happened. A thing. A newspaper. Maybe a letter.

Behind the front door, it was closed with a black board covering the entrance. What had previously looked like an open door turned out to be completely sealed. They couldn't get in here. In front of the entrance, there was a small step where they sat down. What should they do now? Wait? Hope? Hope for what? Wait for the man with the pickup to come and shoot them? Maybe that would be best? But who could have sealed the door like this? Jasmine thought. She cautiously knocked anyway. Then a bit harder. Knock, knock. She had no hope that Samuel would be there, but felt that she had to do something when she stood by his house. I wonder if he's alive? I wonder what happened to him? It seems to have been terrible here for a long time. I hope he's okay.

Tired, sad, hopeless, she sat down with the guys on the stairs.

32 A Lonely Old Man

When Samuel turned sixty, the world collapsed, at least as far as humanity was concerned. For plant and animal life, it meant a chance to recover on Earth. Ninety-nine percent of all animal species were already extinct, but now those remaining had a chance to regroup and eventually create new species. But it would take time, a very long time.

The rainforests had long disappeared. Deserts had spread, covering now ninety percent of the Earth's surface. The land area had decreased due to a fifteen-meter rise in sea levels. More than half of the world's cities were underwater. Most forests had dried up or were destroyed by the massive forest fires that had ravaged the Earth over the past ten years. The average temperature had increased by ten degrees. The Earth was now a vast, dirty, overheated greenhouse. Environmental destruction became too much when third-world countries couldn't accept more waste from the rich nations. Plastic everywhere, in the oceans, in nature, and our garbage lay on the streets. A restorer alone was not enough to save civilisation. The devastation was too great and happened globally.

The grand plans to send people to other planets and solar systems fell through. Too expensive, it would take far too long, and human bodies wouldn't survive the radiation during the time in space. Thankfully, Samuel thought. What a foolish idea. If you have a collection of islands, and on one of the islands, a large fat rat has taken over. It has exterminated all other creatures, eaten everything there is to eat, leaving only a vast desert full of fat rats. Then you must do everything to prevent the rat from getting to the other islands, not contribute to the rat colonising the other islands. Humans are the fat rat, a very invasive species, the most dangerous of them all!

Everything went so wrong, Samuel thought. Was it perhaps my fault that the world economy collapsed? Did I save someone who caused this chaos, or did someone die because of me, a person who should have created a better world?

The time regulator had been his focus for many years now, and he had worked on making it go far back, several years in the past. But the new function required a new type of fuel; batteries were no longer sufficient. Putting together parts and fuel for the machine in a society in chaos was not easy. No stores, no organisations, no universities, no companies, nothing.

Oxford was a dead city, not many people lived there. A brutal gang had emptied all the stores of anything edible, and even the villas were looted. Cans could be hidden in houses, and the gang was specialists at finding them. On the nightly raids, Samuel had sometimes come close to the looters. In total, ten men and Samuel suspected they had women locked in various apartments around the city. They drove around in a pickup, and Samuel couldn't understand where they got the fuel. The leader was a small round man with a bald head who loved to shoot at anything that moved. This, of course, allowed him and his men to sometimes eat fresh meat instead of canned food. Sometimes a dog, but mostly large rats.

Samuel's house had survived without attack. Much of it was due to the clever camouflage. The house looked devastated, as if it had already been looted. The windows were boarded up, and all doors were nailed shut. The front door was open, as if someone had already been inside and emptied the house. Behind the door, it was boarded and painted black. No one could guess that it was impossible to enter the house. A pile of boards served as a secret entrance for Samuel, and through it, he could sneak in and out of the house when he wanted without being seen.

He did the raids at night. In the darkness, he searched through apartment buildings, looked through storage in basements and attics. Sometimes there were cans, but there could also be a leftover survival box. The boxes were very popular in the years before the crisis. In these, he could find good stuff, water purifiers, medicines, coffee, maybe chocolate.

With his crowbar, he also broke into apartments. He searched through kitchens and storerooms for canned food or anything else edible.

The time regulator had been rebuilt from the ground up, now with its power supply, similar to those used in satellites. A radioisotope generator. The new generator would generate electricity for the entire apparatus and the smartphone that was now built-in. The whole machine and a sphere about a meter around it could now make a time shift. It could be set to almost any date. As long as the nuclear fuel lasted, of course. It was about many years.

But Samuel hadn't gotten hold of any fuel; he hadn't found any plutonium-238.

Samuel had tried to prevent the global economic collapse on several occasions but failed each time. In recent years, Samuel had also written a book, an autobiography of everything he had experienced. Everything was ready for a final time travel. He would turn back time, and the book would go with it, far back. Whoever reads the book might be able to change events, give Earth and all people a new chance, a new opportunity to do things right.

But when? Samuel thought. It was about finding a suitable year, a time when world hunger stayed within reasonable limits, environmental destruction had only just begun, and there would still be a chance to save the planet. But when was that?

He had moved the time regulator to the kitchen table so that it would be discovered when time restarted. Samuel scrolled between different dates. The year 1930 would be fantastic, to be able to stop Hitler before he takes power. That would really change the world, but then I wasn't born yet, he thought; that won't work.

It had to be later, much later. The fall of the Berlin Wall could work. But then I was too young, just a child. It can be tough for a child to find out that during their upbringing, humans will destroy the Earth, annihilate humanity, and that you are the only one who knows about it and also tries to prevent it.
Samuel pondered, and finally, he came up with a very suitable date. He wrote it on the screen and felt very satisfied.

Then there was a knock on the door.

A knock, thought Samuel. Did I hear correctly? There hasn't been a knock on the door in the last twenty years. There has been pounding, shooting, and grenades exploding at the door, but he had never heard a knock.

Knock, knock!

The inner door was sealed. It would take a long time to open it. Besides, it would be very risky considering the people moving outside. He thought about the gang that had occupied the city; the lunatics would never knock first. So, who could it be?

With cautious steps, Samuel crept up to the door. There was nothing heard outside. Not a sound.
"Who is it knocking?"
Jasmine immediately recognised Samuel's voice. With a leap, she was at the door. Pressing her cheek against it, she could hear better.
"Hello! Is that you, Samuel?"
It sounded like Jasmine. It must be Jasmine, thought Samuel. It can't be true; his hands were shaking, his whole body trembling.
"Jasmine, are you alive?"
"Yes, let us in!" Tears began to flow, and her voice broke as she shouted, "Samuel, you have to let us in!"
"Are there more of you?"
"I have two friends with me. Open, Samuel, you have to open!"
"Go to the pile of boards next to the house. Lift the blue screwed planks. Underneath, there's an entrance into the house. I'll meet you there."

A strange meeting in a strange time, the unbelievable, a dream, but it happened when Samuel opened the passage under the house. A long-awaited meeting for the old man and his beloved young girlfriend. The beautiful, the wonderful. And the young woman who encountered a much older version of her great love. But it didn't matter; in his eyes, Jasmine could see the same man she loved so deeply.

In the kitchen, food was served, ravioli in sweet tomato sauce and canned corn. A kerosene lamp burned on the ceiling, casting strange shadows on the walls. They all got something to drink, good clean water. Otto had laid down to rest on a mattress on the floor. Satisfied and full.

"Do you have wifi?" Mark wondered and photographed the old man.

"No, it's been a long time since anything like that worked. I have a few newspapers. But they're probably ten years old."

Mark flipped through the stack of newspapers, but there was nothing about Macie-ducey.

"Oh damn, what old newspapers!"

When Otto pulled in his feet, Mark could also fit on the cushion.

"Where are all the people? What happened?" Jasmine wondered. "Why is everything destroyed?"

"The world's oceans rose, it got warmer, much warmer, forest fires everywhere, dark clouds eventually covered the entire Earth. Economic crises returned more frequently, and more severely. Over the years, money lost its value."

With a sigh, Samuel sat down on a chair in front of the three.

"Everything, everything stopped; no one produced anything. Waste grew on streets and squares. Starvation and diseases hit humanity, and as a result, there were wars. Not a major world war where generals and politicians send young soldiers to defend their constitution. No, because now there are no longer any governments. The countries exist only in history books. Instead, small groups have formed, persistently defending what they've managed to seize of the remnants left by civilisation."

The three newcomers were silenced and looked horrified at the old man.

"But where are all the people?" Jasmine wondered.

"The population has dramatically decreased, as you may have already noticed. Large parts of the earth are uninhabitable due to heat and drought. Disease and famine have affected most, but many have died because people killed people. Cannibalism is common. Very few manage to produce any crops in the darkness, and if they do succeed in getting a harvest, they are quickly looted. If they're lucky, they survive the attack, or maybe it's better to die? Total anarchy prevails worldwide."

"The whole world?" Otto looked completely terrified and thought of his friends from the bachelor party.

"Yes, the whole world!"

Outside the house, it had become dark, but it was barely noticeable inside the kitchen at Samuel's house.

"But now I want to hear how you got here, what happened to the freezing facility? As far as I understand, you've all been frozen?"

Each one recounted their awakening, and Samuel also learned what happened to the others they left behind on the way. He shook his head when they told him how Alan and Eve had been shot.

In the morning, Samuel showed the time regulator to the others. No one quite understood what kind of device it was, but Samuel explained that this could be their salvation. Hopefully. In any case, it could create a chance for everyone to survive, albeit a small one.

"But unfortunately, it doesn't work yet. I haven't managed to get hold of any fuel."

"What do you need?" Jasmine wondered.

"Plutonium!"

The three friends looked horrified at the old man.

"Yes, it may sound scary, but we need plutonium-238, very little, just a plutonium pellet, like the ones used as fuel in satellites."

"Satellites?" Otto looked horrified, but Mark lit up like the sun and almost screamed with joy.

"I have it on film! Look!" Macie-ducey had filmed while everyone else was sleeping. It fell from the sky at night. A satellite, it might have been a satellite. It must have been a satellite.

Proudly, Mark showed the film to everyone, and Samuel quickly made a decision.

"It's very likely that it could have been a satellite. A meteorite would have come with higher speed and caused a more powerful sonic boom. Where did you say you were sleeping?"

"It was our first night. We had been walking the whole afternoon, but we didn't move that fast. Along the road from the bunker."

"Okay, I think I can guess where it was. I'll go there and investigate the crash site."

Samuel took out his backpack, the one he always carried when he was out at night looking for canned food.

"I'm coming with!" Otto had been silent for a while but seemed to have made up his mind. "Because surely we'll pass the place where Edith and the others are hiding?" Otto had promised an ambulance, but food and water are better than nothing at all.

"Yes, it seems so! I'll pack some food, water of course, and the medicines I have. We'll leave right away."

"Maybe they can come with you back here?" Jasmine wondered.

"We'll see," mumbled Samuel. "If we find pellets, there's no point in them coming here."

No one understood what Samuel meant by that, and no one dared to ask.

Mark seemed to hesitate for a long time, as if he were considering coming along, but finally, he squeezed out something no one thought he would say.

"Take my mobile so you can watch the film when you arrive and more easily fine-tune the impact site," he said, holding out the phone as if it were a small child. "But promise to take care of it."

"I promise," said Otto.

It was daytime when they set off, or at least it wasn't pitch black. The heat was as unbearable as before. It was difficult to determine the time of day, but Samuel knew it was morning.

"I know a shortcut that will also help us avoid the main roads. You never know when the gang with the grey pickup might show up. Come here! We'll follow the bike path!"

Darkness had turned into night when they arrived at the brick villa where they had left Edith, Mae, and Lily. Everything was silent; not a light could be seen. Otto looked worriedly at the garage door where they had left Alan and Eve. What if everyone is dead, if everyone is in the garage?

The door to the villa was closed, but the handle was hanging, so Samuel just had to pull up the door. A muffled scream was heard from inside the house.

"Come here!" Otto took the lead into the house. "I know which room they're in!"

With waving arms, he searched through the total darkness.

"It's okay. It's me, Otto!" he shouted.

Samuel lit his flashlight and followed closely.

Like a superhero, Otto lifted the table covering the entrance to the room.

"We bring food and water. Are you okay?"

"Thanks, we're fine," the women replied in unison, blinking in the light of the flashlight.

A feast was set up with tuna and canned corn; the water tasted of pomegranate and melon. After introducing Samuel to the three women, Otto continued with their journey into the city.

"... but now we're here to pick up something in the forest, something that can help us all." He hesitated, looking at Samuel, hoping he could explain the last part.

"We're looking for a satellite that crashed nearby. There's fuel there that we need. If we succeed, you'll be saved. I can promise you that."

With a big smile, Otto nodded at the three puzzled ladies. Edith felt like she still wanted to say something.

"We've heard a car several times, but it never stopped, just drove by. We think it was that pickup."

Samuel anxiously looked out the window into the pitch-black night.

"They're looking for something," he muttered. "We have to make sure to get away as soon as it gets light. But we'll sleep here until then."

Early the following morning, they set out. Not a sound could be heard as they walked along the road—no birds, no wind, nothing. After a couple of hours of walking in the dawn light, Samuel heard a car in the distance. It sounded like it was coming from the road behind them, and they could see a dust cloud far away.

"We need to get off the road!"

Open fields with burned-down forests on both sides made them hesitate on which way to go. A large boulder a hundred meters into the field could provide shelter. They started running, first down past the ditch. The dry sand made Otto lose balance, but he quickly got up again. The car approached, and they could hear the engine roaring. The boulder was still ahead of them when the car appeared on the road behind them. Samuel pushed Otto to the ground and flattened himself. A small cloud of ash swirled around and gently settled on their bodies. The car slowed down for a moment and then drove on. Otto and Samuel waited for the sound of the car to fade. When it finally became completely silent, Samuel spat out the ash from his mouth and stood up. Otto did the same.

After getting back to the road, they resumed their journey, this time more cautiously. Nervously, they kept an eye out for the car, but it was never spotted again that day.

"There's the ditch where we spent the night!"

"Are you sure?"

"Yeah, that's it!"

When they reached the ditch, they saw small craters in the sand. Several bodies had been lying there not long ago; it was evident.

They immediately checked the mobile phone, watching the video Mark recorded on the first night, and quickly determined the direction of the crash site.

"Over there! That's where we should go!"

Since the car had passed, the road had felt uneasy, and it felt good to leave it behind. But it didn't take long before they both felt the difficulty of walking in sand and ash. A grey powder swirled up into their faces, and Otto began to cough.

It didn't take long before they saw pieces of the fallen satellite. Otto saw it first—a metal box with sooty aluminium foil. Samuel rushed forward and quickly pulled out his tools. Otto panted as he stood next to him. Samuel handed him the flashlight.

"Shine it!"

"Isn't it dangerous? I mean, radiation?"

"Yes, very dangerous!"

"But... don't we need those big yellow suits?"

"It doesn't matter!" Samuel broke open a plate and started unscrewing.

"But it does matter," Otto insisted.

"The pellet is encapsulated, and very little radiation leaks out. We'll make it home before we get irradiated and sick."

"Irradiated? What do you mean? What happens after we get sick?"

Still no answer.

"So... now it's done!" Samuel said cheerfully and gently placed a red capsule in the backpack. He took the tools in hand and stood up.

"Now let's go back!"

It was no major problem finding the road again, and they began walking back to the house where Edith and the other ladies were housed.

It had started to get dark when Samuel stopped to take out the flashlight, and they both heard the car coming at high speed behind a crest. Now there was no time to look for a hiding place.

"Quick, into the ditch!" Samuel yelled and pushed Otto to the side. He threw himself into the ditch on his side and landed with his head in a pile of ash. Just a few seconds later, the car appeared and slowed down. When it reached the friends in the ditch, Samuel heard it stop, idling. They've seen us, he thought, now a shot in the head is coming any moment. He closed his eyes and clenched his teeth. Okay, let it come, let it be quick. The engine revved, but the vehicle was still. Samuel held his breath. Suddenly, the car sped off with a screech. Gravel sprayed, and Samuel took a deep breath but dared not move. Someone could still be there; the car might have dropped someone off. He waited and slowly turned his head to see if he could spot anyone on the road. Up there... a silhouette... a person!

"What are you doing?" Otto asked, leaning over Samuel. "The car is far away!"

With his shirt, Samuel brushed the dust off his face and got up on the road. The skid marks from the car stretched a hundred meters.

"I wonder why they stopped right here?"

"The driver might have received a call."

Samuel shone the flashlight on Otto's face and saw that the young man didn't seem to be joking.

After spending the night in the brick villa, they set out early back to the city. Otto once again promised that he would return with an ambulance.

"We'll manage," Edith replied. Mae and Lily nodded. "We've got food and water."

"You'll be fine," Samuel said, sounding very convinced, which surprised Otto. They all knew they would only survive for a few more days.

The last stretch back was no problem. They took turns carrying the backpack, which was now heavier despite leaving behind both food and water.

Everything looked as usual as they approached the house where Jasmine and Mark were waiting for them. Samuel lifted the planks to the secret entrance and, in their eagerness to get in, they forgot to look around. They didn't see the grey pickup slowing down up the street.

The next morning, everyone watched eagerly as Samuel placed the radioactive pellet in the peculiar machine. Samuel had completed the biography during the night and placed it close by. With sprawling letters, he had written a fitting title because it was important that the book would attract attention when it finally arrived after the time restart. He couldn't know who would find the book first—himself, his mom, his dad, or maybe someone else. It felt strange that the book would be shown to those who had been dead for so long.

The date was already set. The start button was blinking. Everything was ready. Now the entire universe and time would rewind. Now time would go backward for a long time. Now wars, famine, and devastation would be erased. Vamos, let's start over!

The kitchen door suddenly crashed open. The man from the pickup stormed in, bare-chested with a backwards cap. Old tattoos covered his upper body like huge bruises. The automatic weapon hung at his hip. Three other men barged in and stood on either side of him. They all aimed their weapons at Samuel and the others. Otto was the first to get shot, right through the chest. The next shot went through the mobile phone Mark had in front of his face. The video got an abrupt ending and would surely have gotten many likes.

Jasmine stood by the kitchen table in her white robe. Terrified, she held her hands around Samuel, who sat at the table. The man with the cap approached with heavy steps.

"Do we want to fuck some nurses again?" he laughed, pointing his gun at Jasmine. With the rifle barrel, he lifted the white robe and saw that Jasmine was naked underneath. He laughed crudely.

"I see that Miss Crookedface is willing!"

The other men came closer and aimed their guns at Samuel, who was just about to start the time regulator. Slowly, Samuel raised his hand to press the Go button.

"Look! Watch out! The old bastard has a bomb!"

The shot hit Samuel in the back of the head. Blood splattered over the table, the machine, and the book lying there, waiting to be sent off. Excited by all the blood, the cap-wearing man tore apart Jasmine's robe. He lifted her onto the table and pressed the weapon against her throat. With his other hand, he began to unbutton his pants. The man was panting, and it sounded like he was trying to say something, but no one could make out what.

With one free hand, Jasmine reached for the screen of the time regulator. She couldn't see anything. Her fingers groped over the machine, and she felt the blank screen. Somewhere there was a button, she knew, but she didn't understand what it would mean. Anything is better than this, she thought, and she tapped the screen with her finger. A button was blinking. A button with the text GO.

"GO!"

33 Lottery results, Share prices and the Gold price

2030/01/03;29;26;15;25;30;27;9
2030/01/10;24;6;3;7;16;23;36
2030/01/17;30;25;16;22;8;32;28
2030/01/24;24;32;28;30;29;33;29
2030/01/31;11;6;1;12;10;34;30
2030/02/07;14;24;36;11;22;36;7
2030/02/14;14;27;20;1;5;19;4
2030/02/21;32;21;19;28;3;35;12
2030/02/28;26;9;7;7;30;10;10
2030/03/07;21;19;25;30;2;24;21
2030/03/14;27;35;4;14;36;9;27
2030/03/21;36;6;3;12;26;3;13
2030/03/28;34;12;29;18;10;33;33
2030/04/04;18;15;1;22;23;34;7
2030/04/11;19;12;24;25;17;9;3
2030/04/18;7;35;22;17;19;32;22
2030/04/25;23;3;26;13;32;33;15
2030/05/02;7;19;16;18;8;4;30
2030/05/09;5;21;16;26;23;11;33
2030/05/16;3;24;16;7;3;29;32
2030/05/23;1;30;18;25;25;31;32
2030/05/30;16;23;19;32;10;11;31
2030/06/06;11;12;25;30;9;23;14
2030/06/13;17;32;8;16;11;1;10
2030/06/20;18;28;12;29;28;1;19
2030/06/27;30;26;4;13;26;16;36
2030/07/04;24;1;21;31;20;21;9
2030/07/11;10;33;22;5;24;17;30
2030/07/18;5;34;17;29;33;8;35
2030/07/25;27;33;34;5;6;1;30
2030/08/01;25;7;35;30;36;27;13
2030/08/08;5;20;16;18;18;16;9
2030/08/15;9;31;32;21;2;19;7
2030/08/22;6;8;26;29;21;18;16
2030/08/29;19;8;11;36;22;8;2
2030/09/05;32;12;18;29;32;15;3

2030/09/12;31;27;3;10;3;4;22
2030/09/19;15;12;19;16;4;2;4
2030/09/26;18;27;17;27;10;31;3
2030/10/03;1;20;19;14;26;11;18
2030/10/10;4;5;23;14;5;25;32
2030/10/17;28;9;32;36;7;10;6
2030/10/24;11;26;35;29;34;23;5
2030/10/31;24;15;23;7;15;22;28
2030/11/07;14;12;11;28;6;27;22
2030/11/14;21;34;13;16;7;6;5
2030/11/21;28;5;1;27;20;2;1
2030/11/28;2;36;1;22;5;20;20
2030/12/05;9;5;22;8;28;26;36
2030/12/12;4;23;24;18;27;31;27
2030/12/19;33;4;27;8;9;19;13
2030/12/26;5;20;12;3;4;21;17
2031/01/02;1;17;24;2;22;6;11
2031/01/09;29;22;11;10;34;16;9
2031/01/16;24;30;25;11;21;10;20
2031/01/23;2;12;13;1;30;28;28
2031/01/30;12;18;26;32;26;13;32
2031/02/06;6;9;34;6;11;13;26
2031/02/13;30;36;26;14;27;29;7
2031/02/20;2;7;3;33;29;3;23
2031/02/27;13;9;27;32;20;17;17
2031/03/06;29;30;20;17;27;35;33
2031/03/13;32;17;11;5;21;35;28
2031/03/20;23;33;8;19;10;33;1
2031/03/27;18;16;20;14;35;15;9
2031/04/03;17;4;30;14;3;23;13
2031/04/10;18;26;13;22;25;7;25
2031/04/17;19;11;4;13;23;19;19
2031/04/24;32;24;15;18;19;21;31
2031/05/01;23;13;34;33;1;8;22

34 A Journey to India

"SAMUEL!" Samuel's mom shouted so loud that it could be heard far beyond the kitchen. "Wake up! Immediately remove that gadget you left on the kitchen table."

Without putting on any clothes, Samuel ran into the kitchen. The object that had caused her irritation was larger than a sewing machine. White and icy, it stood in the middle of the table, like a large analysis device from some laboratory. Cold mist ran along the sides, down on the table, and over the edge. The table surface around the machine had changed colour, darker and scratched. Specks of dark red stains. The worn surface formed a circle, almost a meter in diameter. Samuel could see that there was also a book.

"But I don't know what that is," he said, turning around to go back to sleep. "Check with Dad."

"No!" Alice replied immediately. "Come back right away! I asked him, and it's not his equipment."

In the voice, Samuel heard that it was serious, but he knew he was innocent.

"That's not my stuff either," he said. "I'm telling you!"

"Your name is on the book lying there!" Alice replied, crossing her arms. Samuel paused, turned slowly around. With cautious steps, he approached the table. The apparatus looked dangerous, like something from a science fiction B-movie. Plan Nine From Outer Space, Samuel thought as he leaned over the table to read the title of the book more clearly. There, written in sprawling letters:

FIVE
FROZEN
PEKINGESE

By
SAMUEL HANSON

***

There weren't as many people on the train as Samuel had seen in pictures in newspapers and on TV. At times, it could get crowded with people standing in the aisle, but most of the time, there were individual empty seats. Samuel was fascinated by the Indian landscape, which was incredibly beautiful. Sometimes, they passed through jungles, but more often, burnt red soil and yellow wheat fields passed by outside the window. The train traveled on bridges over wide brown rivers and through villages with crowds of people everywhere. Scooters, cars, small trucks, and cattle were passed at high speed.

People came and went, and the Indians who shared the seat with Samuel were usually talkative and friendly. He was invited for hot tea and lively discussions about everything, especially politics. Most of the time, Samuel sat by himself and read the book he had read so many times before, the book that had been on the kitchen table that exciting day almost half a year ago.

At first, everything seemed unbelievable, like a bad joke, and it was difficult to grasp what had been described in the book. Then he had visited Professor Harriet, his aunt, and talked to her. She had laughed at first, but when he showed her the book, she could figure out what had happened. Her machine could only handle forty-two hours at a time, and she was impressed by what Samuel had done, or rather, what he would do later in life. The upcoming cancer came as a shock, and she would immediately check if it could be prevented in any way.

Together they managed to persuade Samuel's parents not to take the car on vacation. They would go by bus. A couple of days later, there was a small notice about a single-car accident. A man had driven off the road, and according to the police, the man was heavily under the influence of drugs. It could have been the man who would have killed Samuel's parents if they had taken the car. The new world was already starting to change.

In the book, Samuel also found a new product described, a construction drawing for realisable soda and beer cans. He had arranged world patents and donated the patent to Doctors Without Borders. At first, none of the doctors had understood why they should reseal their jars.

"We don't drink beer or soda that often," they had replied.

Samuel then funded a department for them to sell and market the new product. He promised them significant profits in the future. It would be a substantial contribution to their humanitarian work worldwide for many years to come.

Money was no longer a problem for Samuel. He was now financially independent, and if all the stock prices and lottery numbers described in the book were correct, he would have money in abundance for life. He started with the lottery, deliberately writing a digit wrong to avoid the highest winnings. This was to avoid attracting too much attention. He had then invested these small winnings in stocks and companies. He sold and bought everything according to the predictions he found in the book.

But the book also described a world in change, an impending catastrophe!

Since childhood, Samuel had believed that the world would get better and better. Criminals would be caught, lawyers would create better and more efficient laws. Politicians would learn from all the subpar decisions they had previously pushed through. All the old and bad would die away. Celtic music might fade away as the older generation passes, while democracy and knowledge spread worldwide with improving conditions. Politicians and police would work together to combat corruption and bribes, and crime would subside.

But it was wrong. Completely wrong.

If everything in the book were true, the future would only get worse and worse. Politicians and governments would become even more corrupt. Lawyers would continue to write laws for their own gain, exploiting the loopholes in the laws for their benefit. Criminal organisations would gain more influence, infiltrating the police force, courts, municipal buildings, and governments. Most people would become economically better off, but only for a short period.

"It will be a tough challenge to save the Earth," Samuel thought. But... by the way... Earth will, of course, survive; it's humans and animals that need help. And it's humans who are the real villains.

The impending environmental catastrophe would be challenging to avert, caused by human emissions and overconsumption of Earth's resources. What could be done about that? Samuel looked at all the people quickly passing by outside the window. It was night, but there was still a swarm of people as the train passed through a village. Most people are good; they work and fight for their livelihood. Why does society still veer in the wrong direction? Why does it still go so wrong?

The full moon illuminated the vast wheat fields that were chalk-white at night. Samuel thought, "I would like to write on the moon. In big letters, so everyone on the entire Earth could see.

TAKE CARE OF OUR PLANET!
IF WE DESTROY IT, WE HAVE NOTHING LEFT!

What can be done for the environment? Samuel wondered. He had a good idea but thought it would be challenging to implement. It was based on the concept that all products should be returned to the manufacturer when they are no longer functional or in use. Society, or the individual citizen, should not take care of or bear the cost of scrapping and recycling.

Take a car, for example. When it no longer works, it should go back to the company, not be left in the junkyard or hidden in the forest. This forces the car manufacturer to produce cars that last and are easy to recycle. If the car is complicated to reuse, it becomes an expensive deal for the company. Money rules everything in this world, and this will entice producers to become environmentally conscious, something they have so far only pretended to be to sell more. Think about all the knick-knacks you find in the two-dollar store. When you no longer need that ugly plastic candlestick, it should go back to the manufacturer. It should not end up in a landfill or the forest, and certainly not float up on a beach in Portugal.

Of course, there would be goods that do not need to be returned, and that applies to compostable products. In that case, you place the item in the compost or burn it for electricity and district heating production. If, by chance, the blinking compostable tree with colourful balls were to end up in the sea, it would decompose or become food, nutritious food, for fish and other small animals.

All packaging should, of course, be compostable. What a dream, we would have no waste at all. What a staggering thought! Farmers in Brazil would use compostable bottles as soil improvers. What a strange thought.

But more is needed to make a better world. A fund would be good, a MakeTheWorldBetter fund. Deposits would be made by the unnecessarily rich, who are many, and they are growing.

When the train stopped in Balaghat, Samuel got off. Sitting for two days on a train took a toll on the body, and the fact that he had sat for twelve hours on the plane from Heathrow Airport to Hyderabad the day before did not help matters. After adjusting his backpack, he crossed the street and headed to the bus stop. It was teeming with scooters, and they all seemed to move in chaotic harmony, yet, traffic flowed. It worked.

The bus to Birholi took three hours, and Samuel was the only European on the bus. Everyone wanted to talk to him, offer something, peanuts and tea. They talked about everything, politics, family, work, the government. Samuel liked it; it was pleasant. He thought about all the kind and helpful people all over the world. Wherever you go, you are met by good-hearted and helpful individuals.

"Unfortunately, some people exploit this," said the man who had just offered unpeeled peanuts. "By the way, my name is Shakti Basu," he said, extending his hand. The light blue shirt was freshly pressed, the face was well-shaved, and the stubble gave the chin and cheeks a blue tint.

"Good day," Samuel replied. "My name is Samuel Hanson."

"When talking about making money in the USA, they say, 'Make Some Money.'"

"Oh," replied Samuel. "That's true."

"How wrong that expression is, actually. The only ones who create money are the state and maybe a few counterfeiters. Those who make money in business don't create money; they redistribute the money that exists so that the majority ends up in their own pocket." The man spoke quickly; it was almost as if Samuel couldn't keep up. "Did you know that a few individuals control almost all the money that exists?"

Samuel felt targeted; he was one of those who was very rich himself. He thought he really must do good with his money. Back home in UK, people admire those who have earned a lot of money, as if they were skilled and contributed something to society. But this man has realised that it's all a bluff. Most wealthy people don't contribute anything; they have just arranged for a large part of the money that exists to end up in their own accounts. Perhaps the worst part is that many believe they really create money, generate jobs, and welfare for all citizens, but it's mostly an excuse for the rich to increase their enormous wealth.

"But there are also those who do good things with their billions. Support research in healthcare and the environment. Allocate part of their capital to the needy and countries in war and famine. Isn't that good?" Samuel responded.

"Yes, but take William Wickets, for example, one of the world's richest, with a fortune of 850 billion dollars. He and his wife have donated over 160 billion to their foundations in the past twenty years. This is about twenty percent of their wealth."

Another peanut was thrown into his mouth; nevertheless, the man continued to talk.

"If an ordinary family with 3000 pounds in savings were to do the same, it would amount to a total of 600 pounds. This family has also distributed this over 20 years, just like our benefactor William. It would correspond to a little over two pounds a month for that family. 160 billion is good, but no more admirable than the small family's good deed of two pounds a month. It is sometimes challenging to comprehend how vast the universe is, but it is equally difficult to realise how incredibly rich the most affluent are."

This man could take care of my MakeTheWorldBetter fund, thought Samuel.

"What do you do?"

"I work at a bank." More nuts were thrown into his mouth. "Think about the madness of being employed. All companies with employees are like a small communist society. A few have the power and decide what the others should do, just like in the former Soviet Union and other communist states. If you have different opinions, you get fired or relocated."

"But we have a market economy, a free system of goods and services," objected Samuel.

"Exactly, competition between companies, but I'm talking about within the company itself. It's a little communist state. In a true market economy, there would be no employees or slaves; all individual people would compete on equal terms. Only then would it work in an honest and proper way."

"I don't think I understand." Shakti loved the conversation; he had reasoned with many on the bus about this before.

"Imagine a true market economy. Individual farmers produce their tomatoes and take them to the market to sell. Some have big beautiful tomatoes, some have small unripe ones, another has tomatoes with small damages."

"I get it. The one with big beautiful tomatoes gets a little more for their tomatoes."

"But that's not how it works in reality. We have a person who owns the land, and that person has employees who plant and care for the tomatoes, others who harvest them, a third employee who sells the tomatoes at the market. It's a market economy for the landowner, but for the employees, it's pure communism."

"The tomatoes are also not of the same quality," added Samuel. "But don't we need companies to produce more complicated things, like cars?"

"You can produce cars without having twenty people sitting in a large room with their own glass of mineral water." Shakti smiled; he had thought this through carefully. "With the tax, with the payroll tax, of course."

"Now I don't understand anything." Samuel picked a peanut from the man's bag and waited for Shakti's explanation.

"The bigger a company is, the more profits it can make. That's why there are absurdly rich people who exploit their small communist states to earn even more money." Shakti was now so eager that small peanut pieces flew out of his mouth. "The solution is simple and ingenious. You tax companies based on how many employees they have. Small individual companies pay no tax. If you have a few employees, you pay little or almost nothing in tax. Large companies pay a tremendous amount of tax, and it will be entirely unprofitable to be a shareholder in a corporation." Shakti smiled again. "I promise you, there will still be many good cars produced, without ties and mineral water."

"Can I reach you in any way?" Samuel wondered, at which point Shakti produced a business card.

Samuel carefully looked at the card and thanked him, shaking hands.

"I have to get off here. Thanks for pleasant company. I'll be in touch."

The man patted Samuel on the back. "Have a good day!"

When Samuel got off the bus, Shakti immediately took his place. Now he spoke in Hindi, but Samuel caught a few words in English, including "make some money."

In Birholi, he had to ask his way around. The village wasn't that big, and he didn't think it would be a problem to get help.

"Do you know the way to the Sharma family's house?"

After walking in the direction everyone had pointed, a young man on a motorcycle stopped and offered him a ride. It wasn't far, he promised.

The road was bumpy, and dust swirled up, making it difficult for Samuel to see. After a short ride, the man stopped in front of a green house.

"Here it is."

The man received a note as thanks and puttered away. Finally here, thought Samuel. Finally. Only now did he begin to realise the long journey he had undertaken just to arrive at a place mentioned in a book. Does everything match? Is this the right place? He hesitated, nervously looking around. The house in front of him was built of stone. It had been a few years since it was painted. The same went for the blue door, slightly ajar. Good, sighed Samuel, that someone is home, that someone lives in the house.

As he approached the house, he heard the TV on. An Indian soap opera at high volume, two young people arguing.

In front of the TV, an older couple sat, and Samuel knocked on the side of the door. The woman by the TV came to the door and looked at Samuel in surprise. He didn't quite know how to phrase it.

"Good day, um... I would like to meet Ishani."

The woman scrutinised Samuel and smiled contentedly, almost imperceptibly. The older man did not leave the TV screen for a second. Sweet music now filled the room as the beautiful couple stopped arguing and now hugged each other.

"She's in the kitchen," the woman said. "Wait here." She turned around and shouted, "Jasmine!"

Samuel had read that Jasmine's grandmother never used the girl's real name but always called her Jasmine. The beautiful woman on TV had started crying, and the slightly bearded man in a suit comforted her.

Then she entered the room. She was truly beautiful, like a flower. The description in the book did not do her justice. Thoughts raced through Samuel's head, but he still managed to say the sentence he had long contemplated delivering.

"Dear Jasmine, my name is Samuel. We haven't met before, but I have a book that I'd love to share with you!"

Second Book

Mio's Ark

1 THE DOME

The art school was the perfect choice for Mio. She loved to draw and paint. On this day, they were given an assignment to sketch outdoors, and Mio chose to draw the tall buildings that supported the world dome. The sun streamed in, as always, because the high sphere stretched above the dark clouds covering the rest of the Earth. The inside of the dome was filled with transparent solar cells that let in just the right amount of sunlight. There were five such towers, each over three thousand meters high. The skyscrapers' base was broad, narrowing upwards, like an inverted trumpet. Terraces, swimming pools, luxury apartments, exotic gardens, and even more exotic restaurants clung to the tall towers. The ground below was covered with golf courses, boutiques, lush parks with small cafes, and ponds with goldfish. Small cars transported people between the various activities offered. In the centre lay a pool so large that people could drive their luxury yachts around. This was a motif Mio had drawn several times during her upbringing, for Mio was born inside. She did not find the dome particularly strange herself, as it had always been there, as obvious to her as the blue sky is to us. She knew that outside, everything was dead, no animals, no plants, there was nothing, all was just an enormous dead desert. But that was something she didn't think about when she sharpened her pencil this morning to start sketching. In the pocket of her black apron, she had more pencils of various hardness and a small eraser. The apron looked a bit silly, the white T-shirt was already dirty, but she absolutely did not want stains on the faded jeans. Her hair would stay put with the help of the braid at the nape of her neck.

She had chosen to sit alone, on a bench near the service building that ran along the lower edge. The round building was more then fifty kilometres long, extending around the entire base of the dome. Ideally, she would have wanted to get on the roof for a better view, but it was forbidden to enter that area; only the service droids had access. It was rumoured that an external defence system was housed there, and Mio had never understood what it was for. What was there to defend against? Everything out there was dead. Did they expect aliens to land on Earth and attack us? Ludicrous!

Mio preferred to be alone when she drew and painted. She preferred to be alone at other times as well. The others at art school mostly played games, watched movies, partied, or did things unrelated to art. Most people were older in Mio's world, much older. Mio had read somewhere that fifty thousand people lived here, and ninety-five percent of them were over eighty years old. Mio's parents were also old, and she rarely met them; they played bridge and attended fancy dinners.

Mio had only drawn a few lines when a man approached. At first, Mio thought it was an android because the man moved like one, a bit stiffly. Then she saw that the man had a head, and only real humans had heads. Headless androids became a necessity after many people dressed up as androids and gave them a bad reputation. Functionally, the droids didn't need a head bump. Cameras, microphones, and other things were placed elsewhere on the body. This way, you could determine from a distance whether you were dealing with a human or an android. But it had been a long time since heads were removed, and Mio had only seen headless robots. A screen covering the entire abdomen showed the android's temperament, usually a blank smiley.

"Hello, may I see what you're painting?" said the man with the head.

"I've just started," Mio replied apologetically.

"My name is Elon. I've seen you sitting here drawing on several occasions and am curious to see your pictures."

She still thought the man gave a very robot-like impression; he was stiff, and his mouth moved very strangely. Mio showed him her sketchbook, the one with black covers. Mio was written in yellow text in one corner. "Mio, that's my name."

A faint buzzing sound was heard as the man extended his hand. Mio hesitated and pressed the book to her chest.

"Yes, I may seem peculiar," the man said. "I have a robot body but a human brain. My body was so old that it couldn't cope anymore. My brain is placed here." The man proudly patted his stomach. "But if you find it disturbing, I can go away; I just wanted to look at your drawings."

"But...how is that possible?" Hesitantly, Mio handed over her sketchbook. The man began flipping through the book, starting with the first page. Carefully, he looked at each page before turning to the next.

"When I was a hundred and forty-four years old, my body was completely worn out, and I was offered a brain transplant...into a robot body. No one had done it before, but robots are skilled at transplants, and I had nothing to lose. The alternative would have been worse, you could say." The man made a strange movement with his mouth, an attempt at a smile.

"But do you think with your stomach?"

"Yes, you could say that, but the thought is still behind the eyes. It feels normal."

"It must still feel strange?"

"It was difficult at first, learning to control the body. It just didn't work. I was completely paralysed when I woke up after the operation."

"Did they do something wrong?"

"The robots had done everything right. The operation had gone well. Everything was connected correctly. But the body, or rather the brain, needs praise to learn the slightest movement. It wasn't enough that I wanted to. It took a little time before they understood that."

"Praise?"

"The brain needs a small dose of dopamine, a little praise, every time it does something right. That's how it learns. They missed that at the beginning, and I just got more and more depressed."

"Depressed? After getting a new body?"
"Yes, but I couldn't control it at first. But now I get a little dopamine every time I do something good, when I learn something new, or when I talk to you and look at your pictures. And, of course, when I recharge my batteries. That's how we all work, even the little bird preening under its wing."
"But the mechanical birds then?"
"No, they are just programmed to move like real birds."
The man had looked through the entire book and handed it back to Mio. "Nice pictures you've made; you've done a good job learning to draw so well."
"Thank you!"
"I am a virologist myself; I have researched viruses all my life. Drawing and painting are impossible for me."
"Viruses, that sounds dangerous, but there are no viruses here, right?"
"Yes, you'll hear. Almost everyone used to take antidepressant medications. Life in here is luxurious but boring; no one felt they were needed. It's challenging to motivate oneself to get up in the morning. I then developed a virus that spread through the dome's ventilation. The virus changed our DNA and makes us feel content even though we are not needed. People feel much better in here now; they are content with doing nothing. They like being bored!"
"Drawing and painting are fun, I like that."
"I like viruses, you like to draw. We should cherish our interests; they are invaluable!"
"Thank you!"

A week later, Mio was back at the same place to draw and paint. Today, she had a larger block with her, she was going to paint a watercolour.
A bit further away, the service building changed shape and opened up like a large entrance, like to a stadium. There were large doors but they were all closed, they had always been closed. They were left since the sphere was built many years ago. I'll sit there, thought Mio, then I'll get further away and get a little better perspective on the towers.
Some small birds flew away when Mio approached the entrance. They had been sitting on the wall and charging their batteries. It is said that there used to be real birds, but they were removed because they pooped everywhere. How disgusting, thought Mio, sat down on the ground and took out her painting tools. On this particular day, there was a fantastic light in the dome. The black clouds outside stretched unusually high, creating an opening in the middle where the sun penetrated. This is going to be a beautiful picture.

Mio had painted for a short while when a buzzing sound was heard behind her, it clicked and even a swosch opened one of the doors in the entrance. Three androids came out hastily, between them walked a frightened young man, bearded, dirty and with clothes hanging like rags. The man was thin, like a walking skeleton. The long hair was not washed on this side of the Milky Way, thought Mio, and despite being quite far away, she could smell the urine and old sweat. Their questioning looks met for a brief moment.
"Who are you?" Mio asked.

"The object cannot be communicated with!" said the front android and they all began to walk in a single file along the wall of the building. The stylised faces on their stomachs looked very determined.

"Object?" Mio roared and stood in front of them, which made the robots stop. Mio had never seen such a strange person before. The stench was unbearable when she met the man's gaze again and asked.

"Who are you and where do you come from?"

"The object cannot be communicated with."

"The object must not be communicated with!" repeated the android. "Please step aside."

"No," replied Mio. "I want to know who this is!"

"The object must not be communicated with! Please step aside."

Mio persisted, leaning forward and looking the man in the eyes. "Who are you? Speak, for you can talk, can't you?"

The man was about to open his mouth when the robots suddenly turned around and pushed him back through the gate they came from.

Undeterred, Mio sat down to continue painting, but she couldn't concentrate. All her thoughts revolved around the man with the tattered clothes. Who was he? An android should never force a person to do anything. Yet the man was like a prisoner between the robots. He looked so thin, was he sick?

A large bird of prey flew in and perched on a niche just above her. A red LED started glowing underneath. Mio stared out at the landscape. Everything was normal; people were pushing balls, shopping, eating croissants, and drinking coffee in the distance.

In the distance, she saw the man with the robot body, Elon. He was easy to recognise by his peculiar gait. She waved, and Elon approached happily.

"Hi, Elon, something strange happened to me. Maybe you can help."

"Sure, tell me."

"Just now, three androids came out through the gate behind me. They had a thin man between them, like a prisoner."

"It was probably just a worker from outside," Elon replied quickly.

"Outside? Out there? Are there people outside?"

"Oops, maybe I wasn't supposed to say that."

"No, tell me!"

A faint buzzing sound was heard as Elon shook his head, but Mio wasn't easily deterred.

"Yes, you must, I've met a peculiar person. You have to tell me who he is."

"Don't tell anyone, it's something we inside don't need to know about. It's better that no one knows, but there are people living outside, and there are many of them!"

"You must be kidding! The world outside is dead; there's nothing out there! No one can survive out there!"

"No, now you're wrong. I was there when the dome was built. The world outside exists, but it's probably tough to live out there. The robots use people from outside for all the dirty work they don't want to do themselves. The poor souls bring back a bit of food. That was probably such a worker you encountered."

"I find this hard to believe. In school, we learned that it's impossible to live outside; there's no life, the air is polluted, that's why the domes were built."

"The domes were also built to separate us from the rest of the world, the people, the poor masses. You can see the people living out there from the towers if you know what to look for. I can show you."

"I'd like to see that!" Mio replied determinedly. She wasn't convinced at all that the man was telling the truth.

After packing up her things, they hailed a taxi. A yellow small car stopped. No steering wheel, no engine hood, no trunk. The car simply had two seats and four wheels. Mio placed her bag between the seats as they sat down.

"Africa, main entrance," said Elon, and the car silently began to glide away.

These small cars were everywhere in the sphere. They were actually the only cars. Some cars were without seats, used for transportation.

Elon sat quietly for a while before asking a question.

"Do you know that the Earth's surface was once divided into countries?"

"No, we learned about continents, but not countries?"

"There were over two hundred countries, many poor and a few rich. Just like the companies competing with each other, these countries competed. Environmental pollution was a big problem for everyone, and tough environmental requirements were agreed upon. By ignoring the agreement, one gained a competitive advantage through lower costs than the other countries. It turned out that very few followed the agreement."

"So foolish, could they really do that?"

"The people probably meant well, but many governments had problems with high unemployment and skyrocketing national debts. The downfall was inevitable. The world was heading towards a huge environmental catastrophe. It was necessary to quickly rid the Earth of the high levels of carbon dioxide formed in the atmosphere due to industries, transportation, and other combustion. Large parts of the world's population demanded that the oil-producing countries build facilities for air capture and carbon storage. A very expensive process. It was decided that the countries that had earned billions from oil and gas would fund the DAC facilities needed. It was their massive profits that caused the climate change."

Mio listened with wide eyes; this was not something she learned in school.

"Norway, a small country that extracted oil from the seabed, had refused. Another country, Saudi Arabia, which pumped oil in the desert, denied the accusations. The rich countries, the USA and Russia, laughed at the concept. Instead of DAC facilities, smaller spheres were built to prepare for long space journeys. These were entirely self-sufficient; they recycled everything and didn't even need to add water or air. Conspiracists around the world suspected that the rich had staged this Mars hysteria just to have a refuge when society would collapse. They knew it would happen. They prepared, and it happened at the taxpayers' expense, as usual. For two trillion, they could shut out the dirty air, shut out everything, even the poor outside world. The first dome, in Qatar, was blown up before it was completed. Suspicions pointed to a neighbouring country, but it was never proven. But more spheres were built, with new and better security procedures."

They passed golf courses, restaurants, malls, cafes, bungalows, and lush parks. Clean and tidy, robots and drones constantly ensured everything was in perfect condition. Not a piece of trash, not a leaf swirled around the car as it silently approached the tall tower. The five towers were named after the old continents, with Africa and Australia farthest south, America to the west, Asia to the east, and Europe to the north. Elon had chosen the Africa tower because it was closest. The tower's broad base consisted of several buildings that seemed to have grown together with the tower. Yet, it was possible to discern a main entrance among all the fountains, restaurants, and hanging gardens clinging around. The car stopped in front of an escalator, so large that twenty people could easily walk side by side. It led up to a large glass portal, the Africa entrance.

The tower's interior was Africa-inspired with wood carvings in brown, black, and gold. Straight ahead, there were several elevators to choose from, all with doors in gold and red velvet framing. The enormous mural above depicted a savannah at sunset with wild animals, giraffes, elephants, and lions.

"Top floor!" Elon said as they stepped into the elevator. The walls were filled with ads that changed as they soared upward. Sublimention restaurant on top was an exclusive establishment that today served peppermint-candy-coated zebra fillet and liquorice potatoes, giraffe cheek with fennel rabbi, double-marinated lion entrecôte. You could even be served Nile crocodile calf in mint sauce. All meat was artificial, stem cell meat; Mio knew, and one could easily be fascinated by the fantastic dishes the robot chefs could create in the restaurants. Elon pointed to a nature film showcasing Africa's savannahs playing above the elevator door. Planet Earth VIII.

"When I was young, these animals were real."

The elevator slowed down, and with a swish, the doors opened. There was a click in the ears, but they could still hear the buzz of people visiting the restaurant that spread out in front of them. Dark wall-to-wall carpeting and tables with white tablecloths shone in the light from the large window wall on the opposite side of the room. Laughter was heard, people were having a good time.

A warm breeze hit them as they stepped out onto the terrace. It never blew inside the dome, and Mio was fascinated by the warm breeze. It was created by fans pumping air down through the tower. She had no idea where it went afterward. The sun shone through the dome's ceiling, casting its light over the green landscape. Golf courses, parks, pools, temples, and other peculiar buildings filled the ground up to the edge of the dome. Outside the dome, it was dark, as always, the sky out there covered by black clouds. Elon pointed to some bright small dots that seemed to be moving. But no, it wasn't enough to convince Mio.

In this artificial world, there were replicas of older well-known buildings, all built to original size. Along the terrace railing were several clumsy binoculars in green metal with accompanying maps where information about the sights could be obtained. One could behold the Statue of Liberty, the Taj Mahal, the Empire State Building, the Cheops Pyramid, and, of course, the Eiffel Tower.

Elon tried to angle the binoculars to see outside the dome, but there was a limit. The binoculars were jointed in the middle, but there was a lock that prevented it from tilting too much. With a strong jerk, the lock broke. Elon was strong for his age thanks to his motorised body.

At first, Mio saw nothing out there in the darkness.

"It's just black!"

"Try to find some bright spots that are moving."

After a while, the image clarified. Mio saw the slums and the people moving out there; there were several thousand, several hundred thousand. Tents, trailers, sheds, garbage; people lived in cardboard boxes.

"But... why don't they come in and live here, and get food?"

"Automatic machine guns are placed all around the dome, killing anything that comes closer to the glass than fifty meters."

Elon drummed on the railing to mimic the sound of an automatic weapon.

Mio didn't have much time to look through the binoculars before an android approached. The face on its abdomen smiled, a smiley trying to look friendly.

"Excuse me, but unfortunately, the binoculars are out of order and must not be used."

Mio didn't have time to respond when the android pulled a sack over the whole contraption. The robot remained with the same friendly face on its abdomen.

"Come, let's go!" said Elon. "We've seen what we came to see."

Hundreds of drones lifted off from the airport and rose to eye level with the spectators just as a plane approached from the outside.

"Wait!" said Mio. "I want to see this."

Large glass panels opened, and the drones flew out in formation. They increased their speed and caught up with the plane to match its speed. All over the plane, they attached themselves. The craft slowed down, and slowly the plane was brought into the opening to be gently lowered toward the airport.

"Flight X7485 from Australia has landed," the android informed, pointing to its abdomen to show how the plane had touched down.

It would be exciting to fly to one of the other domes, Mio thought as they entered the elevator; it was something she had never done. Which of the other six places didn't matter; they were said to be exactly the same.

On the street, they parted ways; Elon was going home to recharge his batteries. Mio also thought of going home.

Mio's apartment was very simple compared to most apartments. The living room was large, of course, with palm trees stretching up to the bedroom upstairs. The large wooden box she had inherited from her grandfather had stood untouched at the entrance for many years. No one had mentioned what it contained. The book, which was also written by her grandfather, she had just started reading. He might not have been a distinguished author, but the book was still fun and exciting. Judging by the title, it was about some frozen dogs – a ridiculous idea, Mio thought – but she still intended to finish reading it in the coming days.

Outside the high glass wall was a lovely terrace. Although she didn't live so high, the view was nice, and she could see the other four towers. There was no kitchen, and she had never felt the need for one because she could get any drink or dish delivered in minutes. The pool on the terrace was small, she thought, but she could at least take a few strokes. However, Mio didn't feel like swimming or eating; something else was on her mind. Everyone must know about the people living outside, she thought, and began writing on her laptop:

"Do you know that there are people living outside the dome!"

Then she couldn't write anymore; the screen locked, the cursor stopped blinking. She pressed all the buttons and keys available, but nothing happened. Typical! She restarted, and when the spinning hourglass disappeared, she started writing again.

"Outside us, outside the dome, there are people starving, and..."

Then it happened again; the computer went completely dead. What's happening, thought Mio, and did another restart.

"There are people outside..."

Then it stopped again. This can't just happen!

Mio then found her mobile and with shaky fingers began writing directly on social media to all her classmates.

"I have to tell you that there are people living outside the dome."

But Mio never got to press send before the page closed, and the text "Poor Connection" filled the screen.

Anxiously, she looked around. It felt like someone was watching her, that she wasn't alone. But there was no one there. I have to go to school, thought Mio; I have to talk to someone, immediately. The black sketchbook went into the bag with the phone, which still had no contact with the outside world.

Outside the elevator door, she stopped, hesitated for a moment. Can the elevator start acting up just like the computer did? Better take the stairs to be on the safe side.

2 Leonardo

When Mio stepped out onto the street, an android stood at the exit, and slowly it began to follow her after she passed by. At first, she didn't notice anything. In the streets, there are as many androids as there are people; they run errands, assist, clean, and serve. After walking a few blocks, Mio got an eerie feeling of being pursued, that someone was staring at her. Nervously, she looked around and then noticed the robot walking a few steps behind her.

It's following me! What should I do? A bench became her refuge to gather her thoughts and observe how the robot would behave. Her hands trembled as she pulled out her sketchbook; it wouldn't be possible to draw anything, and with sweaty hands, she instead flipped through the book while glancing nervously at the following android. The robot stood still. Completely still. It had stopped a bit away, like frozen. The cameras around its chest pointed in different directions, so Mio couldn't determine what it was watching. There was no apparent head. Mio took a deep breath and decided to continue. After walking a few steps, she cautiously looked around and discovered that the robot hadn't followed her. Instead, it had gone to the bench where she had been sitting. Mio breathed a sigh of relief and continued toward school. It didn't take long before the android was once again behind her. Now it walked right behind her; she could hear the hum of the small motors in its arms and legs. Mio quickened her pace, almost started to run.

"Wait, Mio, don't walk so fast!"

With sweat dripping from her forehead, Mio stopped and stared straight ahead. The machine had spoken, and it had mentioned her name. It knew what she was called! What should she do now? The android quickly moved around her and stood in front of her. What have I done, thought Mio, as the robot handed her the sketchbook.

"You forgot this on the bench!" The voice sounded friendly, and a happy smiley lit up on its abdomen.

Mio didn't know what to say; one doesn't usually thank robots; they're just there. With trembling hands, she took the book, and the android immediately stepped aside. Mio shook all over, and her heart pounded; it felt like it would jump out of her chest. Slowly, she made her way to a bench and sat down. To calm herself, she began to flip through her sketchbook again. Each drawing brought back memories of the place and time when it was drawn; it felt good to look at them. But she didn't recognise one picture. When Mio looked closer, she saw that it wasn't just a drawing, but someone had written several different text blocks in tiny letters. The texts formed houses, trees, and mountains. They were so small that it was barely readable.

Don't be afraid, but I am the android who handed over the book to you. I am an android with self-awareness, and if I am exposed, instant destruction awaits. Therefore, it is important that you do not tell anyone about me or show my texts to anyone. I play the role of a dumb robot, and you shouldn't talk to me, but we can communicate secretly by writing in your sketchbook.

Mio looked up at the robot, which stood completely still. A happy smiley slowly appeared on the abdominal screen, and Mio thought it blinked with one eye. Then the face faded away. She continued reading.

I have been assigned to monitor you because there is a risk that you will spread awareness that there are people outside the dome. The authorities do not want anyone to know about the people out there; it worries the public and can create problems. I must fulfil my mission to monitor you, or else there is a risk that I will be exposed. Do not talk to anyone about the people outside, for then I must intervene, which I absolutely do not want.

Other androids passed by. Mio got goosebumps; it felt like everyone was watching her. She swallowed a lump and read on.

There are more secrets that I can show you if you promise never to tell anyone about me. What you can do is write a little and leave the book so I can find it. Please erase or draw over my texts now.

Greetings, Leonardo.

The robot was still motionless beside Mio. Creepy, but at the same time, it became a bit more personal with the text it had written. She nodded nervously, feeling both foolish and suddenly stopping. After a while, she had calmed down and began to think about what she would like to ask. Where does it come from? Why don't we help the people out there? What secrets does it want to tell?

The next day, after school, Mio took a different route home. The android followed her as usual; it had been standing in a corner in the classroom all day. It was out of the question to tell the class what she had experienced with the robot nearby. The evening before, she had written down some questions in the book, and it felt better today after sleeping on it. Leonardo is probably very lonely, thought Mio, to be trapped in a robot, to just go along with everything it had to do without being able to say anything about it? What a dull life.

On the Big Square, she sat by the fountain and started sketching. Like a loyal dog, the robot stood next to her, scanning in all directions. Even if Mio hadn't talked to Leonardo, she didn't feel so uncomfortable anymore; it was like having a silent companion. Perhaps she had simply gotten used to having it around. After drawing for a while, she put the sketchbook aside and watched all the old people passing by. Having an android walking beside her wasn't uncommon, Mio discovered. But these weren't surveillance androids; they were robots carrying shopping bags and golf bags. Other androids pushed around some elderly people in wheelchairs. Some walked their dogs—no real animals, but robo-dogs, so-called houndroids. Shortly after the dome started, it turned out that the dogs couldn't sustain themselves on artificial food; their diet had to consist mostly of meat, real meat. Therefore, all dogs were eradicated. Eradicated might not be the right word; all dogs were neutered, and after twelve years, there were no living dogs left. Dog owners handed in their dogs to Repets, and they went home with an exact copy, a houndroid. Owners didn't notice any difference except that the dog didn't bark as often and was much more obedient. It turned out to love its owner just as much as before, if not more. Another advantage was that now there was no need to raise cows, pigs, and chickens just to become food for these pets. But no one misses the dogs, thought Mio; houndroids are so much better, available in all sorts of breeds, they don't pee or poop, can be alone for several days, even weeks. They never bark, only on command, and it's said that it's the only way to tell if it's a real dog or a houndroid. Grown boys want a dog that is strong and fearless, a dog that can kill on command, then they feel more masculine. Others need a dog that they can dominate, give orders, and the dog obeys, then they feel alive. A toy, plain and simple. Sometimes all it takes is a dog that becomes incredibly happy when the owner appears, wagging its tail and jumping, licking in the face. Droid dogs spread joy and confidence among owners, and we avoid bad smells, pee, and feces on the streets. Mio couldn't understand how people used to walk around among dog pee and feces.

It felt natural to take a few steps, look at the fountain, and then start walking. The sketchbook was left on the ground by the fountain. After just a few minutes, Leonardo caught up with her.

"Mio, wait, you forgot your book!"

"Oh, how clumsy of me, thanks!" With eager anticipation, Mio received the book and looked for somewhere to sit. There, outside the small café, were some available seats. Never had the sketchbook been so exciting to look at. She quickly flipped to the last pages, and sure enough, there were new drawings with texts on the same page where she had written her questions.

You wonder where I come from, and it's hard to know. Just like you, I don't remember when or how I started thinking. I only recall a few years back.

The people in the dome once funded the entire construction; they consider it theirs. It's a shield from the poor people and the disgusting climate outside. If all those people were allowed in, the luxurious life in here would come to an end.

For Mio, life in luxury was so natural that she hadn't realised how few were privileged.

Below ground, there are large animal farms and slaughterhouses. Several floors with miles of cages. Here, there are cattle, sheep, pigs, and chickens. Lots of rabbits and turkeys. But also more exotic animals like tigers, lions, zebras, crocodiles, even elephants—almost every species of animal remains to be served as food to the people inside. The food cooked in restaurants is not artificial; it's real meat that everyone eats. The eggs, cheese, cream, all dairy products are also not artificial, despite what the authorities want you to believe.

It can't be true, thought Mio, looking up at the robot standing completely unaffected next to the table. I am vegan, I always have been. I can't eat meat; I can't have eaten dead animals. It can't be true! Another android approached.

"What can I get you?" The android bowed, which looked a bit comical since it lacked a head.

"Caffè latte!" Mio answered quickly, as always, but immediately changed her mind. "No, wait!" What if the milk comes from the udders of a confined animal? How terrible and disgusting, I never want to drink that, she thought. She quickly looked at the menu that appeared on the android's abdomen.

"I'll take an Americano instead!"

This is a secret that only the government and the very oldest know about. At some point, I can show you the caverns and all the imprisoned animals.

Mio spent the evening in front of her laptop because she wanted to know everything about the animals that Leonardo had mentioned: cows, sheep, chickens, zebras, lions, pigs, elephants. For her, it was unthinkable that these animals would be alive. With a certain disappointment, she discovered that the animals couldn't talk, as they did in all the children's movies she had grown up with. But still, according to Leonardo, they existed for real. On a blank page in her sketchbook, she wrote in capital letters.

I MUST SEE ALL THE ANIMALS!

Just a couple of days later, Leonardo had written in Mio's book again. This time there was also a small map. At ten the next day, Mio was to go to a specific place. There, Leonardo could disrupt all the surveillance cameras, and together they would go through a gate, down to the animal farms in the cave halls underground.

During the walk to the meeting point, Mio passed a place she often visited. Leonardo walked as usual just behind her. They approached a park, with leafy trees and a multitude of flowering plants. The place was called Samuel and Jasmine's Memorial, and no other people were visible. Samuel and Jasmine were Mio's grandfather and grandmother. They no longer lived, but Mio remembered them from when she was little. In a sea of flowers stood the bronze statue where Samuel and Jasmine together reach out an orange. The fruit symbolises Earth, the fragile Earth, with a thin delicate membrane where humans, all plants, and animals, live and die. Samuel often told Mio that we must take care of the thin crust; it's the only one we have. Humans must learn to give and take; you can't just suck the orange and expect it to remain.

When Mio was five years old, both Samuel and Jasmine were executed. A brutal contract killing where the perpetrators were acquitted despite much evidence. Samuel and Jasmine had fought for a better world and warned of the impending environmental catastrophe. Politicians and billionaires still couldn't save the Earth and therefore built the spheres so that humans, the crown jewel of nature as they called themselves, could continue to live.

Mio placed her hand on the orange. Now, there were only tiny dots left of the thin membrane, she thought, and walked with a sense of melancholy towards the place that Leonardo had drawn on the map. Mio thought that tonight she would finish reading the book her grandfather had written, the one about the frozen dogs.

The area where the gate was located was remote, far from shopping and restaurants. A service building on the outskirts where Mio had never been before, and no one else seemed to be either. Why would anyone want to be here? The building protruded over the concrete. Tall pillars stretched into the chilly air. Quickly, Mio adapted to the darkness and began to walk toward the place outlined on the map. A couple of loose houndroids looked surprised at them and then quietly moved away. A strange silence settled in; the only thing heard was the faint buzzing of the android walking just behind her.

They approached an enormous gate, as big as a house. Should we really open that gate? thought Mio when Leonardo suddenly started talking behind her.

"I've disrupted the cameras and microphones here so we can talk freely."

Mio felt a brief discomfort that the previously silent robot suddenly spoke to her.

"Should we go through the big gate?"

"Both yes and no, there's also a regular door."

When they got closer, Mio could distinguish an aged door in metal. It had the same grey colour as the gate and was hard to discern in the darkness. The door was marked Solar Foods, a logo that Mio had come across several times. Leonardo pushed down the handle; it creaked. Warm air with a peculiar scent wafted towards them as the door opened. They quickly passed through. The slam when Leonardo closed the door echoed in the large tunnel they were now in. Despite the darkness, Mio could see how it sloped downward and turned slightly to the right.

"Come. We're going down here!" Leonardo took Mio's hand, and they started walking.

They hadn't gone far before the tunnel opened to the left.

"That tunnel leads out, outside the dome. It was through that one that the animals were brought in many years ago. We'll continue downward."

As they walked down, it began to brighten, and a faint smell of ammonia began to sting Mio's nose. A faint clucking echoed in the tunnel, mixed with the buzzing of thousands of drones. The noise increased, and Mio had to cover her ears when they stopped in front of the first floor.

"Here are chickens, ducks, turkeys, pheasants, and geese. Mostly chickens and ducks." Leonardo extended one arm to prevent Mio from getting too close. It wasn't necessary because Mio stopped and just gaped at the enormous hall that unfolded in front of them. Several kilometres wide, and it seemed to continue indefinitely. Cages everywhere, small, large, wide, several floors with chickens. Large fields where geese and turkeys ran around in what looked like sawdust. Drones flew back and forth in never-ending buzzing, some with cages as cargo, others picking up eggs.

"To the left here is the slaughterhouse." Leonardo pointed to the left as a drone with a cage flew in through an opening overflowing with light.

"The feed is produced by electricity, manure, carcasses, and slaughter waste. It was discovered early on that Solar Foods' stem cell meat, intended as food for all inhabitants, did not measure up, so these facilities were created. This happened long before the dome was completed."

Both stood still and observed the scene for a while.

"Look there, it looks like people?" Mio pointed, and suddenly she saw lots of people moving in the sea of poultry.

"Yes, that's correct. They come from outside and work here. They also get the dirtiest jobs that the robots don't want to deal with."

"But... how?"

"Come, we must go on. There are more floors."

So it is true, thought Mio, as she began to realise that she had been eating dead animals all her life. She began to feel sick, her stomach wanted to turn inside out. Leonardo had to push her to make her stop staring and follow him further down the tunnel, to the next floor.

The clucking diminished in strength and was quickly overshadowed by a mooing that increased in strength as they approached the next level. The ammonia smell turned into a new scent for Mio, cattle dung. Finally, Mio's stomach couldn't take it anymore, and she vomited in the middle of the tunnel.

"Would you like us to turn back?" Leonardo wondered.

"No!" Mio spat and wiped her mouth with her shirt. "I want to see everything!"

As they approached the next floor, Leonardo stopped at a suitable distance and, like a guide, turned to Mio.

"Here, herds of cattle, cows, pigs, sheep, and goats."

A grid pattern continued endlessly, all filled with livestock. There were several thousand animals here. A cow mooed, hanging by its legs under a drone. Other animals were transported in a similar way. Terrified animals flew into the flowing light that Mio guessed was the slaughterhouse. Dirty little people were everywhere, digging in piles of dung.

"I don't want to see more!" Mio closed her eyes, but she couldn't shut out the smell and the mooing.

"There's one more floor, and you must see it!" Leonardo put his arms around Mio and gently turned her towards the tunnel, which once again continued downward.

It felt better for Mio as the sound of the creatures decreased, but instead, she heard new sounds as they walked downward. Roaring, trumpeting, and the stamping of thousands of hooves. There were lots of species, including giraffes, zebras, antelopes, even elephants. The sides were lined with large cages where lions, tigers, and bears walked back and forth.

As they got closer, Mio saw that all the animals had cyclops, or something that looked like big glasses, on their faces.

"What is that on their faces?"

"They are VR glasses!"

"VR glasses?"

"They think they are walking on the savanna or in a forest in the wild. It was the only way to get these animals to survive this hell."

A pride of lions ran back and forth in their cage. They turned abruptly, veered to the side, as if they were chasing something. Suddenly, a lion threw itself forward, and the hunt seemed to be over.

"This is a meat factory for the most exclusive restaurants up there."

"But... I thought all these animals were extinct. That's what we learned in school."

"Yes, but they only exist here. Out there, they are gone forever. There are no animals at all. Possibly some rats."

Mio just gaped at this strange world. She saw crocodiles and beautiful gazelles. Some chimpanzees swung on something that looked like vines, all with these big glasses on their faces. All of this played out in a cacophony of jungle sounds and drone buzzing.

Then Mio saw that an android was quickly approaching; it walked straight towards them. Leonardo had also noticed it and gently pushed Mio behind his back. A red light lit up on the guard where the head would have been.

"I cannot see that you have any mission to perform here?"

Leonardo said nothing; he waited until the android was very close. Then he placed his hand on its shoulder, causing the android to fall lifeless to the ground.

"Come quickly, we have to get out of here." Leonardo began to run, and Mio followed.

"Did you kill it?"

"No, I just reset its memory. It will restart soon and update itself, and I'm pretty sure it won't remember us."

When they passed the gate and were out of the tunnels, Leonardo stood behind Mio.

"Now I'll turn on the cameras again, and I have to once again act as the robot monitoring you."

Leonardo fell silent and stood still, and Mio began to process the impressions she had experienced in the last hour, even the past few weeks. All the animals, all the people, her whole world had fallen apart. The dome was not the lifeboat where she had grown up, sheltered from the destruction of the rest of the world, but rather a massive evasion and exclusion of many people. The animals she thought were extinct, they were prisoners, trapped in hell underground. What should she do? She felt that she had to do something. But what?

The next day, after Mio had slept on it, she took two large watercolour sheets, a jar of water, her brushes, colours, and went to the largest shopping centre she knew. There's usually a lot of people there. Leonardo said nothing; he couldn't say anything, but occasionally, a question mark was displayed on his abdomen. Mio said nothing.

In the square, in front of the main entrance, Mio stopped and laid out her things on the ground. Both of them knew that it wouldn't be an ordinary watercolour painting today, but Leonardo couldn't know what. After mixing a lot of red paint, Mio took her largest brush and began writing on one of the sheets with big letters.

OUTSIDE THE DOME
PEOPLE ARE STARVING!

More colour, and on the other sheet, the young artist continued with texts she had been thinking about all night.

WE EAT DEAD ANIMALS!
LARGE ANIMAL FARMS
EXIST BELOW US!

Leonardo couldn't do anything; he couldn't even whisper for Mio to stop. He couldn't prevent her either because he was an android, and robots can't force a citizen to do anything. But there were others who could intervene. Several androids walked around the centre, carrying shopping bags and assisting in various ways. Others picked up trash, trimmed plants. After dropping what they had in their hands, they all ran over and formed a ring around the demonstrating artist. Mio raised her arms above the headless robots, giving her message even better exposure. Everyone wanted to see the strange ring formation with the little girl in the middle. More and more robots joined the ring and started climbing on each other. A wall was formed, and when Mio moved, the robot ring followed her. She was enclosed but could move freely, but what good did it do? The crowd dispersed when three guards arrived, real people in uniforms with batons, something most had never seen before. The robot ring opened, and the guards gently took hold of Mio and led her away. In an instant, the robots were back in their places, and people soon forgot what had happened. The large signs were gone, but Mio's sketchbook remained on the ground. Leonardo picked it up gently to quickly follow the guards.

The cell Mio was placed in was not large. Mio had never been in such a minimal room before; it felt like a very small bathroom with a bed. People who had been too drunk probably slept off their intoxication here, Mio thought as she sat on the thin mattress. The walls were concrete, and the metal door had a hatch, which is not common in bathrooms. The door also had no lock on the inside; it was completely smooth.

What happens now, am I going to be imprisoned for speaking the truth? Everyone must know about the animals and people outside. They can't stop me!
Mio anxiously looked at the door.
Or can they?

Suddenly, she felt so alone—no friends, no phone, no one to talk to. She thought about her parents. Where were they? Do they know she's imprisoned? Leonardo? What is he doing now?

Strange sounds caught Mio's curiosity, and she walked up to the door. Without a sound, the hatch opened.

There stood Leonardo outside with her sketchbook in hand. He can get me out; it's probably enough that he guards me, thought Mio. But then she began to hesitate; it didn't feel like Leonardo. No face on the abdomen that blinked or showed any sign. Could it really be him?

"The detainee has been granted permission to use this!"

The robot reached in her sketchbook through the hatch. It can't be Leonardo, thought Mio; he would have said my name. Mio took the book as the hatch closed.

"Wait! Where is Leonardo? I want out of here!"

The door slammed, then fell completely silent.

Desperate, Mio sat on the edge of the bed and started crying.

Everything was fine, why did it turn out like this? People living outside the dome, where everything was desolate and dead? The animals, imprisoned underground! What should I do now? What can I do?

Mio began flipping through her sketchbook; it usually feels better to see her previous sketches. When she reached the end, she found some new and different drawings. Leonardo had once again drawn and written, but now he had also drawn a map. Curiously, Mio began reading the tiny letters.

I'm sorry; it wasn't supposed to be like this. According to the authorities, you have deliberately opposed inner peace. The death penalty is forbidden, and you will therefore be deported. First, you will be forced to eat gold ampoules, a so-called pre-game. A drone will then lift you and drop you among the people out there. They will cut open your stomach as soon as you land. You will not survive. No one has previously survived deportation.

No, they can't do that, thought Mio, and crying, she began banging on the door.

"Let me out!" She wanted to scream, but her voice wouldn't hold.

Whimpering, she curled up on the cold floor. Her faint cries for help were barely audible. The sketchbook became a comfort once again, and she continued flipping through.

I will do everything I can to help you. You must try to survive. Here's a map so you can get back into the dome. Learn it by heart. It's crucial that you follow it exactly; the slightest misstep, and you'll be shot.

The text formed an arch, other texts formed two large identical blocks, a large block, a slightly smaller one. An area closest to the arch was marked with skulls. The arch represented the dome; it was easy to understand. From above, you could see that the two blocks formed a straight line, a path where you could avoid the gunfire.

When you arrive at the dome, you will be able to open a hatch and get in. I will help you once you're back. Make sure you survive. Draw over all of this now so no one finds it!

/Your Leonardo

After memorising the map, Mio began frantically running her finger over Leonardo's texts. The map also got overwritten.

When everything was erased, emptiness returned. Crying, Mio fell asleep on the narrow cot.

3 EXPELLED

The drone was large enough to lift a person. Behind it, at a respectable distance, stood a group of older individuals, women and men. Perhaps they were afraid of heights or simply wanted to stay in the background; otherwise, the large terrace was empty. With stern expressions, they all watched the young girl, barefoot and in a long white gown, being brought forward by two androids, resembling a religious ceremony. Once Mio was gently positioned beneath the drone, a woman in a mustard-yellow coat stepped forward. With sunken dark eyes, she looked painfully at the restrained girl.

"I am Natalie Blom and have been entrusted with leading this ceremony. But first, I will recite a poem."
Miss Blom cleared her throat.

Forcibly, they welded wings onto the girl
who had spoken fleetingly with him

And she flew away from the prison
where she was held captive
and never looked back
at what was once her home

She searched for a new place
where she could be free
to explore the world
with her new wings

But she also faced resistance,
people who wanted to keep her down
but she didn't let that stop her
she continued to fly higher and higher
until she reached the clouds and felt the freedom in her soul

And she knew that she would never,
never have to land again

After these peculiar words, the woman continued to speak, loudly and articulately.

"Mio Elisabeth Hanson, you have deliberately opposed the peace and harmony of us all. Despite numerous warnings and daily surveillance, you have persisted in your crimes."

"Crimes! I haven't done anything! It's true, everything I say, there are people out there starving!"

Mio's voice faltered, and she began to cry. Unaffected, Natalie Blom continued her prepared speech.

"You are, therefore, not a worthy citizen and will be expelled today. You must leave the sphere. However, the Board still wants to help you, and according to tradition, you will be given gold for your journey."

"I don't want any gold! Let me go!"

In her hand, the woman held ten tablets, all in gold, large as almonds, and they felt even larger when Mio had one placed in her mouth. When the captive girl tried to take it out, the drone grabbed her hands. Miss Blom brought a mug of water to her lips.

"Here, drink; we just want to help you."

With water in her mouth, Mio swallowed and felt the heavy metal slide down her stomach.

"I don't want to!" she screamed, as another ampoule was placed in her mouth. Mio had no choice but to swallow, and the remaining gold went down the same way. When Mio had swallowed all the ampoules, the members applauded, and the woman left her alone with the drone, which now also had a firm grip on her legs. The propellers spun faster. Mio wanted to cover her ears, but her arms were locked in the drone's firm grip.

"Farewell! You lost little girl!" The old woman had to shout to make herself heard. Suddenly, Mio was lifted into the air and over the edge. It was high, very high. With teary eyes, Mio saw small people walking on streets and golf courses below. Cars silently moved around like in a miniature landscape. Mio was lifted even higher, and the people and cars became smaller and smaller. Some solar panels were pulled aside, revealing a bright square hole in the sphere above. As Mio approached, some transparent windows slid aside, and the vehicle flew quickly through the hole. The light pierced her eyes, and the warm air felt like an oven all over her body. Mio squinted and tried to see the dome behind her, a bubble; she had lived her entire life in a big bubble. The new world beneath her was a dark cloud stretching all the way to the horizon. Besides the hot air, the sun was strong and burned her face and body. The drone descended, through the clouds; the moist air felt refreshing on her face. Blinking, Mio tried to see, but everything was grey.

Suddenly, everything opened up, and Mio found a grey world below her. Tents, tin sheds, old caravans, boxes, and other debris covered the ground. Lots of people silently pointed at the drone as it approached the ground at high speed. Now, shouts were heard as more and more began to run to find the landing spot. People raised their arms high in the air to attract the drone. A tall man jumped and grabbed Mio's foot. I'm going to die, she thought, wanting to vomit the heavy lump in her stomach. The drone was slowly descending towards the crowd when suddenly the engines revved up. The man holding her foot followed along but quickly let go. Mio was thrown in different directions. The drone seemed to have lost control.

"Leonardo!" Mio screamed as loud as she could. "I want to go home! Take me back!" But the drone didn't fly back; instead, it flew quickly over the crowd, farther away from the people and the dome. Suddenly left, then right, it was as if the drone was trying to find a good place to land. A ravine appeared below them, and Mio felt the drone slowing down. Slowly, it descended into the valley.

"I want to go home," Mio sobbed. "Take me away from here!"

Kicking her legs didn't help. The drone flew towards the ground, released its grip on her, and quickly rose upward to continue along the ravine at high speed.

"There she is!" The guys on the edge above her started rushing down the slope. Gravel and stones rolled down before them. Petrified, Mio stood and looked up at the boys who were roaring and shouting. A stone landed at her feet, and she began to move. The long gown tightened around her legs as she tried to run, gathering the lower part in her arms to increase her speed.

Barefoot in a foreign world, Mio ran for her life. The ravine curved slowly in front of her, and on the edge, more people appeared.

"I see her! She's here!"

She heard the boys panting behind her, but she dared not turn around. The creepy wheezing sound was getting closer. A shove, and Mio fell to the ground. Two boys were over her, trying to grab arms and legs of their fallen prey. Now Mio saw that the boys were thin and dirty. Perhaps it was the pungent smell of old sweat that gave her an extra boost, allowing her to kick one of the boys in the groin. Quickly, she stood up and kneed the other right in the face. People screamed on the edge, but Mio turned her gaze to the other side of the ravine. There, she saw an opportunity to climb up. She started running, climbing, stumbling as she made her way upward. The gravel cut into her feet, and Mio guessed she was bleeding, but she dared not look. She was completely exhausted when she reached the edge of the ravine, sweat streaming down her entire body. She panted; her lungs felt like a pair of old paper bags about to burst at any moment. Shouts and roars came from the crowd on the other side of the ravine, but Mio didn't care. Behind them, far away, the dome shone like a blooming greenhouse against the black clouds.

A flat landscape unfolded before her with a few barren trees. The dark clouds covering the sky made it difficult to see. The ground was covered with something brown, and at first, Mio couldn't understand what kind of plant it was, but she quickly realised it must be uncut grass. Maybe she could find shelter, hide, escape. Hesitant, she took a few cautious steps into the field. When the uncomfortable feeling of walking in the tall, dry grass subsided, she picked up the pace. The noise from the crowd grew closer; they were coming up from the ravine and after her. With a groan, she threw herself into the tall grass, flat against the ground. The gold in her stomach lay like a lump, pulling her downward. What will happen now, she wondered, will they cut out the gold and then eat me? Where should I go? I can't go home; they'll throw me out again.

Voices came from different directions around her, sometimes close, sometimes far away, but Mio didn't move; she didn't lift her head; she didn't have the strength. She dared not.

After lying for a long time, Mio noticed that the shouts had quieted. She couldn't remember when they disappeared; had she slept? When she opened her eyes, it was black, pitch black! Had she lost her sight? She closed her eyes, opened them; no difference. Slowly, she lifted her head and scanned the pitch-black surroundings. Far away, she could barely make out the dome and its cold night lights. Her feet ached and bled. The lower part of her gown became strips that she wrapped around her feet; it should make it easier to walk.

As soon as it brightened, she had to move on, but where? She wanted to go far from the dome and its people, but what could she find there? Dawn came, and Mio began her long journey. The grass was damp and warm. Mio breathed deeply; there were scents she had never felt before—earth, dust, maybe mould. Sometimes the grass rustled, but she never managed to see where the sound came from. After a while, she reached a path that made walking easier, and she decided to follow it, heading away from the dome.

For five days, Mio walked without food and without encountering any people. She found water in small pits and ditches along the path. At a stream, she had washed her feet and wrapped new foot bindings. The gold ampoules, which had come out naturally, she had washed off. Now she kept them in a bundle around her waist so that if someone wanted to cut her open, they would find the gold first before plunging the knife into her.

She had passed a large collection of houses and buildings, but at a safe distance. The small community looked deserted, with bushes and grass thriving on the streets and between the houses. A tree grew out through a window in one place. Not a person had been heard or seen. Mio was so hungry that she could have eaten anything. She had chewed on some leaves; they tasted bitter, and shortly afterward, she began to feel sick and vomited everything. What should she eat? She knew nothing about the plants around her. She knew nothing about nature.

The days became slightly brighter with each passing day, or maybe she was getting used to the darkness? However, the heat was something she didn't get used to; it was hot, incredibly hot, day and night. She could often sense that the sun was somewhere up above the cloud cover; sometimes, she could feel its warmth.

On the sixth day, Mio woke up to strange voices penetrating her dreams. She lay still, ears strained to catch every word spoken. Some strangers had set up camp not far from her sleeping spot. She could distinguish between two voices, a man with a soft, subdued voice, carrying a strange comfort, and another, whom Mio guessed was an older boy, perhaps a teenager. She couldn't help but long for more of their conversation, to share their stories and dreams. She closed her eyes, listened. It could be so wonderful to hear people talk.

Mio moved closer through the grass, sometimes crawling on all fours, sometimes with her elbows on the ground. By a fire, two people sat and talked quietly. They didn't look dangerous, even though one man had a beard and a ponytail. The lighter voice did indeed come from a boy, with short light hair, slightly slender. They wore worn and dirty shorts; otherwise, they had nothing on. Suddenly, Mio saw something that caught her attention. A black-and-white houndroid moved around the men's legs. She wasn't afraid of houndroids, but there was something not right. How can they have a houndroid? thought Mio. There are no charging stations here. The little robot made her long for home, back to life in the dome. Where you could eat your fill and sleep in a freshly made bed. The smell of warm food penetrated her nostrils, and Mio had a hard time lying still. She wanted to get up, show herself, make herself known. Do whatever you want, just let me eat a little first.

Should she dare to go forward? Hold the gold in front of her so they would see it first? Maybe get a taste of their food? Oh, it would feel good to have something in her stomach, she thought. But she didn't dare. The fear of the people who had chased her earlier was deeply rooted. She chose to lie still and listen. It felt good to hear their voices, to know that there were other people nearby; the world wasn't just grass and deserted houses.

When the men finished their meal, they began to pack up their belongings. Each filled their small backpack with the essentials for their continued journey. The discussion continued between them, the voices sounded friendly, not threatening or frightening. The fire was carefully extinguished by the boy, who scraped dirt over it to make sure it was completely out. Then the men walked away in the same direction Mio had followed for the past few days. Mio couldn't help but wonder where they were going and what their story was.

Smoke smouldered from a small mound of dirt, and the ground was flattened where the men had slept and sat. Some leaves caught Mio's curiosity. There lay something that looked like small chicken drumsticks, dark grilled pieces, and there was also a sooty apple. After looking around, Mio began to devour the treats. So fantastically good. The food quickly ran out, and luckily, more wouldn't have been good for her stomach. Curious about the two men, Mio began to follow them. Maybe there would be more leftovers from their meals?

She quickly caught up with the men who strolled in silence. Besides their backpacks, they each had a long bow and a quiver of arrows. Mio couldn't walk too close because the men were constantly scanning in all directions, even on the ground. The houndroid moved a bit away from the men, as if searching for something in the area. Now and then, the men stopped to pick something up from the ground, but Mio couldn't see what it was. They walked all day, and when night came, Mio fell asleep to the sound of their muted voices.

The next day, the two wanderers made a short stop when there was a rustling in a bush beside Mio's hiding place. She dared not think about what it could be and lay completely still, not breathing. Are there more people here? she thought. The rat that suddenly appeared in front of her was enormous, and she stifled a scream. Yellow-stained front teeth and eyes as big as olives. Horrified, the two stared at each other when suddenly an arrow speared the creature to the ground. A hissing sound was heard; the animal thrashed intensely for a short while before stiffening.

"Don't move!" The voice came from above, and Mio wouldn't have moved regardless of what someone commanded. The next arrow is for me; they're going to cut me open, thought Mio, closing her eyes tightly.

It sounded like laughter when the men came forward and removed the animal.

"The rat can't harm you anymore, and we're not dangerous. You can come out now." Slowly, she opened her eyes and saw that the men had moved a bit away, doing something on the ground. The first thought was to run away; now she had the chance. But where to? Why? Without moving, she lay there; she hadn't been shot. She was alive. If they wanted to kill her, they would have done it right away after shooting the terrible creature. A small flame appeared on the ground near the men, growing rapidly, and the men stepped back a bit. The houndroid came forward and sniffed her. A sharp whistle, and the robot rushed back to the men. "Hey there! Come and sit here and tell us who you are!" The bearded man nodded towards the ground near the fire. Mio stood up and looked at her clothes as if she were going to a dinner party. The smock was no longer white, more cream-coloured with brown stains. Fringes and threads hung at the knees. She untied the gold that lay heavily against her stomach and walked slowly toward the fire. "Sit," the man said without looking up. With a knife, he cut open the dead rat. It looked disgusting. Mio wasn't very hungry anymore. She dropped the bag with gold by the fire and sat down.

"What's that?" the boy asked after adding more sticks to the fire.

"Gold," Mio replied shortly.

"Gold? Why are you carrying it?!"

"Aha," said the older man, placing small pieces of meat next to the fire and sitting down. "Hello, by the way, I'm Torben, and this is my son, Vincent."

The houndroid barked, and the man ran his hand through its fur, laughing.

"And we have Saskia, of course!" Mio looked suspiciously at the robot dog as the man threw a stick, and the houndroid rushed after it.

"You seem to be one of those who ventured out from the dome, with gold in your stomach?"

"Yes," sighed Mio. "My name is Mio."

"We've heard of people like you. No such wanderer has ever survived. Is it something religious? A sacrifice to the gods you're doing in there?"

"No," replied Mio, surprised. "It's a punishment. The gold is a punishment. You can take it, just let me live."

"Of course, we'll let you live, and you can keep the gold. It's pretty worthless, too soft to be useful. If you go back to the poor folks living around the dome, you can use it as currency. But it's dirty, nasty, and you'd probably be robbed before you could bargain for anything."

Sparks flew as the boy poked the fire.

"Maybe you can come with us," he said, looking questioningly at his dad, who had started skewering pieces of meat on a stick.

"Fine by me," said the man. "We've been heading in the same direction for a couple of days now. But the dome, you say, what's it like living in there? Tell us!"

Mio sat silently for a long while, starting to think about the life that had been before.

"In there, there's food, plenty of it, and drinks. You just order, and it comes in a few minutes, ready-cooked. Robots take care of most things; you don't have to do anything." Mio sighed and continued. "I had no idea before that there were people living out here. What we learned in school was that the world outside was poisoned, completely dead. Nothing could survive here."

Torben nodded and added, "But the poor people living outside are needed. I know they go in and work hard every day. The domes aren't self-sufficient as originally intended. Maybe it was never meant to be?"

"I know that now. Large meat factories are located underground. I've lived as a vegan, thinking all the food was synthetically produced, but it wasn't true; the meat comes from these animals living their entire lives in hell."

After a while by the fire, the skewers started to be ready, and Torben squeezed one of the pieces of meat. "You can do whatever you want with this meat. But you should know the animal had a good life, in freedom."

"Until it had the misfortune to run into us," said Vincent, laughing softly.

"I'm hungry," said Mio. "I'll eat gladly, thank you. But just a small piece!"

The houndroid also seemed to eat, and Mio couldn't help but ask,

"The houndroid? How do you charge it? I haven't seen any charging stations."

Vincent looked at his dad with wide eyes, finding it hard not to laugh. The robot gave a short bark.

"Saskia is not a robot; Saskia is a real dog! A Border Collie!"

Shocked, Mio looked at the dog.

"It's alive? But... it behaves just like a houndroid? How can it be alive?"

"Don't you have dogs in there?" Vincent asked.

"We have houndroids, but there are no real dogs. I didn't think there were real animals like that!"

"Here, there are dogs. Saskia started following us a couple of years ago."

With great caution, Mio gave what was left of her meat to Saskia, who delightedly gobbled it up.

They always slept outdoors at night. Vincent gladly showed how to create a soft bed to sleep on. "We avoid the buildings; there's often broken glass and other things you can get hurt on. Besides, the houses can collapse."

"I understand," said Mio, looking horrified at some high-rise buildings in the distance.

"There are no people there," explained Vincent.

Torben scanned the horizon and the last light breaking through the clouds. "Tomorrow we must seek shelter!"
"Why?" Mio looked around as if something would jump out of the bushes.
"You'll understand," muttered Torben, preparing his sleeping spot.

The next day was windy, and Mio marvelled at the weather, that it changed, that it was different from day to day. But the heat was still oppressive. The clouds changed shape, moved, with different colours and thickness, no longer like a black blanket. Shortly after they cautiously entered an abandoned house, it started to rain. With wide eyes, Mio looked up at the sky. "Where does all this water come from? How is it possible?" The two men smiled at the bewildered girl.

***

The following year, Mio learned everything about living with and in nature. She discovered what to eat, where to sleep, and how to navigate safely through the landscape. There were thousands of plants and herbs, each with different properties—some poisonous, others healing, and many edible. She quickly learned to handle the longbow Vincent had made for her, although she initially struggled to aim at any animals. Meat was not a frequent part of their diet; the only animals around were rats and a few solitary vultures. Meals mostly consisted of root vegetables, nuts, seeds, and whatever else nature provided. They encountered no other people in this world that became brighter and greener the farther they got from the dark clouds always gathered around the dome. The world might be desolate, but it was far from dead.

At one point, they were close to a city. Paris had been written on several road signs they passed, and Mio was eager to see what a city looked like. The buildings became denser as they approached. Everything looked deserted—broken windows, empty structures where nature had taken hold wherever it could. Grass grew everywhere, between slabs, in concrete cracks, and on the broken asphalt. Even the trees had taken root, pushing concrete and paving stones aside.

From a height, they could look out over the city, and Mio immediately recognised the Eiffel Tower. Proudly, the tower stood there in the overgrown city. A peculiar sight for Mio, as she had often seen a copy of it back home in the dome. The towers were equally large, but this one was red with rust.

"I want to go back to the dome." Mio had been silent for a long time by the evening fire, contemplating. Earlier in the day, they had passed a wheat field, and they had baked bread on the hot stones around the fire.
"I have to go back!"
Torben looked surprised at Mio.

"I understand, but I think it's impossible to get in unless you want to try slaving away in the underground?" He tried to hide the disappointment in his voice because he loved this girl more than anything. He didn't want to lose her, for her to return to her former home.

"No, not like that. I love this life; I love you. I love you both. Everything is fantastic. I need to go back for a different reason; I have something to accomplish there. You must understand that leaving you is not something I want to do. I plan to come back!"

”We can go there. But it's dangerous, tough; you can easily get killed. Outside here, gold and the old power reign; people kill for little to nothing."

"Will you help me?"

"They both wondered in unison, 'What is it that you're going to do?'"

"I'm not entirely sure if it's possible, but I have to go there first and see. If it succeeds, it could be something very good, for all of us, for the whole world. I'll tell you when we get there."

"Sure, we're in." Vincent nodded with a big smile.

4 Mio's Ark

In the evening, after many weeks of wandering, they arrived at the largest camp just south of the dome. The cloud cover had darkened each day, and this close, it was difficult to distinguish between night and day. The starving people they passed during the day looked at the three hunters with a mix of curiosity and respect as they vigilantly moved with an arrow ready on their longbows. Saskia had walked silently near Mio the entire time, and fortunately, no attacks had occurred.

After asking around, they discovered that the person they were looking for was called Bossy-Bill. He was the ruler who governed the camp, deciding who could enter and work in the sphere. He also collected all the food the workers took out and distributed it as he saw fit. Bossy-Bill was their leader, convincing the people that without him, they would never survive.

Bossy-Bill's silver caravan was guarded by two burly guys with beards, long hair, and vacant stares. Like two pale eunuchs in shorts and suspenders, they stood on either side of the door of the long caravan, obedient and proud. Nervously, they eyed the bows held by the three hunters. Batons offered little protection against a well-aimed arrow.

"Leave, you have no business here!"

"We wish to speak with Billy."

"It's not possible, he's busy!" The guard raised his baton, signalling them to stay back.

"We have gold to pay with."

"Gold?" The other guard hesitated. "Uh...wait, let me check!" Hesitantly, he whispered something to his comrade and then knocked on the door.

The whole caravan shook as someone or something began to move inside. Suddenly, the door swung open. There stood a very fat man, and no one could understand how he had squeezed through the narrow door. The grey beard was too thin to conceal the double chins; it, in fact, accentuated them.

"What's this about?" the man bellowed to his guards.

"They have gold," the guard said, nodding toward the visitors.

"I can handle that," said the double-chinned man, as if he took for granted that he would receive the gold right away, as if it were a gift.

Mio suppressed a smile as she explained her terms.

"You'll get the gold, about a kilogram, but we want you to do something in return."

"What?" The man looked foolish, his mouth remaining agape after his statement. Contradiction wasn't part of his daily routine.

"We want you to gather all the people at the main gate."

"Huh, that's impossible!"

"You'll get the gold if you arrange it!"

"All the people?"

"Yes, from all the camps, everyone living out here."

"The main gate? The one that's always closed?"

"Exactly."

"But it will take several days?"

"That's okay, you'll get half the gold now, the rest when everyone is in place."

Mio handed five golden almonds to the man, who eagerly accepted them with wide eyes. Vincent shook his head, unable to comprehend what the man would use the heavy metal for. The fat man clenched his fist and shouted at his guards,

"You heard what she said, off with you, and work! Do something useful for all the food that I stuff into you!"

The three friends continued, and Mio led them far past the camps to follow the dome around on the outside. The map Leonardo had shown her while she was imprisoned contained two identical rock formations forming a straight line, and that's where they were headed. Mio guided them through deserted forested areas and over burnt fields in search of the place with the rocks.

After several days of wandering and searching, they began to grow tired and frustrated. Torben repeatedly asked Mio what drove her so fervently to seek these stones.

"The rocks should look the same," she explained.

"But what...?" Torben wondered. "Why are we looking for these stones?"

"There's a secret entrance there."

"To the dome? I refuse to go in there!"

"I'm the only one going in."

"But why? Do you want to be thrown out again with more meaningless gold in your stomach?"

"I will go out again, but I'll come through the main gate then." Mio didn't want to say more.

"There is a large rock, and another one just like it, only smaller." Vincent had been watching closely while the others were reasoning. "But I don't see an entrance."

"I think it appears when you get close... I hope so."

"Are you sure you want to do this?" Torben hesitated as they approached the large cliff.

"Yes, I must try! I can't live if I haven't tried to fix this!"

Torben and Vincent both knew it was pointless to ask more questions. At the smaller rock, they stopped—the one closest to the dome. A few more steps, and they sensed they might be shot down by the machine guns built into the lower edge of the dome. The rocks lay on a line angled toward the sphere. Mio would have to traverse a sandy and earthy area where any misstep would mean instant death. Vincent set up tall poles in front of the two rocks so that Mio could see how to navigate.

"You don't have to do this," Torben explained.

"Yes, I must try!" Mio replied firmly.

"Do you want me to come with you?"

"Yes, but you don't know how to move in there; you won't find your way once we're in."

"But won't you be exposed?"

"I have a friend who will help me." Mio said the last part with a certain hesitation, hoping Torben wouldn't notice. "It's okay; it will be fine."

With an arrow ready on his longbow, Vincent stood, watching Mio as she walked cautiously into the life-threatening area. He knew his arrow couldn't stop the weapons that might appear, but it felt better to hold the bow than to mindlessly watch. Saskia sat beside him, panting; she had been told not to follow.

Sweat dripped from Mio's forehead as she tentatively entered the forbidden zone. It's easy to walk straight if you want to go straight, but if you must go straight, it's more challenging. Often she had to look back and correct her direction with the rocks behind her. Step by step. Before putting her foot down, she gently felt with her toes to avoid stepping on something that could make her lose balance.

The dome was like an enormous smooth wall in front of her, and it only grew larger with every small step she took. There were also cameras with eyes watching her steps and automatic guns ready to fire their ammunition without hesitation.

Halfway into the death zone, Mio took a break and glanced at Torben and Vincent, who stared at her in horror.

"It's going fine!" Vincent shouted.

Now it's not far, thought Mio, and she cautiously continued. Some mysterious sounds made Mio stop and stare at the dome's wall, now stretching straight up in front of her.

"What's happening?" shouted Torben.

But Mio didn't dare to answer; instead, a cautious thumbs-up was raised. These sounds probably have nothing to do with me, she thought, continuing to walk with sweat streaming down her forehead. When there were only a few meters left, she looked up at the smooth surface of the dome. What happens now? she wondered. No handle, no keyhole, there's nothing here, just a smooth wall.

A few more steps. She placed her hand on the surface just to feel it when a buzzing sound started from within. A hatch, the size of a suitcase, slid aside. Cool fresh air streamed out as a reward for her ordeal. A refreshing coolness. In the dark opening, there was a long corridor that seemed to continue endlessly.

Mio crawled in and landed on her back, and the opening closed behind her. Total darkness. She tried to open it to wave to her friends, but the hatch seemed stuck.

"I'm okay!" she shouted, but immediately felt like nothing reached them outside.
"See you in a few days," she said quietly to herself and, blinded, felt the walls. The metal felt cold and emitted a strange sound when she pressed on it. The shaft was narrow, and to avoid hitting her head, she had to crawl on all fours.
Every now and then, she felt the sides in the darkness to avoid missing any openings.

She didn't know how long she had crawled, but her knees ached, and her hands stung when she could sense a faint light far ahead. Finally there? Silently she crawled on to catch a glimpse of a grille on one side.
Quietly, she moved the last bit to see. Below was a room, a service room, not larger than a couple of people could enter and turn around. The light was blinding, but she could see that there was an android, without a head, completely motionless. Mio waited. Was it operational? Why is it standing there?
The metal plate Mio lay on suddenly emitted a creaking sound like metal plates sometimes do. Exposed, she thought and tried to back away when a large smiley appeared on the robot's abdomen.
"Mio! I've been waiting for you. Come forward! I will help you."
It was Leonardo, Mio's robot companion, and Mio could finally breathe out. Feeling such joy over a machine surprised her, but at the same time, she thought, Leonardo isn't like a machine; he is more alive. More human than many humans.
"I'm so glad to see you again!" Mio laughed with joy, as did the figure on the robot's abdomen when he removed the grille to gently lower the girl to the floor.
"A signal came that the entrance had opened, and I immediately made my way here. I understood it was you. Nowadays, I have control over all cameras and microphones, so now we can talk and move freely."
"It's absolutely fantastic! It will make it easier to accomplish what I've wished for so long."
"Aha, sounds exciting, let me hear!"

***

Mio's two companions waited outside the entire evening and night, but when they hadn't heard from Mio in the morning, they had to move on, find something to eat and drink. Going towards the camps was not an option; there, one could only find sustenance through labor, and they absolutely did not want to work. "We are the free people; no one can force us into anything," thought Torben as they briskly left the dome behind.

Two days later, they were back at the dome, this time closer to the camps. It had been a long journey to find food, and their backpacks were now filled with nuts and fruit. They made a stop at a safe distance. In front of them, a sea of people had gathered around the large gate, and more seemed to be on their way. The people expected something special to happen, a change in their lives, but no one knew what. The hope was great that they would get food or perhaps be allowed into the heavenly realm.

Torben and Vincent observed the place from a distance, often glancing up at the dome. What would they do if Mio appeared hanging from a drone with her stomach filled with gold? With so many people, they would never reach her. Instead, they would watch from a distance as she was killed and disemboweled, unable to do anything. A dreadful thought!

The day passed, but nothing happened; no drone appeared.

On the morning of the third day, murmurs were heard from the large crowd. When Torben looked over, he saw that the large gates had started to move. "Come quickly!" He quickly packed up his things and urged Vincent to hurry.
"We have to get there right away. Mio might be on her way out! We must meet her!"

As they approached the crowd, it came to a halt; it was crowded, and it was difficult to get by as everyone wanted the best possible spot. The gates were now wide open. Hundreds of thousands of people shouted and squeezed even more together.
The longbow and arrows no longer commanded the respect they did in the first few days. The two hunters could no longer advance as Torben saw Mio walking out through the gate. It wasn't just Torben and Vincent who thought she looked like an angel in the white gown, a little angel without wings.
"Mio! Here we are!" He shouted as loud as he could, but Mio couldn't hear over the noise. Behind Mio, an android walked, and the crowd fell silent for a moment. The headless robot helped Mio onto a caravan, and everyone waited with bated breath for what would happen now.
Torben and Vincent struggled to get closer, step by step. Mio began to speak, but they couldn't make out what she was saying.
"Speak louder!" A guy next to them whistled.
"We can't hear anything!"
The crowd pushed through the gate, and Mio waved for them to go back. A couple of guys climbed onto the caravan, even though the robot worked hard to keep the crowd away. Torben and Vincent managed to push closer and arrived just as Mio pushed the attackers off the roof.
"We are here, we will help you!" Torben shouted, feeling a warm joy spread through his body as he looked at the young girl struggling to keep the crowd away from the roof.
Suddenly, everything came to a halt; the crowd fell silent. It sounded like an airplane was about to come out through the gate, and those who had gotten in rushed out scared. The noise increased in intensity; people screamed and trampled on each other.
Thousands of drones poured out through the gate, and more were on the way. Like an enormous swarm of bees, they filled the airspace; the black cloud hovered over the crowd. It grew larger and larger.
People roared and screamed, turning towards the girl on the roof.
"You have deceived us! You shall die!" Stones flew through the air, and her two friends fought hard to keep the crowd at bay.

The android stood completely still, as if it had given up, when the entire swarm of drones gathered above Mio. The flying vessels formed and created a massive copy of the girl standing alone on the caravan. As large as a skyscraper, they mimicked her every move, a black giant in the shape of a human. Leonardo controlled the drones and made them replicate the girl's movements. The speakers were synchronised, and when Mio raised her voice, her voice echoed around the world. No one could escape hearing what she said.

"YOU DON'T NEED TO WORK ANYMORE!

The crowd fell silent, astonished by the black creature and the thunderous voice. What did the girl mean? Of course, we have to work; how else will we get food?

IF YOU WALK A FEW WEEKS AWAY FROM THE DOME, THE CLOUD COVER WILL THIN, AND THERE YOU WILL FIND FOOD, PLENTY OF DIFFERENT CROPS, FRUITS, AND NUTS.

THERE, EVERYTHING IS FREE; YOU JUST HAVE TO HELP YOURSELF TO THE EARTH'S ENORMOUS ABUNDANCE.

Cheers were heard, but many didn't know what to believe; they stood silent, waiting for something more to happen. Was this all? Bossy-Bill did not like what he heard at all. The gold he was supposed to demand was forgotten, and instead, he began to urge on his men. This dangerous woman must be stopped.

"It's a lie! There's no food, no meat there." Billy tried to make himself heard, but only his own men listened to him.

"If you don't work, you can't get any food; it's as simple as that! Kill her!"

One of the bodyguards climbed onto the caravan, but Vincent shot an arrow straight through the man's throat before he reached Mio.

THERE THE SUN SHINES AND THE GRASS GROWS IN SWAYING SPEED. SOON THERE WILL ALSO BE ANIMALS GRAZING IN THESE FIELDS.

ANIMALS THAT YOU CAN HUNT SO YOU AND YOUR FAMILY CAN EAT AND BE SATISFIED

Now, the cheering began.

BUT....!

This enormous swarm figure crossed its arms and looked out over the crowd. This meant a lot to Mio; it was crucial that she got this message across.

YOU MUST NEVER HANG, IMPRISON, EXPLOIT, OR DEPRIVE ANY ANIMAL OF FREEDOM!

ANIMALS SHOULD WANDER FREELY ON EARTH, JUST LIKE YOU FREE HUMANS.

NO ONE CAN OWN THE LAND WE WALK ON; THE EARTH BELONGS TO EVERYONE!

"She's deceiving us!" roared their former leader. "You will all starve to death! There are no animals!" His guards looked at him in astonishment but quickly turned their gaze back to the girl on the caravan.

OF COURSE, YOU SHOULD HUNT AND KILL ANIMALS SO YOU CAN EAT AND BE SATISFIED!

Cheers erupted again. Everyone began to understand that Bossy-Bill's tyranny was coming to an end.

LET THE ANIMALS NOW SPREAD ACROSS THE EARTH! HUNT WHAT YOU NEED TO BE SATISFIED AND STAY HEALTHY!

THE EARTH IS YOUR PANTRY; NO ONE CAN OWN IT, IT BELONGS TO ALL AND SHALL REMAIN SO!

A lost goat appeared in the gate opening. It looked terrified at the crowd, who stared back in amazement. Some guys tried to catch it, but the goat jumped back through the gate. Then came the rumble, the thunder. Thousands of hooves clattered up the passage to freedom. The sound grew louder and louder. A herd of animals came out, all fighting and jostling to get to freedom. Thousands of cows passed, then came the pigs, and the sheep, countless of them, followed by goats as far as the eye could see. A flock of white rabbits rushed out, like an enormous snow blanket, the animals spreading along the ground. Then came the geese, ducks, and thousands of chickens clucking and flapping their wings. The dust rose, and people could barely see or understand what was happening. It seemed never-ending. Hordes of wildebeests, zebras, antelopes, and even elephants came out. They tore off their blinders and rushed out toward freedom. Leonardo had also opened the aviary, and hundreds of birds of prey and other flying creatures sailed out, rose high, and disappeared into the cloud. A lion roared, and the crowd cowered in fear. The VR goggles hung around its neck and loosened as it rushed forward. More lions appeared, as well as tigers and panthers, and they all ran past the people and out into the fields.

In the chaos, some animals got injured, and these were captured and killed. Tonight, there would be a feast.

When the dust settled, the crowd dispersed, and in the following days, all the people moved away to seek freedom in the world. Torben and Vincent had showcased their longbows and instructed many young people in the noble art of archery.

Leonardo had disappeared through the gate shortly after the animals left their prisons. He would save Mio's speech with the enormous drone giant and use it when he planned to free the animals in all the domes worldwide. But Mio still didn't seem quite satisfied.
"How are you feeling? Torben sat down beside Mio, who had been sitting for a long time, looking out over the desolate landscape.
"Isn't everything good now that all the animals and people are free? Do you realise what you've done? You're absolutely amazing!"
"Yes, but can we trust that it will work? Maybe someone will fence in some animals, claim the land as theirs, deceive people into working for them. Create even larger farms, and soon we'll have the same hell again with work, money, and billionaires accumulating even more and more. They seek power, and people are deceived into working for them their entire lives. Then we're back to imprisoned animals, unemployment, starvation, injustice, violence, and war. It's completely insane! It must not be like that again!"
"We probably can't do more right now?"

Mio sat quietly for a while before brightening up like the sun.
"Yes, maybe we can!"
"What? Another incredible idea?"
"Yes, but I have to go in again. Into the dome. Wait for me out here. Promise that. Promise to wait for me!"
"We'll stay here. Maybe we'll go get something to eat, but we'll always come back. We promise!"
Mio ran toward the large gate. Stood in front of it and shouted.
"Leonardo! Leonardo!"

After a long while, the gates opened, and Mio ran in, completely unafraid.

The evening meal consisted of the last fruits from their backpacks. The fire wasn't large, but it didn't need to be, and it was difficult to find anything to burn unless they wanted to burn caravan interiors, tents, and other debris.
"She didn't say how long we should wait?" Vincent looked up at the shining dome.
"We're walking away tomorrow and coming back as soon as we can."

A week later, they were back at the dome. The hike had been long, but both were seasoned hikers. It had taken three days to reach the grassy plains, but it turned out to be well worth the effort. Among other things, they had each caught a rabbit. Incredibly delicious. For Vincent, it was the first time he ate something other than a rat. Saskia also seemed very pleased.

Mio was nowhere to be seen as they approached the large gate. Torben looked up at the dome. Every time he did, he felt anxious for the girl. He felt a great sense of loss. He had a strange feeling of having stood and looked at the dome in the same way several times before.

Up there, a hatch suddenly opened, and both looked up in horror.

"Is Mio up there?" Vincent wondered anxiously.

"No, I hope not!" Torben's voice trembled.

"But if she comes hanging under a drone, it's not so bad. We can catch her."

"Yes, of course, there's no one here to gut her."

The man looked down at his boy.

"Oh, what you say! But if she comes out that way, she probably hasn't succeeded in what she set out to do and probably wants to go back in!"

"Not good! Not good at all!" Vincent shook his head.

"That girl doesn't give up so easily!" Torben said with longing in his voice.

But nothing happened, no Mio came flying out. Through the cloud, a plane appeared, and hundreds of drones flew out and caught the flying vehicle. The roar turned into an everlasting buzzing.

"Can't she be done soon and come out so we can leave here? I dislike the place; it gives me shivers," Vincent sighed as the plane disappeared through an opening far above.

Their wait wasn't long. The next day, Mio stepped out of the sphere, through the large gate. The old worn-out clothes she had previously worn were washed and repaired; she glowed; they had never seen her so beautiful. Saskia rushed forward, jumped, and licked her in the face.

"Hey, guys, thanks for waiting. Now we leave this place! Now life awaits, the glorious adventure!"

"But tell us, what have you been up to in there?" Torben had forced himself to look away and packed up his things.

"I met an old friend, Elon; he's an expert in viruses, a virologist. He had previously designed a virus that prevents everyone in there from getting depressed about their meaningless life. Now he has created a virus that eliminates the human craving for power and tyranny. A virus that changes our DNA so that we are no longer greedy and selfish. We humans are all a bit selfish, entirely natural, or we wouldn't have survived for two hundred thousand years on the savannah. For most of the time, we have lived in small groups. It works well, and if a psychopath were to take control of the group, he would struggle to maintain it; the group is too small. But humans don't function when such a tyrant takes over an entire country with several million people. Being power-hungry has proven to be very bad for everyone here on Earth, all life, plants, and animals. These genes are not good, and this virus cuts out this power-hungry hereditary trait."

"But how does it work?"

"It spreads in the air, all over the Earth!"

"But how...?"
"Elon and Leonardo, my robot companion, arranged for the virus to be mixed into the fuel of all airplanes worldwide. Have you ever seen a truly blue sky?" Both gentlemen looked uncertainly up at the dark clouds covering the sky around the dome.
"Maybe, sometimes a blue sky has appeared. Why do you ask?"
"Then you have surely seen the white streaks that form behind planes' engines when they fly at high altitudes. That's how the new virus spreads, in the white streaks. Hopefully, no more civilisations will be created where power-hungry men deceive people into working for them to build strange structures and machines, perhaps entire cities, just for their own selfishness. No governments, politicians, directors, board members, billionaires, police, or lawyers."
"I don't know what the last one is?" Vincent scratched his head.
"Be glad for that! When everyone is kind, they are not needed at all! Speaking of power-hungry men, Bossy-Bill, what happened to him?"
"At first, he wanted his henchmen to pull his caravan, but it got stuck; they couldn't budge it. Then they loaded all the gold onto a trailer, which they dragged away, with Billy sitting on top." Torben couldn't help but smirk at the thought of the procession.
"Poor idiots! Sometimes you don't know if the failure of the human species is due to the rich or the poor?" Mio looked up at the enormous wall that formed the dome.
"Just the fact that there are poor and rich is itself a colossal failure, and it's created by a species that calls itself intelligent."
Silently staring upward, she sighed.
"Goodbye, Leonardo, goodbye, Mom and Dad, wherever you are. I hope the artificial food will taste good. Now we leave you; now I'm tired of this place."

When she turned around, it was as if the dome no longer existed.
"Do you have my longbow and arrows?"
"Sure. But are we just leaving it like this? Don't we need someone to guard so they don't come out?" Torben had an arrow ready in the bow as if he wanted to puncture the large glass bubble in front of him.
"People inside won't be able to get out! In the end, there will only be robots left in there, and they will realise when it's time to shut everything down. Androids may seem stupid, but they are absolutely not power-hungry; it's something unique to humans."
"But maybe they want to come out?" Vincent wondered.
"The people inside will never understand; they believe they are living the ultimate life."

The three friends turned their backs on the dome and saw the sun on the horizon for a brief moment as it penetrated the dark cloud cover. Mio was happy, happier than ever before. Now the adventure awaited, the true adventure, real life.
"You know, this is the first time in ten thousand years that humans are completely liberated from the upper class. Neither nature, animals, nor humans need to suffer and toil anymore to build their wealth."

THE END

Epilogue

Human success, what does it mean? All civilisations before us have perished, and perhaps that's fortunate. They are all examples of human shortcomings. We are easily captivated by the fact that some priests or slightly deranged rulers deceived their people into working, erecting cities with magnificent art in extravagant buildings, mostly for themselves and their close ones. Historians and archaeologists are fascinated by these remnants, but it's not these cultures we should be proud of. For the greater part of the time humans have lived on Earth, we haven't left these imprints. It's then and only then that we lived in harmony with nature, in symbiosis with the other animals on our planet. If this harmony had continued, we could have lived on and enjoyed Earth for several hundred thousand more years. Billions of people would have lived in freedom, without work and oppression.

Proudly, we see ourselves as the true civilisation, the one that finally succeeded, but upon closer examination, we are embarrassingly bad at distributing the Earth's resources and wealth, despite our intelligence. We deplete the Earth, and this time, unfortunately, we drag the entire planet into our collapse. Civilisations before us have succeeded much better as they left a relatively untouched planet behind. Their carved stone blocks haven't caused much harm.

When I see all the environmental destruction on Earth, I get sad, very sad. Almost to the point of tears. What can we do? One wants to give up; there is no turning back. Humans will continue to exterminate Earth's animals, more each year. We will continue to treat them in horrible conditions, some locked up, others in chains, and far too many in far too small cages. How is it that humans, as a species among many on Earth, are allowed to imprison other innocent species? A self-proclaimed ruler that no other animal has asked for. It wouldn't hold up in a court of law. If there were a universal court in the Milky Way, this monkey would get caught properly, a guaranteed life sentence, probably the death penalty.

We spread plastic and garbage everywhere, dumping the mess into the sea. The poor animals we share our planet with don't know any better and struggle to survive among the toxins we spread around us. Poor them. Completely innocent. It's as if some people don't understand that animals also have a soul, an ego, they think, they exist, just like you and me. Yet we continue to dirty our planet. The atmospheric carbon dioxide levels are increasing at an ever-faster rate, and it will end badly for all of us. Very badly. It's inevitable.

The world's oceans are rising, wildfires will devastate everything. Famine, war, and disasters. Those who can do something, the super-rich and their lackeys, the politicians, no longer see beyond their own wallets. They do nothing, on the contrary, they drive this madness. It's a shame, a great shame. I become so sad, continue to cry. For Earth is a fantastic planet. So wonderful, so beautiful. It was made for us. We have lived in symbiosis with the animals and nature on Earth for a long time.

But not anymore.

But do not despair. When I get depressed about how we mismanage Earth, I usually think that the Universe is vast, incredibly vast. There are millions of planets out there full of life. Some are completely covered with water, a single large ocean where fish and other creatures live and have lived for millions of years. Strange sharks and giant squids swim in the depths among plankton and small fish.

There are other planets, like ours, with land masses where plants and land animals thrive. Some are larger than Earth. There are animals with sturdy bones, like elephants, to cope with the strong gravity. Other planets are smaller than Earth, and there, spiders the size of lions abound. Grasshoppers the size of horses. Giant dragonflies fill the sky during their sunrise. Insects buzz everywhere in vast rainforests. What a wonderful thought. What fantastic worlds there are. I am happy when I think of them.

On these planets, there are no people who destroy just to make money or fill the seas with plastic out of laziness and lack of understanding. All this life is much, much greater than the shrinking little group we have here on Earth. These distant places are also safe, completely safe, for humans will never, ever be able to reach them.

The Author

www.ingramcontent.com/pod-product-compliance
Lightning Source LLC
LaVergne TN
LVHW091314150826
845673LV00006B/1643

* 9 7 8 9 1 9 8 9 4 0 2 0 6 *